Off-Season
and Other Stories

Other Five Star Titles
by Jeremiah Healy:

Turnabout

Off-Season
and Other Stories

Jeremiah Healy

Five Star • Waterville, Maine

This collection is a work of fiction. Names, characters, places and incidents are either the product of the author's imagination, or, if real, used fictitiously.

First Edition
First Printing: June 2003

Published in 2003 in conjunction with Tekno Books and Ed Gorman.

Set in 11 pt. Plantin by Elena Picard.

Printed in the United States on permanent paper.

Library of Congress Cataloging-in-Publication Data

Healy, J. F. (Jeremiah F.), 1948–
    Off-season, and other stories / Jeremiah Healy.
    1st ed. Waterville, Me.: Five Star, 2003.
      p. cm.
    ISBN 0-7862-5438-6 (hc : alk. paper)
    Notes: Next season—Proportionate response—Habits—City life—A debt to the Devil—Him, gone? good!—The author—Hero—The safest little town in Texas—Rotten to the core—Off-season.
    1. Detective and mystery stories, American. I. Title.
PS3558.E2347O38 2003
  813'.54—21   2003049086

To Marty Greenberg and Ed Gorman,
with thanks for shepherding
these sheep into a flock.

About the Author

A graduate of Rutgers College and Harvard Law School, Jeremiah Healy was a professor at the New England School of Law for eighteen years. He is the creator of the John Francis Cuddy private-investigator series and, under the pseudonym "Terry Devane," the Mairead O'Clare legal-thriller series, both set primarily in Boston.

Healy has written seventeen novels and over sixty short stories, fourteen of which have won or been nominated for the Shamus Award. Healy's later Cuddy novels include *Rescue, Invasion of Privacy, The Only Good Lawyer,* and *Spiral.* His O'Clare books from Putnam/Berkley are *Uncommon Justice* and *Juror Number Eleven. Turnabout,* a stand-alone private-eye thriller, was published by Five Star in December 2001, and the second collection of his Cuddy short stories, *Cuddy Plus One,* was published by Crippen & Landru in 2002.

A past Shamus Awards Chair, Healy also served as President of the Private Eye Writers of America for two years. In October 2000, he was elected President of the International Association of Crime Writers. He was toastmaster at the 1996 World Mystery Convention (or "Bouchercon") and will be International Guest of Honor at Bouchercon 2004 in Toronto.

Table of Contents

Introduction

I'm really pleased to be writing this introduction, because it's kind of the next-to-last shred of proof (before the collection itself is in shelvable form) that my "non-series" stories are finally going to be published as a group. I've been lucky enough to see most of my John Francis Cuddy private-eye short pieces be collected in *The Concise Cuddy* and *Cuddy Plus One*, with the last story in the latter the first story in my new Mairead O'Clare legal-thriller series under the pseudonym of Terry Devane.

Now, many of the stories in the book you're holding already have been published elsewhere, typically in magazines like *Ellery Queen's* or so-called "theme" anthologies like *Mom, Murder, and Apple Pie*. However, I'd like to comment just briefly on a few that haven't appeared previously.

The title piece, "Off-Season," was a novella I first began about twenty years ago. The problem, then and now, concerns its length. Unlike the science fiction field, there are really no markets for crime fiction that's longer than a short story but shorter than a novel. However, when I wrote "Off Season," I was so green I didn't know that. I still think it's a good plot, though, one which I think would make an excellent TV movie.

An even greater problem of publication occurred with "Proportionate Response," the other long piece in the collection. I wanted to tell a story in which there was some suspense, if not quite a mystery. But, alas, the sorts of markets that do accept longer "mainstream" fiction weren't right for the kind of tale it was.

One of the shortest pieces is "Next Season." It was written by me in English toward translation for a German-language anthology. It also has more of a *Grand Guignol* atmosphere as well, which is very popular in many of the continental countries.

Which brings me to the dedication for this book. Many of you have heard of Martin Greenberg and Edward J. Gorman. However, few of you have probably met these premier anthologists of short mystery fiction. I'd like to dedicate this work to both of them, selfishly for all they've done for me, but more altruistically for all they've done for so many of us in the "mystery scene," a painful pun you will get if you've subscribed to a certain magazine over the years. Marty and Ed, thanks so much for everything.

—Jeremiah Healy
Boston, MA
December 17, 2002

Next Season

I was pulling my fishing boat up from the water and onto its trailer by the bow rope. Behind me, I heard a familiar voice call out, "Karl, do you need a hand?"

Turning toward the sound, I saw my neighbor—if someone living a kilometer away along the shoreline counts as a "neighbor." David held his dog, a friendly golden retriever, by a retractable leash. They walked toward me on the dirt road encircling our lake in front of the few homes built into the steep, forested hillsides around it.

"Thanks, David, but I should be all right."

Dressed in corduroy pants and a fleece jacket against the cool October breeze, he waved his free hand at my swim trunks and tee-shirt. "Don't you ever feel the cold, man?"

I grinned. "Not as much as some, I guess."

Now David gestured toward the dock, where my scuba gear lay in a heap. "At least tell me that you're not going diving?"

I was the only scuba enthusiast on the lake, even during our summers. "The water's still pretty warm, and thanks to such a dry September, the clarity's okay at even fifteen meters, especially on a sunny day like this."

David just shook his head. I thought he might ask another question, but nothing came out except, "Well, if you do need help with closing down camp, let me know."

11

By "closing down camp," David meant preparing the house for winter. "Thanks. I will."

He continued along the path, releasing the leash so his dog could bound eagerly ahead after a red squirrel near the base of a white birch.

I secured my boat to the trailer, then checked the hitch at the back of my Ford Explorer. Over the years since my wife and I had built the beautiful, yellow-pine chalet near the crest of the slope, I'd found that the sport-utility vehicle provided just the right combination of horsepower and gear ratio to haul the heavy, stable boat up a paved driveway angling forty-five degrees from the horizontal.

Getting behind the wheel of the Explorer, I turned my key in the ignition and began inching up toward our garage.

When friends from the city first visited us in the house, they marveled at the anomaly of a gravel public road around the lake but smooth, tarred driveways for the private homes. Sheilah—my wife—reveled in explaining to them that plowing snow from the road often stripped the finer gravel covering the coarser. And both types were necessary for a passable route come "mud season" in April, after the snows melted and the frozen water in the roadbed began to thaw. The contractor who built our house—a husky, bearded roughneck named Hector—was the actual fount of that wisdom, but Sheilah rarely credited him for it. Which, I must admit, later seemed clever on her part.

I reached the halfway point of the driveway, boat and trailer rolling smoothly.

The slope to our house was a microcosm reflecting the entire surrounding topography. Formed as the glaciers from the last ice age receded, Lake Cascade fell away under water nearly as steeply as the hillsides rose above it. Unlike lakes in Canada fed by still-active glaciers that accrete and withdraw annually, ours was gin-clear, not milky turquoise. While fishing from my boat, I could often see a coin on the bottom six meters deep, though the refraction of sunlight under the surface made even Lake Cascade's greater depths invisible from the surface.

But no less perfect for scuba-diving.

At our garage, I did a "K-turn" to maneuver the boat and trailer backward into the covered space, leaving the Explorer facing downslope. After killing the engine, however, I set the parking brake firmly with my left foot, pushing the pedal nearly to the floor. I'd once witnessed a pick-up truck slide down the slope and all the way into the water, and I had no desire to repeat that experience myself.

Exiting the vehicle, I drew in a long, satisfying breath of the brisk air. A truly spectacular day for my last dive of the season. I closed and locked the garage door before walking back down toward the dock.

Sheilah and I had always dreaded closing down the chalet each autumn. She would live there for months at a time during the warm weather while I commuted back and forth to the city and my demanding engineering practice. But our dread didn't come so much because of the little aggravations involved, at least for me. No, I didn't mind pulling the boat, or draining the house's plumbing pipes so they wouldn't freeze, or even removing the roof's gutters so falling leaves wouldn't clog them and crystallizing rain wouldn't split them. The dread was more from sensing another summer gone, another joyous season of loving our house and loving each other in it.

At least until Sheilah decided Hector our contractor also might be a good "fount" for something other than road advice.

I never really suspected anything between them. As I

said, she never credited him with any of the maxims she'd spout to our city friends about this wilderness paradise. And I never would have guessed him to be her type, either.

But then, the cliché does maintain that the husband is always the last to know.

Apparently, though, many folks in the nearby town *did* know. And so it was no real surprise to them when, one Thursday night in June, Sheilah and Hector abandoned our house and his business to run off together in his red Dodge Ram truck. However, Hector wasn't the most reliable of tradesmen, as the other lakeside owners complained that he never contacted them to apologize or refer work-in-progress to other contractors.

At our dock, I went through the mental checklist regarding my scuba gear for the last time till spring. I donned the polyurethane wetsuit, zipping up tight. I checked the pressure gauge on my regulator to be sure I had enough air for a comfortable period of "bottom time." Then I slung the tank and buoyancy compensator rig up onto my back like a very heavy vest, buckling the weight belt around my waist. After spitting into the face-side of the mask and rubbing the protein-laden, anti-fogging saliva around the glass, I adjusted its strap to fit snugly. For insurance, I took two safety breaths from the mouthpiece of the regulator, slipped on my fins, and slid over the side of the dock.

As always, the invasion of cold water into the tiny atmosphere between wetsuit and skin was shocking, but as soon as I began kicking gently and rhythmically, I warmed up again. Dropping deeper, I noticed small sunfish in the shallows yielding to brook trout and landlocked salmon seeking smelt. At seven meters, I was only about ten meters from shore.

As I dove farther down, the fish gave way entirely to the

stark beauty of the glacial lake bed itself. Cracked sheets of slate, some large enough to be blackboards in a classroom. An entire pine tree, ravaged by winds because its roots were sunk too shallow into the exposed, rocky shoreline, its long, delicate needles waving languidly in the water. Boulders, too, huge granite slabs the size of my Explorer.

And, just beyond them, a red mass the size of Hector's pick-up truck.

I finned around to its hood so I could look in the windshield, my favorite position for viewing.

That Thursday back in June, I'd finished work in the city early, and so I decided to surprise Sheilah at our chalet by driving there twelve hours before she expected me. Regrettably, my little surprise boomeranged.

Seeing Hector's truck inexplicably backed into our driveway at 11:00 p.m., I left the Explorer down on the road and walked quietly to the chalet's back door. I let myself in without a sound and picked up the baseball bat we kept in the kitchen against unwanted intruders. I climbed the stairs using the outside edge of each step, so as not to cause a warning squeak. And I entered our bedroom, them lying together in my marital four-poster, dozing in that unmistakable, magical glow after making love.

They hadn't mustered even the decency to use one of the guest rooms.

Sheilah's long, auburn hair lay tousled over the pillow, and Hector snored through an open, snaggle-toothed mouth, his car keys and wallet on my night table. Raising the bat, I struck each in the head. Just a tap, really. Enough to knock them further into sleep, but not so hard as to kill them.

Taking Hector's keys, I started with Sheilah, lifting her

over my shoulder and carrying her down the stairs the way a firefighter might some trapped, unconscious victim of a blaze. At Hector's red truck, I put her into the passenger's seat, then turned the key in the ignition just enough to trigger the ability to raise the electric windows. Making a second trip with Hector proved a bit more onerous, but I managed. Then, placing him behind the wheel, I turned his key more forcefully to start the engine, and I released the parking brake. Closing the door carefully, I got behind the rear bumper and provided my own extra little oomph by pushing hard down the slope.

Probably not necessary, though. The truck gained momentum until it launched itself into the lake, gliding outward for five or six meters before dipping at the front, the weight of the sputtering engine disproportionate to the empty bed. The pick-up then planed like a submarine, paralleling the slope of the lake bottom as it dove silently downward.

The next morning, I went out in my fishing boat, miming someone trolling for salmon as I criss-crossed the area where the truck would have settled. Not even remotely visible from the surface, which made me feel a lot more comfortable that afternoon, during my first dive down there.

And during each later one.

Now, on this final visit of the season, I was hanging in the water nearly twenty meters deep, my face mask almost flush with the windshield. Through the glass, I could see Sheilah's hair, waving vaguely northward like the pine tree's long needles. And Hector's mouth was still open, too.

That June night, the water seeping through the dashboard vents must have "awakened" my wife and her lover as

16

his truck sank. But the drenching of the engine compartment would have short-circuited any wires, so his electric windows could not be lowered. And the resultant hydrostatic pressure on the exterior of the pick-up would have kept even a brute like Hector from being able to open a door toward escape. He did manage to punch a hole in his driver's side window under water, probably with his elbow, but not soon enough.

It couldn't have been an easy few minutes for the tragic couple, the chilling water numbing their limbs as it sought to flood their lungs, their fingernails all breaking off as they must have tried to claw through the windshield.

Over the course of the summer, small fish had made foraging expeditions through that hole in the side window, nibbling on the softer tissues—earlobes, lips, eyes—so that my viewing changed slightly each week. I'm not expert enough to know what effect a winter under there will have on them, but it should prove interesting come spring.

I checked my pressure gauge and watch. Time to go.

Blowing a kiss to my wife and winking at Hector's own empty sockets, I slowly finned back toward the surface, thinking I now had even more reason than usual to look forward to next season.

Proportionate Response

ONE

Raymond Hammett leaned into the next stroke a little, the paddle blade making that satisfying hiss through the water, the afternoon air over the lake so still he could hear the sound. As his paddle passed the side of the canoe at his seat in the stern, Hammett drew it free of the water, the resistance from the lake like a lover's gentle tug. Despite the black flies, heaven come to earth as a sunny Saturday in early June.

Softly, he said, "You'd have enjoyed this, Hildy." And she would have said, "Colonel, you speak the truth." Even after Hammett retired from the Army at age forty-two, his wife called him "Colonel," though they got to enjoy precious little of their hard-earned time together. She died in an air crash on her way back from the funeral of an aunt. At Hildy's own wake, a well-meaning neighbor had tried to tell Hammett how ironic that was. The widower had just stared back at the jerk.

It was that or choke the man to death.

Other people had tried calling Hammett afterward, at intervals of two weeks, then a month, then longer or not at all. Couldn't really blame them, he knew. Probably took a lot for a person to pick up the phone, facing what would be an evening sitting across a dinner table from . . . his face.

The landmine had done a job on it, all right. Strictly speaking, it wasn't a landmine, but a Claymore that some Viet Cong had strapped to a tree trunk and triggered by a tripwire. Took out three troopers and his R.T.O., the heavy radio the last was humping absorbing most of the shrapnel but not the piece that caught then-Captain Hammett on and through the left cheekbone. The medics had done what they could, the evac' hospital even more. But you need something to build from, and the shrapnel hadn't left much. Back in the days Hammett still looked at his face in the mirror, it seemed to him that the long-term effect was something like melted wax where the feature should be, causing the left eye to sag downward.

Goddam good thing I don't need glasses. Hate to see the optometrist bending the frames to try and line up the lenses.

After Hildy's funeral, Hammett had grieved for over two years. What seemed like a reasonable period, but wasn't long enough. Not by a mile. He'd used the "surviving-spouse" settlement the lawyer had gotten him from the plane crash to move back east, picking Maine for the smallmouth bass fishing, and the serenity, and the . . .

"Privacy," prompted Hildy. "Admit it, Colonel. You wanted to be off by yourself. Where nobody had to see you every day."

And I've got that. For sure.

A puff of wind passed over, making the upright fly rod whistle and sing like the rigging on a sailboat. Hammett had used a thin, metal broom-holder and some Velcro strip to fashion a frictiony little clip that secured the rod vertical at its cork handle just north of the reel. Screwed the clip right into the thwart of the canoe, which he knew would offend a purist because the boat was a beautiful, cedar lapstrake, naturally stained a deep, nicotine-yellow both inside the hull and out. But aside from the clip, Hammett babied the caned-seat canoe, taking care not to crash it into rocks or scrape it along the gravelly bottom of the lake's shallows. He even put the ballast rocks (that had to ride in place of a passenger up-front) in a black, plastic battery box with side handles, so he could lift the extra weight from the hull without scratching the finish.

Then the puff of wind steadied and quartered to the northwest, blessedly keeping the black flies at bay. Might make casting a little difficult, though, unless I get in the lee of the far shore.

Looking that way, Hammett spotted a couple of boys, fooling around with diving masks and fins at the water's edge. The lake was clear enough, the snorkeling ought to be pretty good (if a bit cold), though these boys didn't have "snorkels," too. Hammett had liked snorkeling before the Claymore day, but thereafter, the left side of his face couldn't take the pressure of the mask's rubber. And so he'd given up that endeavor.

Among others.

Drawing closer to where he'd pass the boys, Hammett could see them a little more clearly now. One was maybe eight or so, with sandy blonde hair that couldn't seem to make up its mind what color it would be when he grew up. The other boy was a year or so older, his hair more brown, maybe what the younger one's had to look forward to. Both were skinny, the meager flesh stretched over loose-boned frames, but there was something in the way the younger one canted his head that made him seem the leader of the pair to Hammett. You're in the service long enough, you learn to watch for that sort of thing.

"No, Colonel," Hildy would have said. "It's just that you think you know who they are."

And she'd have been right, too. That little point they were swimming off should be about due-downhill through the woods from a ramshackle farmhouse, the name "PEELE" on the side of its rural mailbox. The house kind of slumped at the head of the L-shaped lake road which took a right-angle turn at its foot to service Hammett's and three other cottages. Or "camps," as Hammett had come to realize Mainers called any lakefront properties. Driving by the Peele place, he'd occasionally seen a woman—getting out of an old station wagon or tending the flowerbeds—but no man. Of course, Hammett had never tried to call on the people there, either.

Thanks to the "privacy," don't meet many new folks anymore. And just as well.

The canoe was drawing even with the boys now, maybe fifty yards away. Close enough to be sure it was the two from the farmhouse, even to see the brown-haired one had a purple mask, the sandy-haired one a yellow. That sandy, younger one reminded Hammett of an Australian lieutenant he'd known in-country.

Back when I was a captain. Wonderful guy around the Saigon bars—"Here, have another pint, mate?"—and I'd started to like him. Until I noticed there was something off about the guy. The way he canted his head, too. What was off turned out to be wronger than wrong: the Aussie had caught a six-year-old Vietnamese boy pilfering from their stores. Took a machete to the child, stuck the small, severed head on a post at the entrance to their compound before a superior officer made him take it down.

That was all, too. Just made him take it down and bury it, before any members of the press got wind of the photo-op and arrived with their cameras.

"I don't get it, mate," the Aussie had tried to complain to the American captain. "Proportionate response, right?"

Hammett hadn't thought so.

Shaking off that memory, he eased up on his paddle as the canoe passed the point. Both boys looked toward him, shading their eyes like Indian scouts from the sun behind him. Hammett waved, and the older, darker-haired boy waved back. The other didn't, that younger boy even dropping his shading hand back to join the other, both balled now into fists on his hips.

Raymond Hammett started paddling again. "This distance, Hildy, that brown-haired boy probably doesn't have the eyesight to see my face against the sun."

"Stop waving, you dweeb," said Curt Peele to his older brother.

Dropping that hand to his side, Jeff Peele turned to the boy who was always giving him orders, even though there was nearly two whole years between them. Giving orders like his dad used to before the divorce, which Curt was almost too young to remember. Once in a while their mom would even say Curt reminded her of their father.

When she told them that, though, it somehow didn't sound like a compliment.

Jeff pawed the ground a little with his big toe. "But it's the man who bought the Ward camp."

"So?"

"So, he's like a neighbor, and besides, he waved first."

"Yeah, and you want somebody to see you, waving to a geek?"

Jeff had no answer to the question. Frankly, he wouldn't want anybody to see him doing that, but he also felt kind of sorry for the man, with his face and all. Who wouldn't?

Now that Jeff had obeyed him, Curt was ignoring his older brother again. As usual. "Look at him."

Jeff turned back to the lake. "Look at what?"

"The geek, what the hell we been talking about?"

Jeff strained his eyes, but couldn't see anything special. "What about him?"

"All he does with that canoe is cruise around the lake fishing. Or not fishing. Just grossing everybody out with that geek face of his."

"So?"

"So," said Curt, taking in the little point of land with total scorn, "we want to go swimming and diving and stuff; but we're stuck here."

"Here's not so bad."

"Here's boring."

"So, we can walk someplace else."

"Yeah, right. And get eaten alive by the bugs?"

Jeff took that moment to look down at his leg, swatting a black fly that had landed there. Then he realized there already were three more bites on that same leg, the drops of blood dribbling down from where the—

"Stop messing with those and answer me."

Jeff was afraid he'd missed the question entirely. "What?"

Curt sighed like he was saddled with the dumbest brother in the state. "I said, wouldn't it be cool to go anywhere we wanted to?"

Jeff didn't like the turn this was taking. "Canoes cost too much. Mom said."

"All right. With *his* canoe, we could go all over the lake."

Jeff pawed at the ground some more, his big toe starting to hurt now. "Mom wouldn't like that, and you—"

Curt leaned in toward him, cutting him off. "Yeah, right. And who's gonna tell her?"

Jeff looked down again, realizing his big toe was bleeding, and not from a fly bite.

Lifting the single smallmouth bass he'd kept from the afternoon's fishing, Raymond Hammett left the canoe on the ramp, both paddles inside the hull. Two hand-carved, cedar paddles had come with the boat, seemed no reason not to leave them there as well.

"That's the great thing about Maine, Hildy. You don't have to lock everything up. It's America like she used to be, back in the fifties."

Hammett carried his fish toward the dry sink bolted into a stout maple. He began cleaning the bass quickly and deftly with a Swedish filleting knife—lot homier heft to it than the jagged-edge commando one he'd used in the war. His work today produced a pair of fillets, maybe six ounces each. Skimpy for two, but just right for one with a simple salad and some white wine.

Healthy too, you didn't count the accumulated mercury. But Fish and Game said in one of their circulars that so long as you limited yourself to one smallmouth per week, your own level wouldn't get too high.

Hammett walked up the path through waterfront pines for a hundred feet to the cedar camp. Same wood as the canoe, and same color, too. Old Man Ward had done himself proud building both.

Hammett paused for a moment before washing the fillets at the kitchen faucet. How long before they'll be calling me "Old Man Hammett"?

"If they don't already," Hildy would have said.

Her husband barbecued most things—briquettes rather

25

than gas—but bass was better in a fry pan. Before breading the fillets, Hammett made a salad of Boston lettuce, baby carrots, some smoked cheese diced into cubes, and a tomato. Not a great tomato, but then it was early in the season to have any at all.

Reaching for a canister of breadcrumbs to coat the fillets, Hammett noticed he was running low. After checking the pantry and the fridge, he decided on a drive to the country store in the morning. Coffee, hamburger. Salad dressing, too. And maybe a rib-eye steak, to have with that Zinfandel he'd bought down in Augusta.

Hammett started the smallmouth fillets cooking in the fry pan, thinking about the first time he'd ever tasted red Zinfandel. "Rafanelli" was the name, unfiltered wine from old vines. After his convalescent leave, Hammett and Hildy had been stationed at the Presidio outside San Francisco, and they'd begun driving north to the wine country, stopping once in the town of Healdsburg, where a waiter had recommended this local red with their dinner. After that, Hammett studied up on wine a bit, even subscribing to some of the reviewing magazines. It got to be a joke that if one of the other service couples asked them over to dinner, Hildy would say, "On one condition." And when they'd ask "What?," she'd say, "That the Colonel gets to bring the wine."

Now he laughed a little at that, almost burning one side of the fillets.

A few minutes later and settled in at the dining table, Hammett raised his glass—a nice Beringer sauvignon blanc, $5.99 at that same wine store—and said, "To the lake, to the house, to us."

What he thought Hildy would have liked as a toast, every night.

After Hammett finished dinner and cleaned up the kitchen, there was still a little sauvignon blanc left. He corked the bottle, put it back in the fridge.

Finish the wine on the screened porch after my shower. Maybe hear that owl again, the one with the long, funny call. "Hoo-hoo-hah-*hoo,* hoo-hoo-hah-*hoo*-ah." The last part almost identical to the sound Al Pacino made in that movie, *Scent of a Woman.*

"You mean 'Owl Pacino'?" Hildy would have said, and Hammett laughed for both of them.

This time of year, he showered and shaved at night. Sleep clean, the sheets last a little longer between laundries. Also, you shave in the morning, the insect repellant stings like the blazes. At night you're going to be on the porch, anyway, so you don't need it against the mosquitoes.

Stepping out of the shower, Hammett closed the curtain behind him so the vinyl wouldn't stand wet and begin to mildew. He opened the medicine cabinet and took down the shaving cream from next to the sleeping pills.

Those pills. Hammett had gotten a prescription for them just after Hildy died. Doctor had been real good about it, said they'd last a while. In case he needed one in the future, "if, for example, you should suffer a 'flashback.'"

No doctor had to tell him what "flashback" could be like, though. There wasn't a soldier who'd served in-country that didn't flash back to the worst times now and again. But there were good times, too, and you couldn't close the door on everything without leaving in the cold some of the memories you'd want to have come visit.

Hammett lathered his face, the daubing with his fingers not so different from applying charcoal before a night mission, cut down on the reflected glare off pale, bare skin. The beard to the left of his nose was surprisingly patchy

27

after that Claymore day. In the mirror, of course, the sides were reversed, and he sometimes found himself marveling.

For shaving, you still see the skin, but somehow you've learned not to appreciate the face.

"Just as well, Hildy," said Raymond Hammett, drawing the double-edged razor carefully over the left side. "Just as well."

TWO

"You boys still sitting out there?"

"Yes, Mom," said Jeff, looking at his brother Curt, who himself was looking at the road and petting their dog. Fiver—a mixed breed the size of a German Shepherd, bought from the animal shelter for five dollars—was lying in the dust of the driveway. The boys swatted at the flies, but Fiver just blinked them away without bothering to move because moving rarely seemed to help.

Evelyn Dana "E.D." Peele stepped outside the front door. She watched her two sons, same father but different characters. No, different species, almost. Jeff, the older, was more like Fiver than he was like his brother. Or like his dad, Matt.

For which maybe I ought to be grateful, huh?

But E.D. still felt something was wrong. It was a glorious Sunday morning, even with the black flies, yet her sons were just sitting there. "You both okay?"

"We're okay, Mom," said Curt, eyes fixed on the road, hand stroking the head of the one other creature E.D. was sure he loved.

She looked from one boy to the other. Some kind of "son-spiracy," like over the scuba masks. They'd worked on

28

her for almost a month last summer, saying they knew the country store would put them on sale after Labor Day. And the boys proved right, the masks marked down to fifteen dollars each. Curt insisted on the yellow—the "better"— color, Jeff yielding to him and taking the "dorkier," purple one. The fins were only ten for the pair, but E.D. had drawn the line at snorkels. No, she'd read in the *Kennebec Journal* about a little girl who'd drowned using one on a coastal lake. Seen the news photo of the mother, too.

E.D. shuddered. No photo like that of her was going to be in the paper, not if she could help it.

Though, truth be told, the masks and fins were worth the money I paid and more. Keep the boys occupied when they'd most miss having a father around them. Not that I much miss having a husband around. Matt's kind of husband, anyway.

Most of the time.

E.D. hugged herself as Fiver rolled over. Another father-substitute. Show the boys some of the responsibility they should have—

The dog heard it before Curt did, and Curt before Jeff, she could tell by their heads moving. Car coming up the road from the lake.

Raymond Hammett approached the house he thought the two snorkelers without snorkels called home. Through the windshield of the Jeep Wrangler—"The Colonel likes to stick with a vehicle he knows," Hildy would say—Hammett examined things a little more carefully. "Ramshackle" might give the wrong impression, he decided. The Peele place looked okay in a cosmetic, landscaping way. Flower-beds tended, lawn mowed and raked before it got lost in the surrounding brush and tall grass. But the paint was peeling, and the roofline sagging, and a few shingles were missing in spots where Hammett suspected a man would've replaced each as it got pulled off by wind or storm.

A man. "Colonel, mind your own business, now," said his wife's voice inside his head.

Hammett slowed as he approached the house, as much not to kick up dust from the dirt road as to look more closely at the people in the front yard. Two boys in shorts and sneakers were sitting by a fair-sized male mongrel. Them for sure, too. Look at the way that younger one—the "Aussie"—cants his head. Body language, best identification system there is, at any distance.

Their mother stood framed by the doorway, whisking one hand at a fly. Sturdy woman, but a very feminine gesture. Wearing blue jeans and a print shirt—blouse, Hammett corrected himself—and watching him. Plain-featured, not a face you'd look at twice.

Then Hammett thought of his own. Not a face you'd look at even once, except to stare maybe, in shock or disgust.

The Jeep had slowed so much, the dog started to roust up, woofing at it. The Aussie boy took hold of the mongrel's collar, and Hammett noticed a chain around a big tree. Probably for tethering the dog when the people were all away or inside for the night.

Then the woman waved. Must recognize the car, know who it belongs to, but she isn't turning away. Instead, she's waving. The brown-haired boy, too. Even the younger one.

Raymond Hammett waved back, thinking as he passed the house that the Aussie was smirking a little.

"Poor man," said E.D. to the Jeep's rooster-tail of dust.

Curt muttered from the corner of his mouth. "Geek's more like it."

"Curt, I'll not have you talking that way about anyone, especially somebody as admirable as that Mr. Hammett."

"What's 'admirable' about being a geek?"

"He is not a geek." E.D. let her voice settle down a register. "No one is a 'geek,' period. And his wound comes from the war. Mr. Hammett fought for his country, not like your . . ." Their mother's voice trailed off, but not in time.

"Like our what?" said her younger son, as though he really didn't know.

"Never mind." This attitude of Curt's, the reason I'll have to leave the office early on Tuesday, attend that parent-teacher conference.

But, first things first, "You boys want to take a drive somewhere today?"

Before Jeff could speak, Curt said, "No, thanks, Mom. We're going diving."

E.D. looked at the poor dog, now rolling in the dust against the flies. "Take Fiver with you, let him get some water relief from the bugs."

"Can't," said Curt, tugging Jeff up.

E. D. Peele thought her older son looked a little reluctant, but she also knew he'd never resist his younger brother's decision. "Be careful," was the last thing she said to them as they headed with their mask and fins across the road and down through the woods.

THREE

"Hildy, you'd have loved this place, too."

Raymond Hammett made his way along the aisles of the

31

country store, a bit of everything on the shelves and walls around him. Foodstuffs, hardware, sporting goods—including some snorkeling masks. Even a bulletin board that had index cards tacked to it for "WANTED TO SWAP," "LOST-AND-FOUND," and "CAR-POOLING."

Hammett carried one of those wire-handled baskets on his forearm. Getting the steak and hamburger last, he went up to the counter, where a nice but stringy-haired teen-aged girl was just finishing up with another customer. The cashier's name was "Tessa," Hammett knew, and she had a stringy-body too. Not at all like the woman back at the Peele . . .

Hammett was shaking his head (before Hildy could prompt him) when Tessa turned his way and flinched. Poor girl, she always did that, and there wasn't a thing he could say that would make a difference, because he'd tried everything he knew. And Hammett knew also that he couldn't blame her.

Tessa mustered a smile. "Will you be needing anything else today, sir?"

Hammett thought briefly of all the things he "needed," but instead said, "No. Thank you."

The girl said "Super," yet never once lifted her stringy-haired head until she had to count out his change.

"This is so wicked awesome."

It was Curt who had spoken, but Jeff had to agree. The wind through their hair as they paddled furiously, Curt in the stern clunking the side of the canoe only once in a while now, and Jeff, with slightly longer arms, clearing it every time. There was a great sensation of going fast without noise, like coasting down a long, paved hill on a bike. Even the interior of the canoe was kind of cool, his shoes and mask and fins resting on all this polished wood in funny shapes, the way National Geographic showed a whale's ribs on television.

Jeff noticed the bow of the canoe started to point toward shore, near where they usually went swimming. "We going in already?"

"Just so's I can pee."

"Do you think we should go some slower?"

"No," said Curt.

"But what if there're rocks or—"

They banged into something that made the whole canoe vibrate. Jeff tried in the next few seconds to remember if he heard a crunch sound, like they'd broken the outside. "So now what?"

Curt said, "So now we go around the thing."

They used the paddle blades to push off whatever the problem was, producing a screechy, scraping noise. Curt made the canoe move in a curve, and they got to the sandy shore without any more problems.

And without going so fast.

Jeff got up from his caned seat first, the canoe tipping some, the way it had when they first got it in the water. They couldn't quite beach the bow without him having to wade a little, which was why his shoes were off and Curt's were still on. After Jeff went over the side, he reached for the front of the canoe to pull it up on shore, and the older brother didn't like what he saw.

"Uh-oh."

"What's the matter now?" said Curt.

"The front of this. It's all, like, mushed in."

"So? It's not leaking or anything, right?"

"No. But the man's going to be able to see we screwed it up on him."

"How's he gonna see that?"

Jeff looked at his younger brother. "When he comes down to his dock and looks at it."

"This isn't his dock, dork-brain."

"I mean, after we take the canoe back there."

Curt just shook his head.

"Hey," said Jeff, "we are taking it back, right?"

"You are such a dweeb."

"What?"

"While I take a pee, you're gonna get some brush, cover the canoe up like the Indians did. That way, we can come down here and use it any time we want."

Jeff didn't say anything.

"It's ours now," said Curt, striding up into the woods like he owned the lake and everything around it.

Jeff stood there for a minute, then took his stuff out of the canoe and set his mask by a tree while he put on his shoes.

Trying to swat the black flies headed for his legs. And trying to think, too.

Raymond Hammett watched the sun setting over the far ridgeline. All afternoon, he'd puttered around inside the camp, where the bugs weren't a problem. Once the sun was low, the black flies stopped flying, and you could go out for a nice, Sunday evening of casting in the lingering daylight.

Carrying his fly rod and plastic tackle box, Hammett was almost to the water's edge before he registered that the canoe was gone. He stopped cold, forcing down his anger and looking around for what the ground could tell him.

Footprints. Sneaker treads, from the pattern of them.

Smallish for a man, though. And, you looked a bit closer, two pairs were involved, one a little . . . bigger than the other.

Had to be.

"No," Hildy would have said. "Just 'could be.' No real proof it was the same two boys."

Swallowing the anger rising in his throat, Raymond Hammett marched back up the path to his camp.

FOUR

Turning from the kitchen range, E. D. Peele said, "You boys were gone a long time."

"We got a lot done, though." Curt winked at his older brother.

"A lot of diving you mean?"

"Yeah, Mom," said Jeff, dropping his fins outside before stepping through the door.

"But where's your mask?" she said.

Jeff was transfixed for a moment, then looked down at his empty hand.

Curt said, "Uh, we must've left it down by the lake. The bugs were some fierce."

"Well, you can get it tomorrow."

"Tomorrow?" said Jeff, a forlorn tone in his voice.

"Yes. After school."

"Why not now, Mom?"

"Because dinner's almost ready." E.D. gestured toward the oven. "Tuna casserole, and I want us to eat while it's hot."

"But, Mom—"

"No 'buts' about it. We're eating, period." She turned back

to the range. "Besides, your mask'll be safe. Who'd steal it?"

E. D. Peele couldn't understand why that simple observation would make her younger son burst out laughing so hard he had to run from the kitchen.

"State Police, Trooper Outlaw."

Raymond Hammett stared for a moment at the telephone, wondering how much abuse the woman must take for having a name like that in police work.

"Hello?"

"I'm sorry. My name's Raymond Hammett, and I'd like to report a theft."

"Of what item, sir?"

"My canoe."

"Your location?"

He told her.

"And phone number?"

Same.

"Now, this canoe, can you describe it?"

He did.

"And the approximate value of the item, please."

"I don't know, but given how old it is and the great care the former owner took to keep it in condition, the 'item' probably could be fenced as an antique."

"Well, we don't know yet whether that's likely."

"How do you mean?" said Hammett.

"Lots of times, it's just kids."

"Kids," thinking again of the footprints and the house at the head of the camp road.

"Yeah. Especially the younger ones. They'll boost a canoe like their teen-aged brothers would a car, go joyriding for a while. Then they leave it someplace on the lakeshore."

"You really think that's what happened here?"

"Well, sir, I don't know for sure. But I guess I'd suggest you try looking for the canoe before I do a real formal report on the incident."

"Thank you."

"Uh, and sir?"

"Yes?"

"I were you, I'd wait till the morning light to go looking."

"Thank you," said Raymond Hammett as neutrally as possible before hanging up.

"You think maybe we should sneak down there tonight?"

Jeff floated the question from his one position of honor, in the top bunk of their bedroom. Floated it softly, so their mother in the next room wouldn't hear. And phrased it in a way that might lead Curt to respond positively to the implied suggestion.

The same way Jeff used to ask questions of their father.

"No," came the answer from the lower bunk, sharply.

"But what if—"

"Yeah, right. The geek's going to come out in the dark, trying to find his canoe?"

"Maybe."

"No 'maybe' about it, dweeb. He's not. Probably doesn't even know it's gone yet."

Jeff heard Fiver clanking the chain outside their open window, woofing a little, like some small creature was in the brush nearby. "Curt, the guy goes fishing like every afternoon."

"Hey, we see him once in a while. That doesn't mean he goes out at night, too."

The chain noise stopped. "I don't know."

"And besides, even if he does start looking for the thing, how's he gonna find it, the way we moved all those branches and stuff?"

"I don't know," repeated Jeff, lamely, feeling again like he was talking with his father.

"Yeah, right. You *don't* know, dork-brain." Curt rolled over in the lower bunk. "So quit bothering me and just go to sleep."

Jeff tried hard to do that. He really did.

FIVE

Raymond Hammett thought to himself, This is a lot like walking through the bush in-country.

Before leaving his camp on Monday morning, he'd bloused the tops of his pants into his hiking boots against both black flies and deer ticks. Then he'd selected a long-sleeved, tight-buttoned shirt and the long-billed baseball cap he used for fishing on sunny days. Dousing every exposed area of skin with insect repellant (which somebody had once told him didn't really "repel" insects; it just masked your human scent so they thought you were a tree), Hammett began walking the perimeter of the lakefront. Past an occasional summer house already opened for the season. Past many more that were still shuttered, the owners figuring there was little sense in driving a couple hundred miles only to be hot lunch for the bugs.

But it was pushing through the still-undeveloped parcels along the water that reminded Hammett of being back in Vietnam. He'd always been an officer there, some poor enlisted man having to walk point. Everybody needed to know what to look for, though. The tripwires would be attached to mines and other booby-traps. What you did was cock and recock your head, not moving the rear foot till the front one was planted safely. You shifted your line of sight often enough that way, you might pick up a reflection of moisture on the strand of wire. Or maybe even the wire itself.

Or maybe neither, like the morning the Claymore got my face.

But no need to worry about that kind of thing here. Raymond Hammett had to smile. No, aside from the flies and ticks, Maine was safe.

"Except for canoes, Colonel," Hildy would have said, and her husband stopped smiling.

Bouncing along the potholed road in the school bus, Jeff Peele made sure the books in his knapsack hadn't tipped over and squashed his peanut-butter-and-jelly sandwich, like they once did. Then, quietly, he said, "I don't think we should tell people about the man's canoe."

Next to him on the bench seat, Curt glanced toward his older brother but sideways, like what Jeff had to say really wasn't worth a full-face look. "You mean *our* canoe?"

For the rest of the ride, Jeff didn't say anything else to Curt.

It turned out to be easy to spot. Once you'd been searching for a while, learning the feel of these particular woods.

The leaves were turned the wrong way.

Raymond Hammett circled the little glade of oaks behind a notch of sandy beach between the rocks. "Right about where I saw those boys from the Peele farmhouse swimming," he reminded Hildy.

Hammett went into the glade, stopping by one of the

branches that angled unnaturally away from the sun. When he grasped the branch, it wanted to come away in his hand, revealing a swatch of stained cedar beneath. Thirty seconds later, he'd uncovered the whole canoe and finished his quick inspection of her.

Both paddles were under the thwarts, but her bottom was deeply scratched and her bow worse gouged, like they'd run the little lapstrake beauty into a rock at ramming speed. Mistreated her, and badly.

Then Hammett began to look for sneaker treads. The ground was too leafy, though, and besides, even if he matched a track by the canoe to the ones by his boat ramp, that wouldn't necessarily prove those two Peele boys were the thieves.

"No," Hildy would say. "Just means the thieves were both places, Colonel. Which you already knew."

Hammett shook his head, and that shifting of view let him catch the reflection of sunlight off something made of glass, closer to the lake. Walking over, he knew what it was before he could formally make the thing out.

Stooping, Hammett examined it. No snorkel, and purple, but was it the same mask he saw the older boy with Saturday afternoon? He closed his eyes, tried to picture it. The memory wasn't clear enough.

"Not enough to go confront them, Hildy."

Then Raymond Hammett had an idea.

SIX

"It's not here."

"You sure?" said Jeff.

Curt Peele looked at his brother with all the righteous

contempt an eight-year-old can manage. "Are you retarded, too?"

Jeff didn't see how answering that would help, so he just nudged one of the dead oak branches with his shoe. "Paddles, too."

"What?"

"The paddles. They're gone, too."

"Of course they are, dork-brain. How do you think that geek got back to his camp?"

Jeff never understood why his younger brother always had to answer him with a putdown. Even when they were div—

"Aw, no. No! Mom's gonna—"

"Now what?" said Curt.

Jeff still couldn't speak for a moment.

"You look like you're gonna cry, dweeb."

"My . . . mask. It's not here, either."

Curt looked southward, though the old Ward camp was a good mile from where he stood. "That geek stole our canoe back."

"And my mask."

"Come on," said Curt, repeating himself as he stomped through the woods up toward their house.

Behind the counter of the country store, Tessa flinched. Damn, I wish I wouldn't do that to him, poor man.

He said to her, "Do you have any chain?"

Tessa tried looking him in the eye. The right eye. The left side of his face wasn't so bad, that way. "You mean like a length of chain?"

"Right."

"Sure. We got them on big rolls back there in hardware. You're welcome to take a look, but maybe if you told me what you have in mind . . . ?"

"I need to secure my canoe."

"Secure it? Well, then, we got this braided cable, comes all wrapped in like clear plastic tubing."

"Cable. So, it's lighter?"

"And some cheaper, too," said Tessa. "What we can do for you is form like a little loop at both ends. This vise-thing you pound with a hammer makes those loops pretty much impossible to pull out. Then you can run one loop and the cable through something on the canoe and around a tree trunk. After that, just hasp the two loops together with a combination lock. You following me, sir?"

"I think so. What would it take for somebody to cut through the cable, though?"

"Cut it? Oh, gee, bolt-cutters, I'd guess. Or maybe a hacksaw, only they'd have to cut each one of those braid wires in the cable, and that'd sure take a while."

"I don't think I have to worry about that."

"Oh, so you just need something to kind of keep honest people honest?"

Tessa thought the poor man looked at her like he couldn't understand what she meant.

Her back to the kitchen door, E. D. Peele swung her head around just enough to see who it was coming into the house. "Well, where were you guys, diving again?"

Curt said, "He wishes."

Jeff swallowed hard. "I think some—"

"He lost his mask, Mom."

E.D. turned all the way from the sink this time, grabbing for a towel. "Oh, no." She looked at her older son. He just stared at the floor, so depressed.

E.D. thought about the situation. Admit it: if Curt lost

42

his mask, you really wouldn't feel so bad. But you'd have to replace it, because otherwise he'd just take Jeff's. And diving's one of the few things they do together that your older son seems to enjoy.

"Don't worry, we'll take care of it," said his mother, trying real hard to figure out just where she could squeeze fifteen dollars from this month's cash budget.

As Tessa doled out his change for the cable and lock, Raymond Hammett put the purple diving mask on the counter. "By the way, do you sell these here?"

The cashier picked the thing up by the head strap, making the face part twist a little. "Don't know much about them, but it sure does look like one of ours, yessir."

"I found it while I was taking a walk along the lake."

"With the flies and all? You're a brave man."

Hammett saw Tessa flinch again, probably thinking she'd reminded him of his wound. And she had, but somehow he got over it almost before he realized it.

Hammett took out the three-by-five index card he'd block-printed back at his camp. "I wonder if I could post this on your board over there?"

Tessa read the note. It said, "FOUND: DIVING MASK NEAR LAKE. IF YOU CAN DESCRIBE IT AT THE COUNTRY STORE, YOU CAN CLAIM IT."

She looked up, into his right eye. "Sure. You want me to hold on to the mask, then?"

"If you would."

"No problem."

"Just one other favor?" said Hammett.

"Yessir?"

"I don't want any credit for finding the thing, but if somebody does claim it, could you call me?"

A kind smile. "Sure. That do it?"

A smile back. "I think it will."

Curt told Jeff he wanted to wait till it was good and dark, so they did.

"You ready?" said the younger brother from the lower bunk.

Jeff nodded in his.

Curt sighed. "I said, you ready?"

"Guess so."

"You got Mom's flashlight?"

Jeff said, "You think we're gonna need it?"

"It's night out, dork-brain. How're we—"

"There's a full moon."

Curt stopped. His older brother never interrupted him, but—looking out the window—Jeff was right. For once in his life.

"Okay, so no flashlight," said Curt. "Just slow us down, anyway, and one more thing for you to lose."

"I just thought of something else."

"Now what?"

"Fiver's gonna bark outside when he sees us, and Mom'll wake up."

"No, she won't."

"Sure she will."

"Mom's not gonna wake up because Fiver's not gonna bark. He's our dog, retard. He knows us."

Jeff couldn't think of a comeback to that.

"All right," said Curt, swinging his legs out over the edge of the bunk. "Let's go and get that buck knife Pa left here."

"Knife?" Jeff pictured it, his father unfolding the blade till the whole thing was almost a foot long. "What do we need that for?"

"You think even that geek's so stupid he's not gonna have our canoe tied up this time?"

Our canoe.

"Well, do you?" said Curt.

Jeff didn't answer, but no, he didn't think Mr. Hammett in the old Ward camp was stupid at all.

Sitting on his screened porch in the silence and the dark, Raymond Hammett was swirling the remainder of Monday night's wine around the inside of his glass when he heard the sound of rustling branches down near the boat ramp.

That's what they always told him in Officer Basic before he went overseas, one of the few things that proved to be true there. If I see you before I hear you, then I'm probably dead, because you've managed to sneak up on me. But, if I hear you before I see you, then probably you haven't seen me yet.

And that means you're the one's not going home walking.

Hammett set the glass down and waited until the rustling sound near the water gave way to an abrupt, scraping noise. Then he eased up from his chair and out his porch door.

"It's, like, some kind of . . . plastic rope."

"What is?" said Jeff, crouching down by the boat ramp.

The other voice grew snotty. "I can't see it good enough without the flashlight you said we didn't need."

And I don't need this, thought Jeff. Uh-unh.

Curt said, "Let's see if I can cut the plastic with Pa's knife."

The older brother heard the younger one snap open the blade. Loud enough to carry across the lake, much less a

45

hundred feet or so to the camp. Jeff forced himself to look up the hill, but still didn't see any lights on inside, even with the gritty, sawing sound now coming from beside the canoe. Might be Mr. Hammett's away for the evening, like out to dinner or something.

I wished we'd checked to see if his Jeep was—

"Damned thing!" said Curt.

"What?"

"The geek's got some kind of wire under the plastic. Knife won't cut it."

So, forget about the canoe. "You see my mask?"

"He wouldn't keep it down here, dweeb. That face of his, how's that geek gonna use a mask for diving?"

At the next noise, Jeff nearly jumped out of his skin.

Hammett lowered his hands from his mouth. Their father must have been gone from the scene before teaching the boys how silhouettes stand out in moonlight. Or how voices carry through quiet woods.

No need now for the country store to telephone me, either. Pretty clear who the canoe thieves are.

Raymond Hammett put both hands to his mouth and made the call again. Grinning a little, liking the way his "Owl Pacino" echoed in the night.

Curt said, "It's just a bird, retard."

"I don't think so."

"What do you mean?"

Jeff tried to swallow, couldn't. "You ever hear an owl on the ground?"

The noise came again, closer this time.

"Look," said the older brother, "it's not right to cut the man's chain."

"It's not a chain, dork-brain. I told you, it's—"

A third time. The same noise, but much closer.

Jeff straightened up. "I'm getting out of here."

Curt almost shouted at him to wait, until they both heard the sound again and a flapping noise, like the biggest winged predator in the world was coming for them through the bushes.

And then they both began to run pell-mell along the lakefront.

Raymond Hammett had to clamp a hand over his mouth. It would have been good to laugh, but he wasn't sure the boys were out of earshot yet.

And Hammett had heard enough to tell that the older one was leaning to good, the younger to bad. "Both need a lesson, though, Hildy. And the mask business might not be enough to teach them about . . . proportionate response."

Hammett waited a little longer, then climbed back through the undergrowth toward his driveway. He'd make better time on the road, and there was no need to follow them, since he knew exactly where they were headed.

Her heart in her mouth, E. D. Peele wasn't sure why she was suddenly awake until Fiver's barking registered. Probably just a possum or a porcupine, because he'd already learned the hard way about skunks.

Then she heard the sound of something coming through the woods. Running, and running hard.

Turning to her night table, E.D. opened the drawer the boys were never to touch. Took out the handgun and checked the load, the way Matt always told her to do.

One of the many things he'd always told her to do.

Fiver was near frenzy now. Over the sound of the

47

barking, E. D. yelled toward her sons' room. Got no answer.

And vaulted out of bed faster as a result.

Jeff was afraid his lungs would explode. He tried to remember feeling that way before, just running up the hill from the lake. In the past few years, he'd done that run a hundred times—a thousand, maybe. But he couldn't ever recall being so out of breath, or the tree branches reaching out to whack at him, or the roots reaching up to trip him.

The dog's good, thought Raymond Hammett, lying in the tall grass. But she's even better.

The spunk of her, framed by the doorway. Enough presence of mind to think of the gun and the outdoor floods, though she did forget how the interior lamps would backlight her, wearing nothing but a tee-shirt that barely reached her thighs.

Unh. "Sorry, Hildy," Hammett whispered to himself, the dog going from noisy to nuts, straining at that chain.

Then the two boys breached the woods and came onto the road. Chests heaving, feet stumbling, they had to be scratched up pretty bad, too. Their mother sounded at least as relieved as mad, though Hammett doubted her sons could appreciate any ratio in the mix.

"What in the world are you doing out here?"

Aussie, the younger boy, spoke first. "Tried . . . to find . . . Jeff's . . . mask."

"I thought you already did that after school today."

Younger again. "It . . . wasn't . . ."

"And why were you running so hard? You could've broken a leg, even your necks."

Now the older. "Sorry . . . Mom."

"Well, come over here, let me look at the both of you. And don't ever do anything like this again."

"Mom," said the Aussie, "we—"

"—won't," finished the other brother, and Hammett watched their mother seem surprised, as though he'd done something special or new for her.

"It's okay," said the Peele woman, first toward the dog, still straining against the chain. "It's okay," she repeated, this time to the older boy, before shooing both her sons back into the house.

The dog stopped barking, but stayed alert, woofing a little once in a while as his nose tested the wind.

"He senses me, Hildy. Not sure what I am, just something out beyond his reach that he has to treat as . . . threatening."

Then the floodlights went out, and Raymond Hammett got another idea.

SEVEN

Entering the country store Tuesday morning, E. D. Peele yawned. She hadn't been able to drop back to sleep after all the excitement the night before, and getting the boys up and off to school had turned into a real chore. But given the parent-teacher conference on Curt coming up that afternoon, E.D. wasn't sure she'd have time to stop on her way home. And, since even her younger son was apparently willing to risk his skin looking for his older brother's diving mask, E.D. wanted to be sure she had a new one to give Jeff over dinner that night.

If Tessa had any in stock.

Sitting on his deck—well, kind of reclining, really, in a redwood lounge chair—Raymond Hammett began his checklist. Important things, checklists.

"Wouldn't attempt a mission without one, Hildy."

After looking down at the counter by the cash register, Tessa looked up from the red diving mask in the blister pack. "Didn't you buy one of these last year?"

"Two of them," said E. D. Peele. "But Jeff lost his."

"When?"

"Just over the weekend."

The cashier got a coy expression on her face. Nice girl, Tessa, but she could be aggravating, now and then. "E.D., you see the card on the bulletin board?"

"Which card?"

"Take a look. It's all printed out in capitals."

E.D. walked over to the board, then came back a lot faster. "The lake's where he lost it."

"The person found the mask said he wanted somebody to describe it."

Apparently this was going to be one of Tessa's aggravating times. "Like the new one here, only purple."

A coy smile now as the cashier's hand reached under the counter. "We have a winner."

E.D. looked down at the purple mask, feeling a little knot of money worry unravel deep inside. "Tessa, that's super. Who posted the card?"

Even coyer. "Why?"

"So I can thank him."

"How do you know it was a 'him'?"

E.D. tried to keep her teeth from clenching. "Because *a*

minute ago you said, 'he wanted somebody to describe' the thing."

"Well, *he* also said he didn't want any credit for finding it."

"Tessa, please? I'm going to be late for work."

"Okay, okay. It was the man who bought the old Ward camp."

"Mr. Hammett?"

"If that's his name. He just wanted me to phone and let him know if somebody claimed the mask."

"Thanks, Tessa. But don't bother about calling. I'll do it from the office."

"Easier than visiting him, I guess."

"Easier?"

"Account of . . . you know, his . . . deformity?"

E. D. Peele realized that wasn't how she thought of Mr. Hammett's face.

The telephone rang several times intermittently during the morning, but Raymond Hammett ignored it. As with most tasks, there was a right way to compose a checklist, and that was by the application of total concentration. Picture the mission from beginning to end. Even walk through it in your head, so you know what might be needed.

Dark clothes? Check.

Hamburger? Check.

Pills? Check.

Pliers? Check.

Commando knife?

He thought about that last one a little more. Then Raymond Hammett forced his mind to walk through the end of this particular mission, the possible contingencies nobody could eliminate, and he made a tick mark next to "Commando knife," too.

E. D. Peele hung up the telephone in her office. She'd tried three times, once an hour or so, but gotten no answer. Probably out fishing.

Then she considered thanking the man in person. From what I've seen of him, he's certainly impressive despite the . . . Tessa called it a "deformity," but really it's just a wound, and wounds heal. Not perfectly. Thanks to Matt, I can attest to that. But heal they do, and you can move on from there.

I can attest to that as well.

E.D. drifted back to visiting Mr. Hammett—God, he's not so much older than me, I'd call him by his first name, if I knew it. But directory assistance had only a first initial, "R". For "Robert", maybe. Or "Richard"?

Anyway, I can just stop by casually, after work. Tonight, for instance—no. No, I've got to be at Curt's parent-teacher thing. And besides, that might be his supper hour, anyway. So after dinner, then. Tomorrow, say, and with the boys, so that Jeff can thank him personally.

Sure, that's even better. So why didn't I think of visiting before I tried phoning? It's almost a blessing the man didn't answer.

Because, if he did, I wouldn't have an excuse to go see him, now would I?

E. D. Peele found herself smiling in a way she hadn't for quite some time.

"Okay," said Curt on the ride home in the school bus, now not glancing to the side but turning full-face toward Jeff on the bench seat. "What are we gonna do about this geek?"

"He's not a geek."

"All right, all right. But what're we gonna do?"

Jeff said, "I'm thinking on it," but what was really going through his mind was how much last night had seemed to shift things around between his brother and him. Hard to see why, but ever since I kind of cut him off in front of Mom in the yard there, Curt's been the one asking me stuff instead of making me ask him. Or telling me what we're gonna do.

Only problem with that was, Jeff couldn't think of anything *to* do. Especially since whatever might occur to him would probably mean going back to the man's camp sometime, and that scared Jeff more than Curt—or his father—ever had.

"I've got a surprise for you."

It was Jeff's turn to clear the dishes, so he didn't realize she meant him until he turned around, saw his mother with one hand behind her back,

She was smiling, too, like you didn't hardly see anymore. Then out whipped the hand, and Jeff saw what was in it.

"Well, aren't you happy?"

The older brother looked to Curt, who was shrugging in a way their mother couldn't see.

Jeff said, "Where did . . . ?"

"Mr. Hammett found it."

"Mr. . . . Hammett?"

"You know, that nice man who bought the old Ward camp. He found your mask by the lake and left it at the country store."

"He . . . found it?"

"Yes." E.D. couldn't understand why Jeff wasn't

jumping for joy. "That must be why you boys didn't see it. By the time you went searching, he'd already picked the thing up and brought it in to Tessa."

"But why?" said Jeff.

"Why?" This really was strange. "I suppose because he saw the other masks on display there."

"Yeah," said Curt's voice, "that must be the reason, all right."

E. D. Peele turned to look at her younger son. His voice, maybe, but his father's tone, the one the teacher had talked with her about that afternoon. A tone E.D. didn't like, especially when, as now, she didn't understand what Curt meant by it. But Jeff thought he did. And liked it even less.

Raymond Hammett dressed in the dark clothes before putting the pliers in his pocket and the commando knife in its sheath on his belt. Then he examined himself in the bathroom mirror, the watch cap already pulled down over his forehead. Burnt charcoal from a used barbecue briquette had been applied in slashes under his eyes and across the bridge of his nose.

So the pale skin would blend in more with its surroundings, not gleam in the moonlight.

Hammett could feel himself becoming energized. Like the old days. For the first time in years, he had a mission, something to accomplish. Even the edge of risk to it, small though the personal danger might be.

After a deep breath, Hammett reached into the medicine cabinet, took down the vial of sleeping pills, and shook three out into his hand. Dropping them in the pants pocket opposite the pliers, he moved to the kitchen for the freezer bag of defrosted hamburger.

Then Raymond Hammett made his way out into the night.

"He knows," said Curt from the lower bunk.

"I know."

"He gave that mask to Tessa at the country store so she'd tell him who claimed it—"

"—which would also tell him who stole his canoe."

"Our canoe."

"His canoe, Curt. Period."

"What do you mean, 'period'?"

"I mean everything's even," said Jeff. "We took his canoe, he took my mask, and now everybody's got what's theirs again."

"You think the geek feels that way, too?"

"I told you, Mr. Hammett's not a geek."

"All right, all right." Then Curt did something he never, ever did.

He hesitated.

In fact, it was a good count of five before the younger brother spoke again. "Well, do you think he thinks we're even or not?"

If you'd asked Jeff two days ago, he'd have admitted that hearing such an edge of fear in Curt's voice amounted to a good thing. Now, though, the older brother was already more afraid himself than he'd ever admit to anybody.

Than he'd ever been before, for that matter.

The dog barked at his approach. Nothing you could do about it, of course. A good dog'll let the folks in the house know something's wrong outside.

From his prone position in the tall grass, Raymond Hammett watched the floods come on, despite knowing they'd ruin his night vision for a while. That was okay, though.

He had more than a while.

Hammett watched the Peele woman come to the door again, too. Same spunky attitude, though this time without the gun. Maybe because tonight things were happening a little earlier, even if it was full dark already. In civilized places, people tend to measure danger by the clock.

The woman hushed the dog, who hunkered down into that woofing attitude again. Then she turned off the floods, and Hammett waited.

Waited until everything was nice and peaceful.

That's when he took out the freezer bag of raw hamburger, shaped a glob of it like a baseball, and used his left pinky finger to embed one of the sleeping pills deep inside the core of it. Then, holding the ball of meat ("The 'meat ball,' Hildy") in his right hand, Hammett lobbed it like a grenade toward the dozing dog.

The ball landed almost at the mutt's nose. He started but didn't bark, seeming more interested in the hamburger than how it had been delivered. The dog sniffed once, licked twice, then chomped hard, hoisting the chunk of meat up into his mouth and swallowing with benefit of tongue more than teeth.

Raymond Hammett grinned, checked his watch, and settled in to wait a while longer.

"Mom?"

"What is it, Curt?" E. D. Peele called back.

"Everything okay outside?"

"Yes. Fiver probably just heard a porcupine or something."

"You sure?"

"Curt?"

"Yeah?"

"Go back to sleep."

Half an hour, and Raymond Hammett was surprised the dog's snoring didn't wake up everybody in the old farmhouse. *Glad I tried just the one pill first.*

To be absolutely sure, though, he doctored another glob and heaved it toward the dog, actually hitting a forepaw this time. No reaction from him.

Quietly nevertheless, Hammett moved to the dog's side, waiting a full two minutes more before going to work.

EIGHT

"Maybe it was a bear," said Curt the next morning.

"It wasn't a bear." E.D. looked at her younger son, thinking, *That's the sort of worst-case thing I'd expect Jeff to raise instead.* "We all would have heard Fiver trying to . . . We all would have heard something."

Her older son was examining the chain at its end. "Looks like he just broke through it, like." There was a link bent open on the ground. "Twisted this enough, and it let go."

Looking at what Jeff had in his hand, E.D. had to agree with him. "Good bet. Well, they say little kids and dogs always roam along the path of least resistance."

"What does that mean?" said Curt.

"It means downhill or with the wind." To Jeff, "I'm going to call work and school. You two start by going down through the woods toward the lake, and when I'm off the

57

phone, I'll take the road toward the camps. Keep calling Fiver's name."

Her younger son said, "But what if we don't find him?"

There was a whining tone to Curt's voice that E.D. couldn't remember him using before. "Then meet me at the old Ward camp."

"No."

"Yes, Curt. The man might have seen Fiver, but even if he hasn't, at least we can thank him for finding Jeff's mask."

"No!"

"Yes! Jeff, make sure you and your brother get there."

"I will," he said.

Very evenly for him, thought E.D.

"State Police, Trooper Outlaw."

The phrase "closing the circle" went through Raymond Hammett's mind as he identified himself into the receiver. "I believe I spoke to you Sunday about my missing canoe?"

"Yessir," she said. "I believe you did."

"Well, thanks for the advice. I found it."

"Terrific. Appreciate your calling to let us know."

"Oh, one other thing?"

"Yessir?"

"I'm afraid I also found a sick, stray dog on my property. I've tried the family I think owns it, but first the line was busy, then I got no answer."

"Do you want to give me their name, sir?"

"Maybe I'd better. In case they call in, to report the dog missing or something."

There was a slight tension on the other end of the line, like Outlaw had heard something in Hammett's voice she wished could be checked by seeing his face.

Be glad you can't, Trooper, he thought.

Then the officer said, "The family's name, sir?"

"What're we gonna do?"

Jeff glanced sideways at his younger brother as they walked into the woods. "Look for Fiver, what do you think?"

"But you know he took him."

"Then Mom'll find him before we will."

"But what if he killed—"

"Fiver?" yelled Jeff at the top of his lungs. "Fiver?"

"Oh, thank you so much."

Raymond Hammett nodded. Seeing the Peele woman from the road—or even from the tall grass around her yard—didn't do her justice. Not so much a plain face as a strong one, more character in it than make-up on it. And not shy about rough-housing a little with the dog, getting her cheek slurped in the bargain.

"Noticed him moping around late last night," said Hammett, "like he'd eaten something didn't agree with him. I was pretty sure he was yours, so I waited till a decent hour to call. But first your line was busy, then I got no answer. After that, I contacted the State Police about him."

"I'll call them myself, let them know everything's okay." She looked up at Hammett from a kneeling position next to the dog. Looking right at me, too, with nothing off about her reaction. "I also want to thank you, Mr. . . . Hammett, right?"

"That's right. Raymond Hammett."

"What do you go by?"

The retired colonel found he was unprepared for her question but wanted to answer it right. "Your choice," he said, and tried a smile.

59

She smiled back. "I like 'Raymond.' "

"So do I."

That's when they both heard running feet slapping the gravel of his driveway.

Jeff's legs gave him a better stride, so he got to them sooner, though if he'd stopped to consider it, he'd have had to think long and hard to remember another time when he'd beaten his younger brother in a race. Understanding what he saw might take even longer.

There's Mom, getting to her feet from petting Fiver, who's rearing up on his hind legs and waggling his paws like he's begging for food. And there's Mr. Hammett, too, standing close enough to her he could touch a shoulder. Somehow, his face doesn't look so bad up close, like I imagined it worse from the canoe and the Jeep than it really was. And Mom has that smile again, like from when she gave me the mask last night after dinner, only more—

That's when Curt caught up and went by, running hard to Fiver, who started jumping all over him, almost knocking the younger boy down.

E. D. Peele said, "Jeff and Curt, I want you to thank Mr. Hammett for finding Fiver."

"Thank you," said Jeff, thinking, Wow.

"Thanks," said Curt, not thinking anything beyond how glad he was to have Fiver back.

Their mother's face returned to her older son. "And thank Mr. Hammett for finding your diving mask, too."

"Thanks, Mr. Hammett."

"That's all right. I lost my canoe a couple days back, forgetting to secure it at my boat ramp." The man stopped, but not a hesitation. "I know how easy it is to lose something, not to mention how happy you can be, getting it back."

And somehow Jeff knew that was all the man would say about the subject, now or later.

His mother waved a hand. "You boys take Fiver back to the house. I'll be along in a minute, then I'll drop you at school on my way to work."

As they walked up the driveway, the dog running figure eights around and between them, Curt said to his brother, "I can't believe Fiver just ended up there."

"Me neither."

"So, how do we get even?"

"We don't," said Jeff.

"But—"

"Look, Curt. That man was ahead of us all the way, from the minute we stole his canoe on. I'm not ever—repeat, *ever*—doing anything like your stupid stunt again."

"But—"

"No buts. Period."

"Nice-looking boys," said Hammett.

"But a lot to handle alone."

E. D. Peele suddenly looked at him, then flinched and looked down. "I have to get to work, Raymond."

"Before that, what do you go by?"

"Well, my full name's 'Evelyn Dana Peele,' but everybody calls me 'E.D.' for short."

" 'E.D.' or 'Evie'?"

A smile without a blush. "Your choice, Raymond."

Hammett nodded. "Thanks, Evie."

She nodded, too, her next words tumbling out in kind of a hurry. "Look, how about if my sons and I say a proper thanks by having you to dinner tomorrow night?"

"Dinner?"

"Oh, nothing fancy. Maybe chicken, if you like that. And

potatoes and a green vegetable?"

Raymond Hammett felt Hildy prompting him but somehow not talking to him. "On one condition, Evie,"

"What's that?"

"I get to bring the wine."

The two of them smiled and nodded until each felt a little, well, giddy.

Habits

"As my brother Earl would put it," said Joe Bob Brewster from the rocker on his porch, "you're having a day of bad bio-rhythms."

Chief Lon Pray looked up from the window of the town police cruiser at Joe Bob, a paperback book open in his lap and a sleepy hound dog named "Old Feller" twitching his tail under the chair in time to the rocking of his master. Pray couldn't recall ever meeting Joe Bob's brother, who'd moved away before Christmas a year before, but he had been introduced to a couple of the Brewster sisters, and they varied from Joe Bob's carroty hair and stocky frame about as much as one pumpkin from another. Unfortunately, though, issues of family tree—or Yule Tree—weren't what brought Pray back to Joe Bob's dusty front yard for the second time that December morning.

The Chief said, "You still haven't seen anything, then?"

"Uh-unh," from the man in the rocker. "You ain't turned up nothing from all those roadblocks?"

"Nothing like the three that hit the bank, anyway."

"Well," said Joe Bob, "I sure didn't hear them running down behind the house here," flicking his head to the rear,

Three men, in masks, had hit the bank just as it opened that morning. Pray had seen his share of armed robberies while working as a detective on Boston's force up north.

63

But instead of a getaway car with a wheelman out front, these guys had run across the street and down a path through the wooded hillside half a mile above Brewster's ramshackle home. They'd apparently stashed a pick-up truck on a fire road about midway down the slope, because the one witness who'd had the courage to run after them saw it pulling away in the distance when he reached the fire road himself.

Only thing was, Pray had contacted his patrol units within two minutes after the bank manager had called it in, and the county sheriff within two after that. This part of the state—which Pray had found himself just by driving south from Massachusetts one brutal February until he started feeling warm—had paved routes laid out like a grid pattern at intervals of roughly three miles, so setting up roadblocks had been both practiced in the past and easy in the present.

Except that while quite a few pick-up trucks had been stopped, none had contained three men, their handguns, or thirty-six thousand in cash.

"Besides," said Joe Bob, "Old Feller would of tore them to pieces."

Pray tried to refocus. "What?"

Joe Bob seemed hurt, leaning down to scratch his dog between the ears. "Old Feller got wind of three strangers barreling in here, Chief, he would of tore them to pieces."

"Right." Pray tried to keep the sarcasm out of his voice, especially given that he hadn't seen the hound burn twelve calories total in the five months he'd been driving past the Brewster house to the restaurant where he took most of his meals.

"Well, if you do see or hear anything, call the office."

"You gonna go around to everybody else you already talked to once?"

"Can't think of anything else *to* do," replied Chief Lon Pray, putting the cruiser in gear and pulling away.

"Like I told you before, Chief," said Mary Boles from behind her bank desk, a nice holly wreath centered on its front. "It had to be somebody who knew we had extra cash on hand to cover the mill's Christmas bonuses."

Watching Boles—a plump black woman in her forties— Pray fidgeted in the "customer" chair, finding it uncomfortably like the "client" chair in his divorce lawyer's office back in Boston. "Isn't that pretty widely known, though?"

"In town, yes. Even in the county. But robbers from any distance away? I don't see how they could know that today was one of maybe three times a year there'd be enough cash in the vault to be worth stealing."

From Pray's experience, armed bank robbers were the most dangerous felons around exactly because they *didn't* know very much, or plan very well. But, he had to admit, so far these had planned well enough to fool him.

"Mary, can we go over what happened in here this morning?"

"Again?"

"Please?"

"Okay." The manager seemed to compose herself for reciting a particularly distasteful poem. "I'd just opened the front door from the inside, and Eugene was just unlocking his drawer at the teller's cage, when the three men burst in."

"And Josh?"

Boles blushed at the bank guard's name. "In the bathroom, like I told you before."

"Then what?"

"These three men came busting through, like they knew

the precise moment I'd be opening up."

That didn't seem to Pray like much of a clue, but he nodded to keep Boles talking.

"The one man, he stuck a gun in my face and walked me backwards to the vault. The second one rushed past us, and I heard him tell Eugene not to press any button, or he'd die with his finger on it."

"What about the third man?"

"He ordered me to open the vault, which of course was where we kept the money after the armored car dropped it off yesterday."

"And you did."

"Open it? Damned right, with that spooky first man pressing his gun to my cheek." Boles went to rub the spot.

"Mary, the man who stayed on you, he never spoke?"

"No."

Pray always felt uncomfortable asking, much less re-peating, the next question, but it was necessary. "And you don't know the race of that man?"

She shook her head. "Like I said before, they all wore masks and gloves, long-sleeved shirts and pants. But from the voices of the two who spoke, I'd say they were white, so I'm guessing two grains of salt didn't ask a peppercorn to join them."

Pray grinned, getting the impression Boles was trying to make him feel at ease for having to ask the question at all. People rarely behaved so considerately up north when probed by touchy questions.

"Anything else, Chief?"

"Yes."

"What?"

"Eugene."

"I had to send him home," said Mary Boles. "Poor boy was shaking like a leaf."

"How about Josh, then?"

"Mary has her habit of opening on time," said Josh Stukes. "I have mine of relieving myself just then."

Pray blinked at the doughy, fiftyish man with sandy hair. "You couldn't wait till the first few customers came through?"

"Chief, you never worked in a bank around Christmas, let me tell you. There ain't never a time nobody's coming through the doors, so one time's as good—or as bad—as another."

"Give me the sequence again, then, as you remember it."

"All right." Stukes pointed toward the rear of the bank lobby. "I was just finishing, and the flushing kept me from hearing anything. When I opened the door, I got the muzzle of a Ruger forty-four stuck in my face."

"And you knew it was a Ruger . . ."

". . . account of that's what I have next to my bed, for home protection." Stukes pointed again. "This feller with the cannon walked me over to where they already had Eugene and Mary, kneeling on the floor, noses against the wall, and I joined them."

"And that was it?"

"Mary already had the vault opened by the time I got out there, and all I heard was the one feller telling us to all be quiet and nobody had to get theirselves shot. So I was quiet as a little mouse." Stukes suddenly grinned, but not pleasantly. "Speaking of mice, you gonna talk to Eugene again?"

Very evenly, Pray said, "Yes."

"Hope for your sake he changed his undies first."

"Chief, I really don't know what else I can tell you about that frightful experience this morning."

Lon Pray watched Eugene Cornwell cradle a small dog in his arms. The dog was a little mop of brushed hair and cute as a bug, the living room decorated tastefully even without the handsome tree and draped bunting of pine branches.

"Eugene, I won't know what'll help me either till I hear you tell it again."

Cornwell closed his eyes, then opened them. "Very well. I was behind my cage, just opening my cash drawer for the morning and arranging the currency and coins, as is my habit. Suddenly, I heard a stampede sound from the front door. I looked up to see these horribly dressed men barging past Mary, one stomping up to me and pointing a monstrous gun right here." Cornwell's index finger reluctantly left the dog and tapped the owner's forehead over his nose. "They say your whole life is supposed to flash by in front of you? Well, I swear my only thought was, 'Who would take care of Florinda?' " Cornwell's finger returned to the dog, and his forehead dipped to touch the same spot on the dog, who licked appreciatively.

Pray waited a moment. Then, "You did hear the men speak?"

"At least one of—no, *two* of them. But I was too terrified to recall anything they actually said."

After striking out again on race, age, and idiosyncrasies, Lon Pray concluded with, "Anything else you remember?"

"Yes," said Eugene Cornwell, "I remember that the reason I relocated here after college in Richmond was to be able to feel safe in a small town."

"That was still pretty brave of you, Luis."

Pray noticed that his words made the thirteen-year-old in the Atlanta Braves jersey stand a little taller, the wiry dog at his side whuffing.

"Without Mrs. Boles and her bank, we do not have our life here."

Pray knew that the Cortez family had moved in over the store they were running after Luis's parents had decided the migrant life left a lot to be desired. But he also knew how impossible becoming shopkeepers would have been if their loan request had been turned down.

"Luis, can you tell me again what you saw?"

"Sure thing. I am outside our store, washing down the windows from the dust that seems to come during the night from nowhere. I hear the sound of people running, so I turn to see three men crossing the street from the bank, guns in their hands but not shooting at anybody. I drop my window brush into the pail, and I wait until they cannot see me before I run after them."

"You get any kind of look at their faces?"

"Like I tell you before, they have masks over them, and gloves on the hands, too. But the way they run, I think they must be white."

"Why?"

Luis Cortez scuffed at the dust with the toe of his sneaker, causing the dog to stick his nose down there and paw the ground himself. "Because they do not run so very well."

Pray tried not to grin this time. "Go on."

"I am coming after them down the path through the woods. I can hear them in front of me, making noise with their feet and hitting the branches with their arms, maybe, but not talking or nothing. Then I hear the sound of a car engine starting, only when I get to the edge of the fire road, I can see that it is a pick-up. By this time, though, the truck is too far away to see anything but that it is dark in color."

Which was what Pray had put out over the radio to his officers and the sheriff's deputies. Too bad half the vehicles in the county were pick-up trucks, and half of those were blue, black, or brown.

"Nothing else, Luis?"

The boy and his dog pawed at the ground in unison. "Just that when I tell my mother what I did, she slap me hard enough to loosen a tooth."

Chief Lon Pray tried to tell himself that, as a parent so close to Christmas, he wouldn't have done the same thing. Tried and failed.

"Anything?" said Pray.

Edna Dane, one of two uniforms on the roadblock, reached into her cruiser, a short ponytail bobbing against her neck under the Stetson. Coming out with a clipboard, she looked down at it. "We've had fifty-five vehicles so far. Twenty passenger cars, three semis, two buses, five panel trucks. The balance were pick-ups, seven of them 'dark in color.' We called them all in to Dispatch. None with more than two men in it, and no wants or warrants on any of the trucks or occupants."

Pray squinted past the other uniform, standing hip cocked with the butt of a riot pumpgun resting on his thigh. The pavement was otherwise empty in the noonday sun, people either working or doing holiday shopping at the mall ten miles away.

Dane said, "I'm guessing you haven't had any better

70

luck at the other roadblocks or you wouldn't be here with me."

Pray turned to her. "You grew up in town, right?"

"Born and bred, except for four years of Criminal Justice over to the university."

"Answer me this, then. Three men hit our bank at opening, and then run for it instead of driving away. But they get into a pick-up on a fire road barely ten-feet wide that would leave them no way out if just one of our cars—or hell, a county surveyor even—happened to be on the road at the same time. Now, why would a gang risk that?"

Edna Dane smiled, and Lon Pray thought he could see the teenager she'd have been a few years back shining through. "I guess if I knew that, Chief, you'd have stopped fifty-five vehicles this morning, and I'd be worried sick over what you didn't find."

Chief Lon Pray stopped at his own house—a small ranch he rented on the edge of town—to let the dog out, as he did each day around lunchtime. Everybody else in the area just seemed to let their pets roam free during the day, and probably, Pray thought, in time he would, too. But back in Boston, before making detective, he'd tried unsuccessfully to comfort one too many kids kneeling in streets, crying uncontrollably while they in turn tried to will their pets back to life after being hit by passing cars.

And Lon Pray didn't think he could tolerate that happening to Grizzly at this time in his life. In Pray's own life, that is.

After his divorce, most of the marital property—house, car, even their TVs—went to the ex- or her lawyer. Funny, Lon realized as he unlocked his back door. You thought of her as "Sally" in Boston but down here as "the ex-." I wonder if other guys—

Which is when Pray was knocked nearly flat.

"Grizzly!"

The combination German shepherd/Irish wolfhound had already bounded by him, loping around the yard like a race horse around its paddock. Watching him, Pray couldn't stay mad. Grizzly had been the first creature in his life after the divorce, and the chief knew that, in a very basic way, the dog kept him sane.

By the time Grizzly got the pent-up energy burned off, Pray already had washed out his water bowl and filled it with fresh from the tap. Placing the bowl down in the yard, Pray watched Grizzly pad over in that slightly prancing way he had from the Irish side of his family. Lon decided to let the dog run free for another ten minutes, then grab a sandwich-to-go at the restaurant before wracking his brain again on why the robbers had planned their escape as they had.

And why the roadblocks hadn't turned them up.

But meanwhile, he'd take a page from Joe Bob Brewster's book and just sit on his porch, giving himself an early Christmas present by watching Grizzly enjoy the habit of midday exercise.

Driving by the Brewster place, Lon Pray gave a thought to stopping and asking Joe Bob a third time if he'd spotted anything, but the man was holding up a newspaper instead of the usual book, just the carroty hair visible above the top of the paper. Pray thought, Joe Bob must be deep in thought, too, because he wasn't rocking, and Old Feller wasn't in his customary position but rather a full yard away from the chair.

It was five minutes later that Pray, ordering his trademark ham and cheese on wheat with mayo, suddenly registered what he'd seen. Then he put it together with what he'd heard, both as answers to his questions and as statements that had seemingly been offered gratuitously.

And, sprinting to his cruiser, Chief Lon Pray thought he'd figured it out.

Twenty minutes later, the man in the rocker was still holding the newspaper, and Old Feller was still lying a good three feet away.

Which was fine by Lon Pray, now crouched behind a tree rather than sitting behind a wheel.

Pray waited for three minutes more, until he heard the shrill whistle from the back of the house. Then he leveled his Glock 17 and yelled over the sound of breaking glass. "Let that paper fall from your hands without lowering them!"

Old Feller looked first toward Pray, then to the rocker. The paper trembled, but didn't fall from the fingers holding it.

"Be smart!" yelled Pray a little louder. "Nobody's been shot yet. Don't make yourself the first."

From the back of the house, Officer Edna Dane's voice rang out with, "Clear in the house. I say again, the house is clear."

Pray yelled a third, final time, "Last chance to see Christmas."

The paper then wafted down, the hands staying in the air and about even with the carroty hair and the face below it that was almost, but not quite, Joe Bob Brewster's.

Chief Lon Pray said, "Just a day of bad bio-rhythms, Earl."

"Chief, I was beginning to think I'd have to hit you in

the head with a hammer."

Lon Pray watched the Santa coffee mug shake as the man holding it shuddered in his rocking chair. "You did everything you could, Joe Bob. It just took me a while to catch on."

"I mean, I lead with my brother, I flick my head toward the house, I even go on about Old Feller and 'strangers.' But all you do is kind of grin and drive off."

"Joe Bob, I just didn't get what you were telling me till I drove past half an hour ago."

"When my brother Earl was out here."

"Right. I'm guessing he wasn't too pleased with your mentioning his name to me."

"He thought he had a tight plan, all right," said Joe Bob, taking a slug of coffee. "Him and the other two hit the bank, then run down to the fire road. One gets in his own pick-up that they left there, the other runs with Earl almost to my place. Old Feller didn't kick up any fuss when his owner's brother happens to stroll around from the back and ask how I'm doing. Then Earl tells me that him and his 'friend' are gonna be in the house for a few days, waiting for things to cool down before they call their third friend to come back and pick them up."

"Along with the guns and the money."

"The money Earl never showed me, but he sure did wave that gun under my nose, and I knew I couldn't say anything direct-like to you, or he'd have shot through the window there and killed the both of us."

Pray said, "So you tried to tip me, Earl didn't like it, and he came out onto your porch here to impersonate you."

"Which was pretty smart of him, what with my habit of sitting out here." Joe Bob took another slug from the mug. "Only my book wasn't big enough to cover his whole face, so he had to use a newspaper, which I doubt you've ever seen in my hands. That was what tipped you, right?"

"That plus some other things. I wondered how out-of-towners would know about the mill money and the fire road. I also wondered why the third man in the bank never spoke."

"Simple," said Joe Bob around another sip of coffee. "Old Mary Boles might've recognized his voice."

"Another thing was, when I drove by a little while ago, your brother wasn't rocking in the chair like you do."

"Earl tried that, but his rhythm was all off, and he caught Old Feller's tail underneath."

"That's the last thing."

"What is?" said Joe Bob.

Pray gestured toward the sleepy hound. "Old Feller wasn't switching his tail under your chair, and that seemed to me oddest of all."

"Habits."

"What?"

"Habits," said Joe Bob Brewster. "We all have them. Sometimes they hurt, but sometimes they help, too."

Chief Lon Pray found himself nodding in time to Old Feller's tail.

City Life

As the fire engine wormed its way through the stubborn downtown traffic, Jill had to stop walking and wedge her Western Civilization text between her thighs in order to clamp mittened hands over both ears. At least back in Tuckville, the volunteer department could drive fast and had sirens that sounded like sirens, not electronic synthesizers like a Klingon Bird of Prey uncloaking and swooping in for the kill. Too much, you know?

After the noise diminished to a tolerable level, Jill dropped her hands, retrieved her book and continued moving, or trying to move, jostled this way and that by the streams of Tuesday afternoon pedestrians. Freaks with spiky Mohawks, fat mothers and their snot-nosed kids, blue-hairs that ought to be in nursing homes instead of slowing down everybody in the real world, bums panhandling. All of them crowding the sidewalks, the sidewalks that were too narrow because the mayor's sanitation crews hadn't bothered to clear off the last snow, and the weatherman on the radio was predicting another storm for that night. Great. Going to college in Boston was exciting, especially meeting different guys and eating in restaurants and living in your own apartment, even just a studio, but sometimes it left a lot to be desired in the quality of life department.

Like having classes in dilapidated tenements some commission or other designated a "landmark". Believe it. Jill could barely hear half of her professor's lecture, the radiator next to her rattling and banging all the time. That was okay, though. She was just taking the course because of something called a "distribution requirement," like she couldn't just take electives of her own choice the way she did in high school. I mean, really, you'd think they'd treat you more like an adult in college than high school. At least the guy was dreamy in a mature kind of way, like an older brother rather than a younger father, so the seventy-five minutes passed a lot faster than the boring two hundred years of boring history in the boring book.

After class she would like to have gone out with the other kids, but she was due at the health club, and had to beg off. Another bummer, boy, having to work part-time to pay for the tuition her old man couldn't cover. At least she got a job near the school, in this glitzy spa. Jill knew she was sexy, even if her hips were spreading a little from the starchy food in the dining hall. At the interview she thought she'd come on to the owner just right, enough to show she was friendly, but not so much he'd think she was easy. Just right, you know?

The boss, Barney, was a heavyset, balding guy with a moustache. Jill figured he opened a health club just so he could watch girls in leotards do aerobics and Nautilus because the club didn't have space for anything else. Barney was in a hurry to get going, so he reminded her to hustle people out at 10:30 p.m. so she could lock up by 11:00. Yeah right, like she'd be there a minute later than she'd have to be. She worked only Tuesdays and Wednesdays, but sometimes everybody would be gone by 10:15, so she could close down early.

At five, the yuppies started pouring in, the men in their suits that looked like Brooks Brothers but weren't, the women wearing business outfits but with sneakers and leg warmers. Affected and yucky. I mean, how unfeminine can you look if you try? Still, a lot of them, at least the guys, were in good shape, and there were worse things in life than helping some of them fit themselves into the equipment and show them what muscles to use by sense of touch. Especially—

Then she saw Purple Gloves and groaned inwardly. His hair, black and oily, was in a crew-cut, but the hair grew down his neck like an ape's. He wore black gym shorts and a nerdy t-shirt from some California winery and black high top sneakers. But the worst thing were the gloves. They were like handball gloves, or maybe even *bowling* gloves, eeeeewwwww, with padded palms and no finger parts so his fingers stuck out. He'd been in each of the last two Tuesdays and Wednesdays, even though the training manual says you're supposed to work out only every other day. Jill was convinced Purple Gloves was trying to get up the nerve to talk to her, but so far she'd managed to be reading *People* or using the phone every time he'd come close to her. He seemed to know what he was doing on the machines, so at least he didn't ask her for help.

The hours wore on, the yuppies changing over a few times depending on how long they stayed at their jobs to impress their bosses. A wicked-preppie blond guy wearing blue and gold Notre Dame shorts was circling the machines, doing sequential sets of declining weights. That was probably how he built and maintained his great muscle tone, not to mention the endurance even declining sets demand. Around seven some couples came in together. Then the androids who spend most of their time posing in the mirrors rather than exercising. Jill took two new women around, demonstrating the functions and planning a program for them. It was easy work, and once in a while she'd look up, catching Purple Gloves glancing away, as though he'd been copping a peek at her. Great. Why doesn't he just go home?

If he has a home.

By ten twenty, the place was nearly empty, just the two women stretching to warm down, Notre Dame doing one more circling set, and Purple Gloves, kind of using one machine. Kind of, because Jill was sure he was just killing time till the others left, till it would be just him and her. And she didn't see what she could do about it.

The two women changed to street clothes in the locker room and stopped by the desk on their way out. Jill tried to stall them by re-explaining all the facilities and membership options the club offered, the women becoming slightly impatient and finally cutting her off with a "we'll be back" wave.

That's when Notre Dame saved her life.

He strolled over, wiping a towel across the perspiration on his face. "Excuse me, miss, can I see a membership schedule?"

She said, "Sure," handing him the flyer and liking his voice and the way the tendons on his forearms wrestled under the skin.

As he looked at it, he bowed his head closer to her and used the towel to muffle his voice. "That guy. The one in the purple gloves. He a weirdo or what?"

Jill whispered, "He's in here a lot." She gulped. "He scares me."

Notre Dame acted like he was pointing out a line on the form. "How about I do another set? That way you won't have to lock up alone with him."

"Oh, that'd be great! My name's Jill."

"Jill. Mine's Paul. Just nudge me when you're ready to roll."

At 10:30, Jill made a ceremony of announcing everyone would have to finish up soon. Purple Gloves reluctantly went into the locker room. Paul followed him in, but preceded him out, moving over to Jill carrying an Adidas bag.

Jill said, "He's still showering?"

Paul nodded. "It's the weirdest thing. The guy goes through this ceremony of taking off his clothes, then folding them up, then taking things like soap and deodorant out of his bag one at a time and lining them up like little soldiers. I'm telling you, I think he's psycho."

Jill smiled. "That's okay. I feel safe enough. Now."

Paul smiled back. He kept smiling as Purple Gloves came out of the locker room and slouched past them without a word. Jill walked through the place anyway, making sure everything was okay. As she secured the front door, Paul asked her if she'd like a lift home.

"Oh, I'd love one, but it's only a couple of blocks."

"It's still pretty cold out here, and I don't mind."

Paul had a Mazda RX-7, the sharp older model before they yucked it up and made it look American. He even opened and held the passenger side door, closing it behind her. When he got in the other side, she said thanks. He said he liked being polite.

They drove the four blocks to her apartment building, snow flurries swirling and Jill debating how to ask him to come up. As the car drew even with her door, Paul double-parked next to a Toyota. Jill finally just said, "I've got some red wine. If you're interested?"

"Thanks, but this time of night, I'd never find a parking space. And, I've got a big meeting in the morning." Then he leaned over and kissed her. Not particularly passionate, just strong and natural. "Besides, this way we'll both have something to look forward to next time."

Jill got out, liking the confident but not aggressive way Paul had about him. Before closing the door, she bent back into the car, beckoning him toward her. He edged over the stick shift, and she kissed him this time, saying "Thanks for the ride."

"I just like doing things for people."

Jill noticed Paul didn't drive away until she had the downstairs door to her building opened. As he tooted and moved off, an image flickered in the corner of her eye, as though a shadow had moved halfway down the block. She hurried up the stairs and into her studio apartment, slamming both bolts home.

A glass of red wine calmed her down. She poured another, sitting with it in front of the make-up mirror while she lowered her eyelids and repeated, in different registers, "But I don't have a roommate."

Wednesday morning was Jill's one chance to sleep in, except for the weekends, for God's sakes, and she took it. About two, she bundled up for the trek to classes, dreading the thought of Purple Gloves later but hoping Paul might at least stop by.

It was ten degrees colder than Tuesday, three inches of new snow on the ground. As she reached the end of her block, she saw a police car, bubble lights rotating but no siren—thanks for something—blocking the end of the alley behind her apartment building. Some people stood around in two's and three's, talking and craning their necks to see around the top of the cruiser. She walked over to them. Down the alley, some police officers in uniforms and men in brown jumpsuits milled around, their breath coming out in milky clouds as they gestured and joked.

An elderly woman's voice said, "I saw him. When they took him out of the garbage can, *I* saw him. Frozen stiff, he was, but all bent like a jackknife. No hat, no gloves, nothing. A derelict, he was. Must have been a derelict."

Frozen bum. Yuck. Jill trudged on to class.

Jill thought about mentioning Purple Gloves to Barney when she relieved him, but decided against it. Next to tight hard bodies, Barney liked member dues best, and he wasn't about to throw out a paying customer who hadn't really bothered her just because she didn't care for the color gloves the guy wore. It was more than that, and she knew it, but she also knew she'd never be able to make Barney see it, so why bother, you know?

At least things moved along on Wednesday night, the temperature keeping attendance sparse. There was no sign of Purple Gloves, but there was no sign of Paul, either. The Wednesday regulars came and went, a few saying hi and bye to her like she was a parking lot attendant. About 10:00 the place had emptied out, completely, and Jill thought she'd be able to bag it early, I mean good and really early, for once. She went through the locker rooms, nobody left. As she was flipping off the lights, the front door blew open, an icy blast chilling her. She whirled around.

Then she smiled. "Paul!"

"Hi." He wore his business suit tonight, a muted plaid that looked like it might really be from Brooks. He had his hands in the pockets of his overcoat, no Adidas bag tonight. "Still interested?"

She put her fists on her hips and exaggerated her stride, kissing him lightly on the lips. Just enough to whet his appetite for later. "What did you have in mind?"

"How about dinner, then your place. If we wouldn't be disturbing your roommate?"

Jill lowered her eyelids the way she'd practiced in the mirror. "But I don't have a roommate."

"At least not yet." Then Paul grinned ruefully. "I probably should've have thanked that creep last night."

"Well, whatever he was thinking, he didn't come in tonight."

"No surprise there. When I dropped you off, I thought I saw something in the bushes."

Jill's heart fluttered. "You know, I did too, but I figured it was my imagination."

Paul shook his head. "No, no you were right. The guy followed us, or maybe he already knew where you lived. Anyway, I went around the block, slow, and I saw him sneak into your alley."

"No!"

"Yeah. I got out of the car and kept an eye on him. The psycho was nearly up to your building when I caught him from behind. Never even heard me coming."

"You're kidding!"

"Nope. His neck snapped just like I thought it would, too. Kind of weak and sickly, not a real good crack, you know?"

Jill stared at him.

"Jill, you okay?"

"You . . . you killed him?"

"Sure." Paul pulled his hands out of his pockets, tossing two crumpled purple gloves onto the counter. "He was a psycho, would have bothered you forever. They're like that. This is the city, girl. You gotta do things like that for people. Especially people you like the way I like you."

Jill didn't say anything.

Paul said, "So, you feel like Chinese?"

A Debt to the Devil

A Rory Calhoun Story

Don Floyd led me into the Memorial Chapel as though he'd been there before, despite his mentioning on the drive over from the Lauderdale Tennis Club that he wasn't Jewish himself. Given the short time I'd lived in South Florida, much less at the Club, the building we entered looked more to me like a Spanish villa than a funeral parlor, what with exterior walls of yellow stucco and orange humpy tiles on the roof. But around us a lot of grave markers dotted the flat, green meadow.

In a small vestibule, we signed a visitors' log, Floyd—in the deliberate cadence of his native Georgia—introducing me to people as "Rory Calhoun." Back in the early sixties, my mom had developed a permanent crush on that B-movie star, and so after she married his surname-sake and I came along, my given name was a foregone, if embarrassing, conclusion.

Floyd and I began to follow the flow into the chapel proper. It was a big, square room, with rows of oak benches like Catholic pews but upholstered on the seats, a Star of David carved into each end post. A seven-spiked candelabra stood centered at the front of the room, a large-lettered prayer entitled the "Mourner's Kaddish" to one side, a similar mural of the Twenty-third Psalm to the other, which kind of surprised me.

And, underneath the candelabra, a blonde-wood casket. Closed, which didn't surprise me.

Most of the benches were full already. I followed Floyd—eighty-plus and white of hair, but still as spry as he was sharp—into one of the back rows. As we sat, a woman moved with purpose toward a podium near the Kaddish mural. Identifying herself over the microphone as a rabbi, she announced she'd be reading the Twenty-third Psalm first in Hebrew, then in English. Tuning out the initial version, I began to wonder exactly why I was there.

You see, I'd gotten a college degree before going on the professional tennis circuit. After a few years of touring, however, a chronic knee problem and a mediocre first serve relegated me to satellite tournaments, especially those on clay, where stamina and strategy could carry a player past the first round. During the stretches I couldn't play, I'd apprenticed myself to private investigators for the day-labor money they paid. In fact, I'd just gotten my full Florida investigator's license, though I didn't understand—

Floyd nudged me in the ribs. "Rory?"

That's when I realized the rabbi was now reciting the psalm in English, most of the people in the chapel joining in. I mouthed the words, feeling strangely reassured by the chorus rising up in honor of Solomon Schiff, a man I'd seen on the courts at the club but only barely met.

After we all finished, the rabbi gave a short, thoughtful eulogy for "Sol," noting that he wasn't exactly a regular at "Shabbat" services, but still supported his faith in tangible ways. Then she invited any who wished to share a "remembrance" to succeed her at the podium.

A man who turned out to be the publisher of *Florida*

Tennis magazine made his way there. He spoke with humor and grace about Sol Schiff's career as a college champion and solid amateur before the era of open tennis began with Rod Laver at the Longwood Cricket Club. Then he toted up Schiff's long history with the U.S.T.A.—the United States Tennis Association—and Seniors' Sectional and National Tournaments.

A few members of our club followed, including Don Floyd—its unofficial "mayor." All recounted different anecdotes about playing with Schiff or instances of kindness the decedent had shown to people over the years. The phrases most repeated were "fair opponent," "man of his word," and "tough negotiator."

I was kind of surprised no family spoke, then realized that a man in his seventies like Solomon Schiff might not have had any direct survivors. But as a woman in her forties moved to the podium, a hush fell over the room.

Floyd leaned into me a little. "She's the one who wanted you here today."

The woman identified herself as Naomi Schiff, Sol's niece. Her curly hair was black, only a few strands gray. When she began speaking, you could hear sniffling and outright sobbing for the first time during the service. Schiff herself kept swiping a hankie at her eyes, but the voice was strong and clear.

And more than a little angry.

"My uncle was known to all of you, but he was loved by me. After my father died, Sol took me in as his own. He fed me, he educated me, he helped me finance a business of my own up in New Jersey, where we lived until Sol moved down here permanently twenty-two years ago. At every stage of my life, there was a step where I would have faltered if he hadn't taken my hand in his and led me the right way. Though he never married and had no children of his own, Sol was everything anyone could ever have asked for in a parent. Only now he's been taken from me. From all of us."

Schiff gripped the edges of the podium with both hands, bringing her lips very close to the microphone, although she spoke her next words most softly of all. "As some of you know, my father . . . committed suicide. I made my uncle promise then that he'd never do that to me. Well, I'm the one making a promise now." She turned to the casket. "Uncle Sol, I will not rest until the person who killed you is strapped into Florida's electric chair."

Don Floyd leaned into me again. "That's why she wants to hire you."

Naomi Schiff said, "You look more like Tom Selleck than William Conrad."

Stars of the television shows "Magnum, P.I." and "Cannon." "Is that a compliment?"

"Not really." She shrugged. "Selleck was good-looking, but Conrad gave the impression he was just good."

Schiff and I were walking back from the graveside toward the Memorial Chapel. The services over the coffin were mercifully brief, workers in tan jumpsuits and wraparound shades lowering it into the ground via green straps attached to a perimeter frame of chrome. Some mourners, Don Floyd included, used a small shovel to take handfuls of pale-colored earth from a wheelbarrow and sprinkle it into the hole before the workers began disassembling the frame and straps for the next person needing them. Then Floyd went back to his car so Schiff and I could talk by ourselves.

We reached a little glade in the cemetery with half a dozen markers and a polished marble bench that read

"Clarstein" on the edge of its seat. Schiff said, "Why don't we sit? I somehow don't think the Clarsteins would mind."

"All right."

Settling onto the stone, she smoothed the black dress down over her thighs almost to the knees. "I've never done this before."

"Talked with a private investigator?"

"Yes."

I didn't want to blow Don Floyd's cover. "I'm assuming it has something to do with your uncle's death?"

Schiff looked at me more closely. "Mr. Calhoun, how long have you been at the Lauderdale Tennis Club?"

"I've lived there about a month."

"So, you knew my Uncle Sol."

"He was a non-resident member, so I more knew *of* him. Who he'd been, how people viewed him."

"Meaning, as an icon."

Give it to her. "My impression."

Schiff sighed, scuffing the soles of her shoes on the slate flagstones beneath her feet. "Tennis was everything to Sol, and he was everything to me—though once he moved down here, we lost track a little of each other's lives. You follow what I said in the chapel?"

I didn't want to tell her that Florida had switched from the electric chair to lethal injection, so I just said, "Yes."

"Well, my father—Sol's brother—suffered a series of . . . 'Reversals,' he called them. 'Just business reversals, honey,' I remember him saying to my mother. Until one day when I was seven years old, and he blew his head off. Which sent my mother into a mental institution for the rest of her life."

"Ms. Schiff, I'm sorry."

A frustrated wave of the hand. "But my uncle got me through it, Mr. Calhoun, and through everything else, from dating boys to negotiating contracts. And now somebody's killed him."

"Word around the Club was he surprised a burglar."

Schiff ratcheted down a notch. "That's the theory the police fed me. But his place had been ransacked, and as I tried to clean up the mess, something else occurred to me."

"What?"

"That maybe the killer was searching for something. So many things got broken, it's hard to say if much is missing."

"I don't know exactly where your uncle lived."

"On the Intracoastal Waterway. Near 'Las Olas Boulevard,' I think you call it?"

Kind of Fort Lauderdale's Rodeo Drive, but toned down rather than tonier. Several engineered isles stuck out from Las Olas into the channel with canals cut between them to maximize the amount of "waterfront" property.

I said, "Are the Lauderdale police still investigating?"

"According to them, the case 'remains open.' "

Which could mean anything, but in my limited experience usually suggested there was no active suspect. "Why do you want to hire me?"

Schiff shrugged again. She seemed an "in-charge" kind of person, and I got the feeling "shrugging" wasn't something she did often or enjoyed doing at all.

Schiff said, "Sol was everything to—God, I'm repeating myself, aren't I?"

"Under the circumstances, I'd say you're entitled."

She passed her left palm over her face. "Thank you, Mr. Calhoun. To answer your question, though, I'd like you to approach this opposite to the way the police have."

"Meaning?"

"They're assuming it was a burglary gone wrong. If it was something else, I want to know that."

She fixed me with eyes I'd hate to negotiate against myself. Then I realized that, in a sense, I already was.

Schiff said, "And I want to know who killed the dearest man in my life."

I looked over her shoulder at a painfully blue sky, made the more so by a few clouds scudding past, pushed by the maybe ten-mile-per-hour breeze that lifted the petals on the cut, graveside flowers all around us.

As though they were still living plants, reaching toward the sun.

Naomi Schiff said, "Mr. Calhoun?"

"I'll give it a try."

Don Floyd started his car, pulling out of the parking area of the chapel. "Did Naomi tell you there was a reception— the Jewish people call it 'sitting Shiva,' I believe?"

"She told me." I shifted in the passenger seat. "Don, if what happened at Solomon Schiff's house wasn't a burglary, is there anyone I should talk to?"

Floyd frowned, then stopped for a traffic light. "Nobody who'd wish him harm, Rory. But there are some who knew him better than others."

"For instance?"

"Sol's business partner died—not like his brother, though. This was complications from a stroke, some five years or so back. The partner's name was Bourke, spelled B-O-U-R-K-E. Casey Bourke. His widow still lives at the Club. Karen?"

"Haven't met her."

"Sweet lady. Then there's Sol's . . . girlfriend."

"You don't say it like you mean it."

The light changed, and we moved forward. "Well, she's quite a bit younger. Early thirties, I'd say. In my view,

Karen—the widow—might have been a better choice, but Sol was kind of strongheaded that way."

"You sure that there *wasn't* anything between Schiff and this Karen Bourke?"

"Romantically? Hard to say for certain, Rory, but you know how the Club is."

I pictured it. Eight condominium buildings, four stories each, arrayed in a wide fishhook pattern around twenty clay—actually, Har-Tru—tennis courts. Every building was a squared-off horseshoe with its own common-area patio, and the entrances to each unit were visible to pretty much anyone who bothered to look. Also, there was an "Olympic Village" atmosphere I'd sensed about the place within days of moving into my apartment there. Gossip would be hard to avoid.

I said, "What's the name of this girlfriend?"

"Shirlee—that's with two 'E's' instead of 'E-Y.' I don't remember her last name, but I can tell you which building she's in."

"Meaning, also at the Club?"

"Right."

"Anybody else, Don?"

"For you to talk to, now?"

"Yes."

Floyd seemed to mull it over. "Well, I don't know were they real friends, but Luh-nell Kirby comes to mind."

"Can you spell that one for me, too?"

"Sure. L-Y-N-E-L-L. Big and black, with an even bigger serve."

"And this Kirby . . . ?"

Floyd seemed to stifle a laugh. "Sol was in his seventies, Lynell his sixties. They were pretty evenly matched, but Sol always beat him."

"Just as a regular opponent, or tournaments, too?"

"Tournaments only, I believe. You see, Sol was a real competitor. Nothing pleased him more than to play down and win."

In most tournaments, older entrants can "waive" age limits and "play down" in a lower, presumably tougher age bracket, but younger ones can't play up. Otherwise, so the thinking goes, they'd trounce their seniors.

"How did Kirby take that?"

"About as well as you'd expect a former colonel in the Army Rangers to accept defeat in anything."

I made simple, mental notes on all three people. "Don, thanks."

"You want, we can swing by the reception. I'm pretty sure Karen and Shirlee will be there, and maybe even Lynell as well."

"Not a comfortable time for interviewing people." I reached into my pocket. "Besides, Naomi Schiff gave me the key to her uncle's house, and I'd like to see it before talking with them about what happened there."

"Then you want to visit Sol's place?"

"No." I returned the key to my pocket. "No, just drop me back at the Club so I can pick up my own car. There's a stop I ought to make even before the crime scene."

I'd used the prize money from my last satellite victory to buy a two-year-old Chrysler Sebring convertible at a rent-a-car fleet auction. It was candy-apple red, with a tan interior and top. Given the stalling of my tennis career, the flashy wheels soothed my ego.

I parked outside the Fort Lauderdale Police Headquarters on West Broward Boulevard. The building is gray with blue piping detail, enough palm trees and flower beds around it to confuse you on its function.

Inside, I showed my investigator's license to the dour woman behind the first floor Information counter, but she wouldn't buzz me upstairs to the Homicide Unit, telling me instead to have a seat on one of the gray plastic scoop chairs in the lobby.

A few minutes later, a different woman came through the security door to the left of the counter. She had a golden tan that I thought came more from gene pool than sunbathing, with slightly darker hair drawn up in a high ponytail that just reached the collar of her blouse. Slim and somewhere in her high thirties, she had the kind of cheekbones that would wear well.

"You are Rory Calhoun?"

A slight edge of Spanish on her words. Standing, I said, "Yes."

"Lourdes Pintana." She extended a hand, and we shook. "Can I also see your ID, please?"

I took it out again, remembering that a lawyer in town had told me Pintana was the sergeant in charge of the Homicide Unit.

She took her time studying the print on my license before giving it back. "And what does a private investigator want with us?"

"Just some time. And permission, maybe."

Pintana studied me harder than she had my ID. "It is a nice day. Let us walk a little."

I followed her outside, thinking she spoke precise, "no-contractions" English like the Castro refugees I'd met on the circuit. Pintana seemed to think the parking lot was safer than the sidewalk, because she simply began strolling between the rows of vehicles. I fell in beside the woman, shortening my strides to match hers.

Pintana said, "Your meter is running, no?"

I took the hint. "I've been asked to look into the murder of Solomon Schiff."

A sad smile. "Let me guess. The niece?"

"Her name's Naomi. She seems to feel you all may be looking in the wrong direction."

"It has been known to happen." Pintana kicked at a loose stone like a soccer player might a ball, sending it under one of the parked cars. "But this time, I think not."

"Because?"

She crossed her arms. "No motives among those he knew. Solomon Schiff seemed to live his life around a tennis court. He was retired from active business, had a young girlfriend with no other boyfriends, and a nice house on the Intracoastal that would tempt many who believe in the redistribution of wealth."

An academic way of putting it. "So, a burglary gone sour."

"*Sí,* and almost a refreshing change of pace." Pintana looked up at me. "We get so many domestics, so many 'senior suicides,' so many drug killings, that the occasional felony-murder invigorates us."

"But not quite to the level of solving this one."

"Solving it? What fingerprints and fibers we found one could have predicted: Mr. Schiff's, Shirlee Tucker—that's the girlfriend. There were marks on the victim's wrists, like somebody wearing gloves held him by both in a struggle, with traces of velvet left on his skin."

"A burglar who uses velvet gloves?"

A nod. "And the body was found face up on the floor at the foot of his bed. When the official cause of death came back 'heart failure,' it was not a surprise."

"Anything from the autopsy that was?"

Pintana crossed her arms. "I do not think it 'surprising' for a man in his seventies, but Mr. Schiff had cancer."

"Where?"

"Everywhere. Metastasis run wild."

I tried to match that up with the man I'd seen play tennis. "It didn't show."

"Some people are stronger than others."

"Schiff knew this about himself?"

"For about six months, according to his doctor. The victim declined the alternative treatments of chemotherapy and radiation, choosing instead to 'tough it out.' " Pintana shook her head. "In his situation, I might have felt the same."

We were almost at my car. "Okay if I visit the house?"

"Schiff's, you mean?"

"Yes."

"I do not see why not. We released it as a crime scene two days ago."

I stopped at the Sebring's rear bumper. "Thanks for the help."

Pintana continued for several steps before turning and looking at my convertible. "This is yours?"

"It is."

Sergeant Lourdes Pintana looked it over, then did the same for me. "Take my advice, Mr. Calhoun. You will not make a very good living by trying to follow subjects in secret."

Solomon Schiff's house was on the second Isle south of Las Olas. The sprawling ranch looked like one of the older homes on the street, especially given the number of places being bought and then torn down for the construction of mansions, two of which were in progress. I parked in the driveway behind a jaunty teal Toyota, which I assumed was Schiff's.

The key his niece had given me fit the top and bottom locks on the front door. When I swung it open and stepped into the foyer, the muzzle of a black semiautomatic was aimed about belly-high on me from ten feet away.

The woman holding it said, "Sol always told me to aim at the fella's belt buckle and fire till he falls."

Slight southern lilt to the voice, hands shaking a little.

Keeping my own hands open and shoulder high, I managed to speak past a cottony tongue. "Even good advice isn't always right."

"Come any closer, and we'll both find out."

I decided to give her a moment. She was thirtyish, with dark, full hair cut just off her neck. The tank top showed about a third of the kind of breasts that make South Florida the true "Silicon Valley," and her Capri pants looked to be painted on her butt and legs. I remembered Don Floyd saying Schiff's girlfriend was much younger.

She blinked first. "Well, aren't you going to tell me who you are?"

"A man given a key to this place," I said, wiggling it for her to see.

"Oh, hell," the woman said, lowering the gun. "Why didn't you say you were from the realtor's?"

"I'm not, but if I can show you some identification . . . ?"

"Sure." She let the gun rest against her thigh as we moved together. Her eyes were hazel and just a little too far apart for smart.

"A private investigator? Like, really?"

"Really."

"Oh, wow. And you're even cute."

"And you're even Ms. Tucker?"

"Right, right. Shirlee Tucker. But with two 'E's.' My mama couldn't spell real good. So, what are you doing here?"

"I've been hired to look into Solomon Schiff's death."

"Ugh. Tell me about it. I was the one found him."

"Where?"

"Just like on TV, huh?"

"Let's start there, anyway."

Tucker led me through a living room that seemed sparsely furnished except for shelving that held more tennis trophies than books, but then Naomi Schiff had told me there'd been a lot of breakage and that she'd cleaned up the house. By the time we reached the bedroom, Tucker's gait, enhanced by the fit of her Capris, had started to hypnotize me.

"In here."

I moved past her in the open doorway, something musky coming off Tucker that I didn't think originated in a bottle. The room was fifteen by twelve, a king-sized brass bed against one wall, a master bath through another. There were no sheets or pillows in sight, and just an overhead light fixture hung down from a ceiling fan.

"Where exactly was Mr. Schiff's body?"

Tucker now moved past me to the footboard of the bed, which had a pattern of sturdy, vertical pickets between lateral top and bottom pieces the diameter of bar rails. She grasped the top rail as support and lowered herself to the floor until she was face-up and lying flat, head toward the bed and feet toward the door.

Tucker said, "Sol was like this?" the lilt making her statement sound like a question.

"How about his arms?"

She moved hers to a more exaggerated version of my

"Don't Shoot" in the foyer, her fingernails almost touching the base of the brass footboard.

"What else did you see?"

Tucker did a partial sit-up, now resting on her elbows, which pushed the doctored bust more aggressively forward. "His bed had been slept in," now a coy cocking of her head, "but not with me."

"Meaning with somebody else?"

"I didn't get any perfumy smell. Ugh, Sol's was bad enough."

When people die, their muscles relax and release a lot of unpleasantness. "You didn't see anybody else?"

"No. And Sol had pajama bottoms on."

"Bottoms, but no top?"

"Right, right. That's how he dressed for bed when I wasn't here."

"How do you know?"

"Because," the head now cocking the other way, though to the same effect, "when I was with him, he'd sleep naked."

Not exactly logical, but the last part struck me as pretty probable. And probably enjoyable.

Tucker said, "You're thinking about it, aren't you?"

I decided not to lie. "Yes."

Her tongue came out, moistened her lips. "Me, too. Minute I saw you in the foyer back there? I was hoping it wouldn't come to shooting you."

Reassuring. "Had you and Mr. Schiff been sleeping together much recently?"

A frown, like that wasn't my next line in her script. "No, truth to tell. Oh, Sol was no great shakes in the sack, but he was—Sol liked to call himself 'inventive.' "

"Inventive."

"Yeah. Loved going into the sex shops, buying me things like teddies or bikini thongs." Tucker stretched the top of her Capri pants to show me some red lace. "These, for instance."

My throat felt a little tight. "How about sex toys?"

"Oh, he had just a drawerful of those." Another frown, directed toward the bureau. "But I think his prudy niece must have gone and thrown them all away when she cleaned up the place, account of that's what I wanted to take back with me, and they aren't there now."

I couldn't see somebody ransacking the house for one of those. "Shirlee, did Mr. Schiff have anything in the house that somebody might have searched for?"

"Searched for? You mean like treasure or something?"

"Jewelry, cash, anything somebody else might want."

A third cocking of her head. "Just me."

Actually Tucker's answer gave me several ideas. "Did Mr. Schiff ever take any photos of you?"

"You mean, like, nudie shots?"

"Yes."

"No. No, Sol was into gadgets, not cameras." Yet another nice cocking of her head. "Of course, you don't look like you need any of those things to please, and this floor's getting awful hard."

The floor wasn't alone in that. "Maybe some other time."

"Oh, I get it." Full sit-up now. "Like when you're 'off-duty,' right?"

Clearing my throat, I agreed with Shirlee Tucker, who recited her phone number, including how easy it was to remember the last four digits because "you just have to keep subtracting by '2' for each?"

100

★ ★ ★ ★ ★

I had a resident decal pasted on my windshield, so the security guard at the Club just waved me through the main gate. As I drove around the fishhook road toward my building, Wingfield, I spotted the man I believed to be Lynell Kirby walking toward the clubhouse with a tennis bag slung over his shoulder and that purposeful stride that I've always associated with doctors on their way to major operations and players on their way to important matches. Instead of continuing all the way to Wingfield, I parked in a guest slot for Lenglen.

Every one of the club's residential buildings is named for an historic tennis player, and there's a twenty-foot mosaic of each legend—in this case, Suzanne Lenglen of France—on a peach wall in the respective courtyard. Lends a nice air of tradition, a sense of permanence that I hadn't found anywhere else in the Lauderdale area.

Jogging, I caught up with Kirby as he reached the pool area, which, along with the tiki bar on the patio, overlooks the front five courts. "Colonel Kirby?"

The man turned. Six-three, great muscle definition in arms and legs, no gut. From fifty feet away, you'd be off thirty years on his age, but up close, his spring-coil hair was spritzed with gray, and his eyes had that faraway look of some older guys I'd known who'd fought in Vietnam.

"You look familiar," he said. "We serve together somewhere?"

"No," though I nearly added a "sir" to it. "I'd like to talk with you about Solomon Schiff."

"Police or reporter?"

"Neither." I took out my license.

Kirby barely glanced at it. "I've got a match in ten minutes, and that's all I'm thinking about right now. You've got

101

the time to wait, I'll be happy to talk with you afterwards."

"Seems reasonable."

You can tell a lot about people from the way they play tennis. What I could tell from watching Lynell Kirby was that Don Floyd's implication was dead-on: The man did not like to lose.

He was playing an athletic younger woman who had the kind of game you associate with Chris Evert: steady, deep, and enough pace to never let you rip at it. Even on Har-Tru, which slows the ball down and causes it to sit up, I figured Kirby—a lefty with a powerful serve, but whose strokes were "by-the-numbers" mechanical—to have trouble staying with her.

I was wrong.

Kirby never quit on a point, and he had a sharply angled crosscourt forehand. His slice backhand showed good bite, and his topspin "approach" shots down the line were often winners in and of themselves. Plus Kirby was quick if not graceful, volleying the ball solidly.

After seventy-five minutes by my watch, he'd beaten a good player half his age by a break each set: 6–4, 6–3.

They shook hands, the woman leaving almost immediately by one of the fence doors. Kirby toweled off his face and neck, then beckoned me to come down under the awning separating his court from the next one, also empty.

When I reached him, Kirby said, "Sorry to be so curt with you up there," gesturing toward the elevated pool/patio area, "but I was trying to keep my mind on the game."

"No problem. I do the same thing."

Kirby yoked his towel around his neck, then sank into

one white resin chair under the awning as I took another.

He said, "Didn't catch your name before."

"Rory Calhoun."

"Rory . . . you were on the tour."

"It's nice to be remembered."

"Saw you at the Lipton twice—call it the Ericsson now, but it's still held on Key Biscayne." Kirby grinned. "Of course, you'd know that."

"Probably won't be a difference for me anymore. Bad knee."

A judicious nod. "Comes from all that hard court you kids had to play on. Clay keeps the body young." Then Kirby straightened in his chair. "You said something about Sol, though, right?"

"His niece has asked me to look into his death."

The eyes grew shrewd, and he moved his head some, assessing me, I thought.

Finally, Kirby said, "Man was killed by a burglar, probably to feed a drug habit. What's there to look into?"

"She'd just like to put some concerns to rest."

"Like what?"

"I've heard you knew Mr. Schiff pretty well. Could he have had anything at his house somebody would be searching for?"

Kirby settled a little deeper into his chair. "You think somebody intentionally targeted Sol, and not just his place as a good candidate for loot?"

Loot. "That's what I'm trying to find out."

"Well, I guess I'd challenge your premise, then. Sol and I were more friendly opponents than friends."

I knew what he meant. "You didn't socialize off the courts?"

"Or really even on them." A faraway look in the eyes

again. "You ever in the service, Rory?"

"No."

"I always was a scrapper, even scrambling to stay alive. And that's how I play tennis, because I never learned as a kid the way Sol did, with the right racquet and good coaching showing me the proper strokes. Sol was like a ballet dancer between the lines, always moving himself in balance to the ball, always under control. Like there was this overall . . . choreography for every match, but he was the only one who got a peek at it in advance."

I knew what Kirby meant about that, too. The sense that you were playing the opponent's match instead of just the opponent. "And so?"

"And so it was damned frustrating to go up against him. I had ten years on the man, and he'd play down just so he could be the champion in his seventies *and* my sixties. The king of the geezers."

"You couldn't beat him."

"I never beat him. There's a difference."

"Meaning you were getting closer."

"That's right. Last tournament, I was up 4–2 in the third. Even had a matchpoint at 5–4. I couldn't quite put him away, but next time out, I believe I would have. And I think he believed it, too."

What we all do, psyche out our opponents to psyche up ourselves. "Still, it must have galled you to lose all those—"

"Let me save you some time, my friend. Sol Schiff could be a prima donna and even a royal pain in the ass. But if I killed him in his bedroom, how would I ever have gotten the chance to beat him on a court?"

"How did you know that?"

"What?"

"That he was killed in his bedroom."

A grin, the fingers on his right hand flicking upward one at a time. "First, newspaper article. Second, Shirlee Tucker—his 'principal squeeze,' my grandson might call her—can't shut up about it. Third, the Tennis Club is like a primitive culture, and the drums tell us things."

At which point Lynell Kirby began to paddle his palms on his thighs like they were bongos.

Karen Bourke wasn't hard to find. She lived in a two-bedroom, two-bath flat in the third building past the club's security gate, diagonally across from the tennis center. Greeting me at her front door, Bourke listened to why I'd come to bother her and said it was no bother at all. By the time we sat down in the living room, it was "Karen" and "Rory."

Though she had to be in her sixties from what Don Floyd had told me, Bourke was another one whose appearance gave lie to her age. Blonde and slim, with blue eyes and an eager smile, the only telltales that she was over forty were little crow's feet of lines around the corners of her eyes.

From laughing or crying, I thought, with no way to judge which.

"Rory, I'm really sorry about Sol."

I nodded. "Forgive me, but did I see you at the Memorial Chapel?"

"No." Bourke seemed to go inside herself for a moment. "The excuse I gave people is that I had committed to play doubles in a tournament near Palm Beach, but the real reason is . . ." She looked up to a shelf over my head. "I've become a little tired of funerals."

I twisted around to see a framed photo of two men, both in their fifties, dressed in business suits with lapels from the seventies. "Your husband and Mr. Schiff?"

"Yes. That's Casey on the left. I took that photo of them in their office, just after they'd closed the deal that made all of us functionally rich."

"Anything happen to change that, Karen?"

Bourke looked at me oddly. "To . . . change it?"

"I've visited Mr. Schiff's home. No palace, but—"

"—compared to this place, it looks as though I've come down in the world?"

Bourke's words came out sandwiched between smiling lips, but I got a sense of strength and resolve buried deep within her. "Basically," I said.

The smile softened. "I don't blame you, Rory. No, I'm sure my condo here isn't worth a tenth of what Sol's house would bring as a teardown, given that waterfront lot it's on. In fact, Casey and I owned a pretty similar place, but after my husband died, I sold ours to move here." Bourke looked back at the framed photo. "When you're alone as a woman, it's nice to have people around, and living here at the Club gives me a community to be part of. An . . . identity, if that makes any sense to you."

It did. I remembered back to my knee first failing me, and the pang of wondering whether I'd ever be part of the circuit—or any gregarious, sorority-fraternity experience— again. And, to be honest, I wondered if I hadn't moved into the Tennis Club for just the same reason Karen Bourke had.

She said, "But you're here about Sol, right?"

"Right." I tried to refocus. "I guess what I was getting at is whether you were on good terms with Mr. Schiff?"

"Good terms." Bourke looked down at her lap for a moment, then smiled, but very sadly. "Sol wasn't just Casey's partner: They were best friends as well. One was barely

Jewish, the other never missed Mass. But they had tennis as well as business in common, and they played champion-ship-level doubles for years until Casey's stroke. After that, Sol would visit every day, sitting at my husband's bedside, making conversation for both of them. And when Casey died, Sol made sure I had the kind of financial advice that let me—and still lets me—never worry about money." Bourke looked up now, the strength and resolve I'd heard in her words now shining through her eyes as well. "So, yes, I'd say Sol and I were on 'good terms.'"

Impressive speech. "Karen, anything in his home that somebody might have torn it apart to find?"

"To find? Like what?"

"That's why I'm asking."

"Sorry, Rory, but I can't help you there."

I decided to risk our first-name basis. "How did you feel about Shirlee Tucker?"

My question seemed to genuinely throw Bourke. "*Feel* about her?"

"Did you . . . approve of their relationship?"

A laugh, one that I thought would go on before I sensed Bourke realizing it already had lasted a little too long. "Sol never married, Rory. What he did romantically was hardly any of my business."

"I don't think you've answered my question."

"Well, then," said Karen Bourke, standing, "I guess that's the only one I haven't."

After losing a professional tennis match, I practiced a little ritual whenever I had cash to spare. I'd rent a car and drive around to clear my head. I don't know why, but having to concentrate on steering, accelerating, and braking would help me analyze what had gone wrong as well as push myself toward improving next time out.

Now I just cruised some of the major streets around the Club, letting the Sebring kind of have its head as though it were a stable horse taking me for a slow, aimless ride. Maybe the last question I asked Karen Bourke is what let me notice something about the strip malls lining Oakland Park Boulevard as I headed east toward the beach.

Several of them sported sex shops.

I pulled into the parking lot of the second one. Shirlee Tucker had told me that Solomon Schiff was into kinky sex, but not recently. And Karen Bourke had dodged that issue entirely.

I thought about it, then drove back to my apartment to check the Yellow Pages and pick up my camera.

It was a single-lens reflex Canon, which is about all I understood of what the guy at a photography store in Chicago had explained to me years before. But I'd just reached the semis of a satellite near there, and I wanted my girlfriend of the weekend to have a decent camera to capture me winning the title. I lost both the finals and the girlfriend, but not the camera, and once I began doing daywork for private investigators, I'd invested in a telephoto lens as well.

Spending Naomi Schiff's retainer in what I hoped was a responsible way, I sat outside her uncle's house on the Intracoastal until I caught Shirlee Tucker arriving in her teal Toyota. I got three good head-and-shoulders portraits of her, one with the sunglasses off. A few hours later, I snapped two close-ups of Lynell Kirby as he picked up a pizza at the Big Louie's on Andrews Avenue. Finally, I caught Karen Bourke the next cloudy morning from the balcony of my unit as she walked onto Court 10 for a singles match wearing neither shades nor a baseball cap.

I drove to the Walgreen's and patiently waited for their one-hour photo service to prove itself, then I took the prints and began making the rounds of the sex shops I'd found in the phonebook.

"You're not a cop?"

I looked at the guy in the fifth place. He wore a palomino toupee, kept a dead cigar clamped between his teeth, and had breath foul enough to blister paint.

I said, "Cross my heart and hope to die."

"My loyal customers expect some privacy when they shop here, you know?"

I took in just the "impulse" items near his cash register. "I can see that."

"But you say this is about a killing?"

"That's right. And I'd rather not have the police drag you down for questioning, only to leave your loyal customers in the lurch."

His eyes told me I'd pressed the right button.

"Okay, let me see your photos."

As I'd done four times previously that day, I laid them face up in front of him on the counter as though I were dealing blackjack. He waited to see all three people before pointing with his cigar. "Her. Yeah, last week sometime."

"What did she buy?"

The dead end of the cigar went toward the "bondage" wall. "One of those sets there, on the left."

"Why," said Shirlee Tucker, the one-trick pony again cocking her head coyly from the bar stool, "you want to play with them?"

I'd called her, asking if she'd meet me at Lord Nelson's

Pub on Southwest 2nd. Given the time of day, the bar was ours.

I centered my pint of Boddington's on its coaster. "Actually, what I'm wondering is why you were buying a pair of velvet handcuffs last week when you told me that lately Solomon Schiff hadn't been much into lovemaking, much less anything kinky?"

Tucker drew on the straw sticking in her Sex on the Beach, which made me shift a little uncomfortably on my own stool.

She said, "Do you like watching me . . . drink this?"

"More than we can go into now, but I'd still like to know—"

"Seemed funny to me, too," Tucker, looking almost thoughtful. "But Sol asked it as a favor, and when I wanted to know why—if he wasn't going to use them with me?—all he said was, 'It's to repay a debt to the Devil.' "

"A what?"

"A debt to the Devil." Tucker waved with her drink. "Look, I didn't get it, either. Only, like I said, Sol asked me as a favor, so I went out and got the cuffs for him."

"What did he do with them?"

"Beats me. I know this: He'd never asked me to tie him up before, and he never asked me to cuff him last week after I gave the things to him." Then Shirlee Tucker drew on her straw again. "If you like the idea enough, though, we could always just . . . buy another pair?"

Exercising significant willpower, I left Tucker at the bar and drove around some more, trying to sort through what I'd learned. Solomon Schiff dies of heart failure, apparently trying to defend himself against a burglar. Only his devoted niece Naomi doesn't completely buy that, and she hires me to find his killer. Shirlee Tucker seems almost detached from her lover's recent death, Lynell Kirby seems to regret only losing the opportunity to best an unbeaten opponent, and Karen Bourke seems to think her dead husband's partner was the salt of the earth. Besides, Sergeant Lourdes Pintana tells me the autopsy confirms a struggle but also found that cancer would have killed Schiff if his heart hadn't given out first. And the only thing I've discovered that somebody could have been ransacking his house to find—even assuming Naomi Schiff was right about that part—is a pair of velvet handcuffs that Shirlee Tucker says—

I stopped in the middle lane of Route 1, and the poor guy driving his family around on vacation behind me smacked into my rear bumper.

The damage to both cars was minimal, though it seemed to take forever to exchange licenses and registrations. I assured the tourist that I'd tell my insurance company I'd caused the accident.

Even if only indirectly.

"Karen?"

She turned toward me on the club's patio, apparently on her way from a match back to her condo. I'd debated just following her there, but I figured to let her choose the ground.

"Rory. More questions?"

"Actually, more answers."

"I don't understand."

"I'm pretty sure of what happened, Karen, but I'd like to talk with you about it first."

Bourke stared at me, then rolled her head on her shoulders, as though her neck was stiff and she wanted to relax before serving. Or, in this case, probably before returning serve.

Finally she said, "Can we walk?"

"Sure."

I'd guess the perimeter of the fishhook road around the club's buildings is about half a mile. We hadn't gone more than a hundred feet, that sweet pong of female sweat wafting off her, before Karen Bourke said, "Why don't you start?"

Okay. "Your husband and Solomon Schiff were partners—both businesswise and tennis, but friends as well. They hit it big twenty-some years ago, big enough for both sides to be completely comfortable financially. But, as they say, if you don't have your health . . ."

Bourke nodded beside me, biting her lower lip. I waited a moment as a couple on their way to play greeted us cheerily.

When the couple had moved out of earshot, I continued. "The rabbi at Mr. Schiff's funeral said he wasn't terribly religious, and you confirmed that. On the other hand, a lot of people there felt Mr. Schiff had been a tough negotiator but a man of his word. And one of the promises he'd made—to his niece, after her own father had committed suicide—was that he'd never take his own life."

"Sol told us about that."

"Before you all reached . . . consensus?"

"Rory, I don't know what you're talking about."

"After your husband's stroke, he was bedridden."

"Yes." Bourke got quieter. "Casey couldn't walk, much less play tennis. Lying on his back every waking hour, the sores that . . ." She shook her head.

"Did you talk about . . . ending things?"

"Casey was very religious. Even if my husband could have taken his own life, he wouldn't have. And I certainly couldn't do it for him."

"But Solomon Schiff could."

Karen Bourke looked at me, that strength back in her eyes. "Casey begged him, and Sol deflected it, tried everything to cheer my husband up. But the doctors told me there was no hope of improvement, and with that Kevorkian man being prosecuted up in Michigan, they were scared of acting themselves." She seemed to steady herself. "So Sol and I both did some . . . God, 'research,' I'd guess you'd call it, about how to 'simulate' heart failure, which is a pretty typical complication from a stroke. And one night, when we'd all come to peace about the decision," Bourke's pace of speaking accelerating, "Sol took a pillow and pressed it over Casey's face and smothered him."

After a few more strides, I said, "But Mr. Schiff first . . . negotiated a return promise, right?"

"Right." Bourke looked down at her tennis shoes now. "Sol told me about the promise to his niece. He made me agree that if he was ever like . . . in a situation like Casey's, that I'd do the same for him."

"Only Mr. Schiff wasn't—"

"—paralyzed?" She grunted, but not like a laugh. "Just by that promise. And by his pride, I suppose." Bourke looked at a court we were passing, two older men playing scrappy singles. "Sol was sick with cancer. He kept it from most people, and he still played well. But Sol himself told me that opponents he used to beat soundly were now creeping up on him, and he was afraid he couldn't maintain his game much longer."

I thought back to Lynell Kirby sensing the same thing.

"And Mr. Schiff couldn't tolerate that."

"No. And I also think that, after seeing Casey the way . . . confined to his bed for so long." Another shake of the head. "I think Sol didn't want to wither away in a hospital somewhere with tubes sticking out of him."

"So to keep his promise to his niece, and to cover the mercy killing, you made it look like a burglary."

"He made it look that way. Slashed his furniture, smashed his things." A sad smile. "Except for the tennis trophies, of course. He couldn't bear to hurt those."

I'd registered that at his house. "But why stage it like a homicide at all? Why not have it look like just plain heart failure?"

"We talked about that, too. Sol had his pride, Rory, as I said before. And the man who could play three matches a day felt his overall level of conditioning would make it hard for people to believe that his heart would simply "give out" in his sleep. Sol thought some kind of trauma—like 'struggling with a violent burglar'—was necessary."

"And the velvet handcuffs?"

"We actually tried it first the week before without anything. A 'practice session,' Sol called it. But each time I . . . pressed the pillow onto his face, even with me sitting on his chest, he'd flail away with his arms." A sadder smile. "The instinct to survive, I guess. He hadn't had that . . . problem with Casey, on account of the stroke."

"And so Mr. Schiff came up with the idea of the handcuffs, so he'd be restrained—"

"—we ran the cuffs through the brass rods at the foot of his bed—"

"—and it would look as though the 'burglar' had held his wrists while wearing gloves."

Just a nod now. "And he had me carry away all his . . .

marital aides, so the police wouldn't think of anything 'velvet' *but* 'gloves.' "

Bourke's story was consistent with the facts.

Almost a laugh from her now. "You know what Sol called it?"

"Called what?"

"His agreement with me, that I'd do for him what he'd done for Casey."

I said, "A debt to the Devil?"

Bourke stopped cold in her tracks. "Who told you about—?"

"It's more what I'm going to tell everyone else."

She stared at me now. "Everyone?"

"That Solomon Schiff died while trying to protect himself from a violent burglar."

I'd have walked Karen Bourke back to her condo, but after giving me a desperate hug, the woman excused herself, saying she really had to be alone for a while.

Him. Gone? Good!

Darragh Galvin walked down the corridor toward her apartment door, juggling the grocery bag and notebook computer as she fumbled with her key case.

DOOR. SHE? FOOD!

From the corridor side of the wooden six-panel, Darragh could hear squeaky mewling mixed with mad scratching just above the saddle of the threshold.

"Pooky, it's me. Leave some of the paint on there, huh?"

Darragh said basically the same thing every day when she arrived home from work, but that had never stopped him yet, and she didn't expect tonight would be any different.

The key finally turned in the lock. As the apartment door swung open, Pooky dashed out, the orange tabby doing a lightning-speed figure-eight around the corridor.

What Darragh called his "Dance of Welcome."

As soon as she was inside the apartment, Pooky came dashing back, rubbing his face against her calf, nearly hard enough to knock his "Mom" off-balance.

"God, you'd have made a good football player, Pook."
Dropping the computer into a living room chair, Darragh

moved to the kitchen, just a little galley, really. The grocery bag containing her Valentine's Day fixings went onto the counter by the microwave. Then Darragh bent over the stacked plastic trays under the counter, taking out a small can.

SHE. FOOD? ME!

"Minced turkey, one of your favorites."

Reaching down with her free hand, Darragh felt Pooky rise up on his hind legs, pushing his head into her palm. "Glad to see me, right?"

She opened the can. "Even with an extra claw on those front footsies, you'd have some trouble doing this for yourself."

Pooky rubbed his face against Darragh's calf again as she used a dessert fork from the utensils drawer to mush the soft food into the dry cereal left over from the morning meal. When the blend looked right, Darragh set the dish on the linoleum next to the refrigerator.

Watching him tear into his dinner, she thought, God, I love you, Pookmeister. Almost as much as . . .

Darragh moved into the living room, stopping at the framed photo of a smiling, dimpled and clefted male face on the mantel over the fireplace. Thom—with an "H," he'd said to her the first time they'd met, in a bar near the theater district. From across the room, he was good-looking enough to be an actor. Darragh was wondering about that when she noticed him noticing her, then wending his way toward her stool. But Darragh knew she was attractive, too—the red hair, the green eyes—and Thom's opening line to her ("Are you in a play around here?") showed just the right combination of awareness and compliment. In fact, Thom was the right combination in a lot of ways: stockbroker, six-feet tall, medium build but great legs and buns from his tennis days. Other than being a little fixated on money, there was really only one problem with the man.

He was still married.

But separated, as he'd told her, upfront with it that first night. The problem was, the divorce could be messy, since his wife ("Emily"; never did like that name, "*Em*-ily") had an invalid mother and infantile attitudes about a lot of things, like investing for retirement through buying seven lottery tickets a week. Put simply, Thom had to keep their affair under wraps until his lawyer could drive a "rational" deal that would free him to plan a "rational" future.

A future that, "rationally," would include Darragh. If she didn't botch the relationship by pushing too hard. (Darragh didn't count her gentle hints about when the divorce was going to become final). Besides, it was often more convenient "entertaining" Thom at her apartment rather than insisting on visiting his ("*Em*-ily might have hired a private investigator to 'stake out' my place, luv; I never know what that woman will do next"). And, in this age of sexually-transmitted plague, there certainly were obvious advantages to seeing a "married" man.

Which reminded her of what would happen after dinner. Feeling a delicious shiver, Darragh moved back into the kitchen and the grocery bag on the counter, carefully lifting out the veal chops and fresh broccoli and especially the amaretto/chocolate torte in the shape of two joined hearts.

Thom Wexford sat in his office, spending what he expected would be his last Monday behind the desk. Computer terminal for stock quotes and trades, television screen for CNN, even a VCR. for those dead times. "Dead" times? A snorted laugh.

Did I actually just think that?

Then, focusing with his right eye, Thom looked at the tennis trophies in the glass case against one wall. Quite a few of them, too. High school through college and on to the club, nice little display to act as an icebreaker with new clients, even impress them some with what a Renaissance Man he was. Most never noticed that the last trophy was dated almost five years before. Oh, Thom still played tennis, but he never won trophies any more. Not since the injury to his left eye.

A fluke, that, I must say. Volleying at the net, the ball caroms crazily off the frame of my opponent's racquet and hits me. Result?: Eighty-percent loss of vision by the time I'm tested at the hospital.

That injury soured Thom on the sport for a while. On everything for a while, including hucking the stocks. Drifted from one brokerage house to another, never regaining the touch he'd had with the market, like the touch he'd had with the racquet. *Depth perception, damned important factor in tennis.*

Nothing wrong with his other perceptions, though. Like spotting Darragh across the bar that night six months ago, her falling for him like a ton of bricks. He sensed that lying to the girl right away about his being separated would prove one of those strokes of genius he had from time to time.

"Stroke?" Tennis pun, that.

And Darragh was a red-headed tiger in the sack. Nice change of pace from the ever-duller Emily's rather weak service (there's another; they do creep into one's vocabulary, eh?).

Emily, Emily. Obsessed with her wheel-chaired mother

and her absurd lottery tickets and her dovetailed belief that good people—daughters who looked after their parents, for example—would be rewarded. As with hitting a jackpot, for example.

And damned if she didn't. Last Wednesday, the four-million dollar bonanza. Pre-tax, a couple hundred thousand a year for the next two decades. Rationally invested, that would throw off . . .

Then Thom frowned. One problem with the rosy financial forecast. Emily's definition of "good people" didn't include husbands who were getting a little something on the side. And Darragh wasn't exactly the first. No, Emily hadn't found out about all of them, but the one last year who'd actually telephoned her—*telephoned* her, can you imagine the gall?—was enough. Or too much, really. Ultimatum time, Emily called it. One more, Thom, and I'm kicking you out. Which wouldn't have mattered much to him, honestly.

Until last Wednesday, that is.

Yes, the lottery jackpot changed everything. Now Emily was a bit too good to let go, or continue to betray, or risk being betrayed to. As, for example, by a certain redhead scorned.

And Darragh would feel just that way, no matter how he might try to let her down easy. She was more cloying every day he saw her, dropping broader and broader hints (read, "prods") about when his "divorce" would "finally" go through. Not to mention her escalating demands about their spending more time together.

Like Valentine's Day, for example.

Fortunately, Emily's mother happened to have been born on February 14th, and throughout their marriage Thom "understood" that his wife just "had" to spend that evening sitting next to the wheelchair. Which was just fine, when your "affairee" believes you're already "separated" and therefore free to spend the most romantic of calendar days with her.

No, any risk of Darragh contacting Emily out of pique or revenge or . . . whatever was simply too much, given the stakes. And like any good stockbroker, Thom had learned how to deal with risk.

And its . . . management.

Smiling now, Thom Wexford leaned forward, going over the checklist on his desk one more time.

SHE. SMELL? MEAT!

Darragh Galvin went over the recipe one more time. "I have everything in there, Pooky. What do you think?"

The cat rubbed his face against her calf, but Darragh was pretty sure he was reacting more to the veal than the marinade mixed in the casserole dish. Covering the dish with some aluminum foil, she placed it carefully in the refrigerator. "Fire's next, Pookster. Want to help?"

Just a squeaky meow. Darragh was always amazed, a cat as big and strong as her tabby with such a little voice.

Probably because I had him fixed.

Walking to the mantel in the living room, Darragh looked at Thom's photo again, feeling her heart skip. It was the only thing of his she had in the apartment, him warning her constantly of the dire consequences to the divorce proceedings should *Em*-ily find out about their relationship. But that was tolerable, so long as it was only temporary. And even though Pooky could leap like a gazelle—onto furniture, the kitchen counter, even this mantel—he never wrecked anything, so the photo was safe here and easily remembered for hiding should somebody other than Thom come visiting.

Darragh picked up the brass rack holding the fireplace tools and carried it around the corner into her bedroom. One of the real advantages of an apartment in the city's older buildings: a fireplace in both the living room and the bedroom, the latter just right for romantic evenings. There were disadvantages, too, however. Like cranky heat from rattling radiators, a fire escape looming outside the bedroom window, and rent higher than the Himalayas. When the landlord told her what the apartment would cost, Darragh decided she'd have to economize on furnishings, like not having two sets of tools when only one fire would be going at any given time.

WALL. HOLE? FIRE!

Edging Pooky to the side with her foot, Darragh set the tool rack on the hardwood floor next to her bureau. She removed the spark screen and began laying the crumpled newspaper, fatwood sticks, and split logs for the fire that would accompany the one she hoped to kindle in the four-poster behind her.

A pen in his right hand, Thom Wexford made a little tick mark next to each item on the checklist.

Fingerprints? All over the apartment, but since I've never served in the military, or been arrested, etc., mine aren't on file anywhere. *Tick.*

Telephone records? Inconclusive, since I've always used payphones or someone else's extension here to call Darragh. *Tick.*

Alibi? Shouldn't need one, but just in case: stop by the

Civic Center, buy a standing-room-only ticket for tonight's Agassi-Sampras match. Then set the office VCR to tape the program, allowing me to see all the details tomorrow morning as though I'd been there. *Tick.*

Flowers? Darragh will expect *some*-thing. I mean after all, it is Valentine's Day. Easily bought, however, functionally anonymously, from a sidewalk vendor. *Tick.*

Witnesses? Shouldn't be a problem. Old building, no doorman. Seven other apartment doors along her corridor, but the tenants kept to themselves, and going up to Darragh's place, he'd never so much as seen one of them. Or been seen by them, which was more to the point. *Tick.*

Photo? Just remember to take the whole frame from the mantel and put it in my briefcase. No other trace of me there. *Tick.*

Murder weapon? Nicely provided by occupant. Smile. *Tick.*

Window? Easy enough, with a facecloth from the bathroom linen cabinet. *Tick.*

Cat?

Thom Wexford thought about the little wretch. Darragh named it "Pooky," but Thom would have preferred "Pukey." And the disgusting hairballs weren't the worst transgression the thing committed. No, the absolute nadir was the way Pukey hid around the corner of the living room, against the fireplace. Its mutant, six-clawed front paw raised in the air, somehow sensing in its feline way that Thom's reduced vision limited his ability to spot the ambush coming.

Tearing open my ankle every time I walk from Darragh's bathroom toward the kitchen after taking a shower. Slashed with that paw the way I'd take a tennis ball on the rise, come to think of it. Sweep the ball cross-court for a winner in a three-count movement. Cock the arm. Sweep the ball. Follow through.

Except tonight, perhaps a backhand was called for instead.

Returning to the checklist, Thom Wexford spoke softly to himself. *"Cat?"* Broader smile. *Tick.*

By the time Darragh finished laying the fire—using the heavy brass poker to angle the unlit logs—she realized Pooky had left her for another go at the food dish. Just as well. She needed to take a bath before Thom arrived, and she hated to close any doors on the cat, because he always wanted to see what he was missing. Thom insisted on the bedroom door being shut when they made love, of course. And, to be honest, she didn't think the guy was exactly nuts about cats, especially given Pooky's tendency to attack him after a shower.

Darragh suppressed a giggle. She had to admit, it was kind of funny to see a grown man like Thom hopping around, holding his bleeding ankle, cursing.

But she always found a way to make it up to him.

WATER. HIM? GO!

"Hello, Emily? . . . Yes, I'm still at the off—. . . I remember that it's her birthday. That's why I'm calling. . . . I certainly do. The tennis match at the Civic Center. . . . Probably not before eleven. . . . Fine, you have a good time, too. . . . Right, bye."

Wearing only her robe, Darragh opened the bathroom door, a little surprised that Pooky hadn't been waiting outside it. She drew the sash tight around her waist and walked toward the kitchen, turning the corner by the living room fireplace.

LEG. HIM? NO!

"Carnations, please."

The scabrous man hunching over the large white containers of flowers looked like one of Snow White's dwarfs as Thom Wexford called to him from the driver's window of his BMW.

The man walked across the sidewalk to the curb, but carrying a bouquet of roses. "It's Valentine's Day, buddy. How's about getting her these instead?"

Thom thought about it. "How much more than the carnations?"

"These here are ten, the others six."

"Then the just the carnations."

Thom was quite certain the dwarf muttered something with the word "bastard" in the middle, but, under the circumstances, didn't dare make a fuss over it.

"Oh, there you are."

From his position next to the living room fireplace, Pooky blinked up at Darragh, then began licking his raised right forepaw. "Caught you in the act, didn't I?"

The tabby blinked some more, the soul of innocence. "Just you behave with Thom tonight. It's special." And Darragh moved into the kitchen, clanging pots and pans to make the holiday even more so.

"Will this chardonnay be all, sir?"

"Yes."

The clerk rang it up. "A fine selection for Valentine's Day, if I may say."

"Thank you."

And it was, a fifteen-dollar varietal from the Alexander Valley. But no sense in stinting on something he'd be enjoying.

Whether shared or alone.

SMELL. HOT? MEAT!

"You like this, huh, Pook? Well, maybe if you're real good, a couple of scraps will find their way into your food dish."

Darragh took the squeaky meow for agreement on the subject.

Parking his car several blocks away, as usual, Thom Wexford walked with the chardonnay in his briefcase and the carnations under his arm. Getting to Darragh's apartment would be the tricky part, but good luck: No one at the main entrance, or on the elevator, or in the corridor of her floor.

Perfect, perfect, perfect.

DOOR. HIM? BAD!

"Happy Valentine's Day, luv."

What Darragh said was, "Oh, thank you, Thom." What she thought was, Just carnations? Well, that's probably all the florist had by the time Thom got out of work.

He inclined his head toward the kitchen. "What smells so good?"

She told him.

Then he leaned into her, his lips barely brushing hers, then crushing them a little, his tongue slipping through here and there. "Can dinner wait?" he whispered.

"If you can't."

Smiling, but not completely happy about the schedule reversal, Darragh took the flowers to the kitchen, arranging them in a vase.

Thom looked around the room. No sign of the cat. Probably have to chase the little wretch off a pillow in—no. No, there's Pukey, peering around the side of an armchair like one of the Marx Brothers in a movie.

Over her shoulder, Darragh said, "I think they'll look best up on the mantel, to the doorway side of your photo."

"So long as they remind you of me, luv."

Thom watched her move his photo from the center to the left, so that the frame and the vase balanced each other on the mantel. Have to remember the photo. *Tick.*

Which was when he realized something. No fireplace tools. Almost said as much, too, until he realized something else.

Only one other place in the apartment they could be. *Tick.*

Grinning, he moved up behind Darragh, pressing his pelvis into her rump. "Let's take the wine in with us."

UP. FLOWERS? TASTE!

An hour later, her head resting on her lover's shoulder, Darragh said, "I hate to hear Pooky scratching like that."

Sipping his chardonnay in the after-glow of making love, Thom thought, Better thy door than me. Then he looked around the room. The flaring, flickering light from the fireplace made the bedposts seem to dance against the multipaned old windows, especially if he closed his right eye. Rather like a surreal scene from hell through the reduced vision in the left.

When he opened his right eye again, the brass of the poker seemed to glint like gold, reminding him of Emily's jackpot. The gold he couldn't risk losing.

"I have to leave you for a moment, luv."

"Oh, but it's so nice, cuddling like this."

"Sorry, but nature calls."

WATER. GO? NO!

In the bathroom, Thom took a clean facecloth from the linen cabinet and used the flushing of the toilet to mask his re-entry into the bedroom. At the tool rack, he wrapped the facecloth around the handle of the poker to mimic a burglar's glove. Then, hiding the weapon as much as possible behind his bare right leg, Thom tiptoed to Darragh's side of the bed, where one of the floorboards creaked just a bit.

Without opening her eyes, she said, "I didn't hear you coming."

Thom raised the poker over his head. "That was the idea, luv."

HIT. SHE? BAD!

Very carefully, Thom Wexford leaned the poker against the side of the bed near Darragh's body, slipping the facecloth off the handle. She'd made only a low, grunting noise when he struck her, and for all the blood on the sheets and pillow, there was none on the facecloth itself, though some had spattered up and onto his chest. Hmmmmmmmn.

Thom moved to the window, using the cloth first to

open the lock and then to lift the window. Cold February air, but he'd be out in it only a matter of moments.

Climbing onto the fire escape, Thom wrapped the facecloth around his fist before punching out the small pane above the window lock, so the glass would fall inward and break on the hardwood floor. Climbing back in and being careful to step around the glass shards, he lowered the window again.

A last glance around the room before heading to the shower to clean up. Poor Darragh Galvin, another tragic victim of urban burglary gone violent.

Grinning, he headed into the bathroom to shower off the drying drops of blood.

WATER? DOOR? HIM!

In his left hand, Thom Wexford carried the wineglass he'd used back toward the kitchen. Flexing his right forearm, he liked the way the facecloth felt, now wrapped again around the handle of the poker. Rather like a racquet's grip when he'd towel it off during a match, and the perfectly ironic way to avenge all those ambushes by the fireplace.

Thom had considered going after the cat before showering, on the off chance that some of its blood also would spatter up on him. But showering first meant he wouldn't have to remain at the crime scene for a dangerously extended length of time to search out the little wretch.

Because Thom knew just where Pukey would be. Standing inside the doorway to the living room, against that fireplace. Mutant forepaw up to slash at me after my shower.

Yes, well, not this time, eh?

Thom stopped for a moment as something he hadn't anticipated occurred to him. What kind of burglar would kill a cat, too?

Then Thom grinned again. A very *bad* burglar.

HIM? UP! WAIT.

Quite simple, really. The lower creatures are supposedly quite sensitive to emotion, so walk naturally, as if I didn't have a care in the world. Left, right, left. Only instead of leading with my right ankle, I'll bend down a bit and lead with a nice, firm backhand. The cross-court ground-stroke, with topspin. Rip the little wretch's head off its neck.

A three-step movement. Cock. Swing. Follow through.

HIM. READY? NO!

"Damn!"

The poker made a slight crunching noise as it glanced off the wall at the base of the fireplace, chipping some of the plaster onto the floor.

"Not there, eh? Well, that's one life you've burned, Pukey."

Knowing he couldn't risk more time in the apartment searching for the little wretch, Thom began to straighten up.

HIM. SOON . . . NOW!

Thom Wexford's peripheral vision began registering something, but far too slowly for even his honed reflexes to react to it in time.

The pain! "Oh, God!" Searing, indescribable pain from

his right eye. Screaming, he dropped the poker and the wineglass. Brought his right hand up to the socket, felt only wet mush there. Then, terrified, brought his hand over to his left eye. It could deliver only a blur, but a red blur. Slippery against his fingers.

"Oh, God! No. No!"

Naked, and screaming still, Thom headed toward the fuzzy mass of a front door he could barely make out with his left eye. "Help! Doctor! Help me, oh God, help!"

Thom managed to undo the lock and burst into the corridor, his screams reverberating as though someone had loosed them inside an echo chamber. Doors were opening, blurs now of lights and bodies, flooding into the hall.

"No. No!" Thom stumbled against the tenants grabbing at his arms. He pulled away, trying to find the elevator, even the stairs. Other voices yelling, his own mind seizing through the pain into just an internal mantra: "God. Blind? No!"

Everyone seemed unaware of the creature watching it all from the threshold of Darragh Galvin's open door, licking something from its right forepaw and almost . . . smiling?

Him. Gone? Good!

The Author

Just around the corner—a little bit more . . . and there, Steve spotted her again. She really stood out in the registration line at Records Hall, and Steve could overhear her comment to the guy behind her about what a shame it was, Teddy Kennedy being involved in that scandal on Martha's Vineyard the previous summer. The last words she said were, "Well, it's 1969. If Nixon could get elected last year, I guess you really can't trust anybody anymore."

Good, Steve thought. *A challenge.*

A challenge in more ways than one. She was a dead ringer for Katharine Ross, wearing blue-jean bellbottoms and flat sandals, her flower-print peasant blouse providing background for cascading, sun-streaked blonde hair. And cross-registering from Douglass for a class on the Rutgers campus meant she had some sense of adventure, too.

After passing in her form, she moved toward the exit door. A wave to the guy got a "Take it slow, Diane."

So now Steve had a name as well.

Slinging his backpack over just his right shoulder, he began to follow her. Fairly closely, too, because a lot of the people around them—both boys and girls—had shoulder-length blond hair. But Steve was sure Diane wouldn't remember him from the registration line. Face it, he stood at only average height, with flat brown hair that kept falling into his eyes whenever he moved his head. And Steve was also kind of skinny, always glad to be able to bulk up his clothes when sweater-weather came to "the banks of the old Raritan." His dad had said that to him three years before as a freshman when he dropped Steve off at Pell in the Quad, and son had been afraid to ask father what it meant, not understanding until he attended a football game at the Heights and heard the alma mater sung drunkenly after an unexpected victory against Lafayette.

Steve watched Diane turn onto George Street, and for a moment he was afraid she might be shacking up with a guy in one of the river dorms, like a lot of students everywhere were doing. But no, Diane bobbed and weaved through the people on the Clothier side of the street, passing Frelinghuysen and its parking lot and walking toward downtown New Brunswick.

Maybe she was going to walk all the way to Douglass, which would complicate things. Then Steve relaxed as Diane finally crossed the street and went into The Pub.

Probably old enough to drink, so she's heard a lot of lines before. Which made her even more of a challenge.

"Anybody sitting here?"

Diane looked up at the guy with the brown hair in his face. Kind of skinny, but a nice voice. "Help yourself."

She was having a glass of Chablis, Almaden. Ever since turning twenty-one, Diane treated herself to a drink after accomplishing something she hated, like standing in a stupid line to sign up for a Rutgers course. Just so there'd be some guys to meet who wouldn't be moaning at a coffeehouse about getting drafted and sent to Vietnam. Or be pouring a pitcher of beer over her head at a frat house on College Ave. God, what Diane wouldn't give for just one intelligent, groovy, maybe even artistic—

"My name's Craig, Craig Powers."

She looked over at the guy, who had his hand out. Clean fingernails, and he didn't bite them. She shook with him. "Diane."

"You look smart," said Craig.

Diane realized he was still holding her hand, but strangely enough, she also realized she didn't mind. "You at Rutgers?"

"No. I'm here for a signing, out on Route 1."

Diane was sure she'd blinked stupidly, but tried to recover by saying, "A signing."

"Of my book. I'm an author." Craig dipped into his backpack, came out with an orange flier like you'd get at a peace rally. Only this paper had the guy's name and face on it above a little bio of how he'd graduated Princeton and gotten his first novel published at age—

"You wrote a novel?" Diane said, feeling a little ping deep inside her.

"Two actually, but only one's out so far. The production time at the publisher is almost a year. Once you hand in the manuscript, that is."

"How did you get a novel published?"

"Well, my dad's the head of this printing outfit, and they work with a lot of publishers. So, when I wrote the book, he used some of his contacts to get an editor to look at it, and . . ."

"Wait a minute," said Diane, looking down at the flier again. "Anybody can hoke up one of these."

Craig shrugged. "There a bookstore within walking distance?"

Steve let her lead him to Reed's, maybe another block

east on George Street. It was an ancient place, with a loft overlooking displays of stationery items and hardcover books. When they got to the right shelf, he also let Diane pull the book by "Craig Powers."

Steve watched her open it to the back jacket, where his photo appeared over the same mini-bio as was on the orange flier. He also watched her eyes widen as Diane realized that.

"This," she said, "is way beyond cool."

Steve made a ritual of looking at his watch. "Tell you what. How about if I buy that and inscribe it to you?"

Her eyes got wider. "You serious?"

"Sure, but . . ." he glanced at his watch again. "I have to get back to my motel out on Route 1."

Diane smiled then, just the way Steve hoped she would. A little lilt of the head, a subtle shift of the hips. "Think we'd have time before your signing?"

He smiled back, confident now. "I'll make time."

Steve lay on his back under a sheet in the motel room. Pretty standard place, but then "standard" also meant anonymous, as he'd come to prefer, dodging the draft.

Steve glanced over at Diane, lying on her stomach, face turned toward him. God, after flunking out of Rutgers halfway through his freshman year, he'd never have dreamed of making love with so many college girls. But going back to work in his father's printing business—even with his tail dragging between his legs—had provided unexpected . . . advantages. Like earning enough money to buy a car and stay on the run from Selective Service. Like learning how to fiddle things, especially when that geek from Princeton, Craig Powers, got a first novel accepted.

It had been child's play for Steve to slip a few extra

proofs of the book jacket from the production line and superimpose his own photo for "Craig's" on them. Steve had even read the sappy story, just in case any of the girls asked him about it.

But so far, none of the four had. He'd bedded each with the same scam. One from Columbia, the second from Temple in Philly, a third from Monmouth College down the shore. And even Diane, who'd said he could inscribe her copy—the book he'd re-jacketed in Reed's an hour earlier—"afterwards."

Well, now it was afterwards, all right. Steve reached over, ruffled the hank of blonde hair hanging over her open right eye.

That was the bummer, of course. Having to kill them.

He'd disposed of each body discreetly, using the trunk of his car as the "hearse." And the different newspapers had chalked every one up to "just another runaway, off to join the hippies."

Yes, killing the girls was necessary, to protect him from being caught in his scam or caught dodging the draft. But maybe even more to protect his own sense of identity.

His new identity as . . . "the Author."

Then Steve laughed, hard enough to shake the bed. Diane had been right in that registration line.

You really couldn't trust anybody anymore.

Hero

ONE

Frank Rossi sat in his swivel chair by the telephone table at the gallery end of the jury box, watching the "real cop" testify from the witness stand. As a court officer, Frank was by statute entitled to police powers himself, like the right to carry the Glock 17 on his right hip. And he went to the firing range every Friday to make sure he could hit what he aimed at. Because that same statute also said a bailiff could arrest a perp if he saw something illegal go down on the street. Only problem was, any time Frank'd be on the street, he'd be wearing civvies instead of his uniform, and fat chance Angela Rossi's only son would risk his life to bring in some scumbag.

You can picture yourself as Sylvester Stallone playing Rambo, or even Rocky, but when you're more like Sly as the fat sheriff in *Copland*, who'd you be kidding, huh?

Frank liked being a court officer well enough, though, despite the low pay. After all, it was an eight-to-four job with plenty of dead space in it, and no cameras in the courtroom to catch a poor civil servant on the doze. Most of the dead space came from a trial being less like your slick, bang-bang movie and more like a theater play the actors and all were still rehearsing, with lots of stops and delays in

139

the action. If endless testimony and truckloads of documents counted as "action." But Frank thought the different people he got to see made up for all the bullshit.

Take this trial, for instance. *Commonwealth vs. Dennis Doyle.* Or Dennis "the Menace," which was Doyle's mob nickname. Frank actually enjoyed seeing the Irish Mafia get roasted for a change. Doyle himself was a big guy, kind of role you'd give Brian Dennehy with the broad shoulders, beefy face, and wavy hair. Every tooth in his head perfect from birth or dentistry, Doyle had to be in his sixties trying real hard not to look a day past fifty, and pulling it off. Of course, he pulled off a lot of things, running most of the rackets on the South Shore, but according to the prosecution, the Menace had made the mistake of whacking somebody by his own hand in Frank's county. Doyle claimed he was framed, which was par for the course, given that somebody had to have pumped three slugs into the victim. Frank had seen the crime-scene photos of the body when they were put into evidence and passed around the jury. Not pretty pictures, either, and even Dennis the Menace with all his money got denied bail on the charge back at his arraignment.

Which was about all the poor prosecutor had won, far as Frank could tell. Assistant D.A. Ellen Duchesne was short and fat, with a whiny voice that made her seem not exactly up to the task at hand. You'd cast her as Rhoda's sister from that old sitcom, feeling sorry for her every time she opened her mouth.

Mainly, though, you'd feel sorry for her because of the tap dance the defense attorney was doing on the prosecution's evidence. Frank had to admit, he ever got in felony trouble himself, be nice to afford Aaron Weinberg in there pitching for him. Medium height with a beard, the guy was kind of a bald Al Pacino. Sharp dresser, yeah, but sharp as a tack, too. And genuinely "courtly" to everybody, not like those assholes on O.J.'s "dream team."

Weinberg managed to look noble even when he was talking with Doyle's number-two guy, one of those thirtyish, executive types with a quarterback's build that every mob seemed to be bringing up as the next generation. Edward was his name, but Frank thought of him as just "Eddie," account of the guy reminded him of Eddie Haskell from the old *Leave It to Beaver* show. Doyle's Eddie would sit in the first row of the gallery, directly behind the defense table, though he was gone from the courtroom a lot, probably running errands for his boss. Eddie had the good fortune not to be indicted for this particular homicide, as he was driving Mrs. Doyle home from some kind of charity function at the time.

Which brought Frank to the most interesting part of the case, at least from his standpoint. Mrs. Lisa Doyle. About five-six in sensible heels, but with great legs that seemed to vibrate as she walked down the center aisle of the courtroom. She always took the gallery bench right behind Weinberg, so the Menace could see her by turning only halfway in the defendant's chair. And so the loving couple could kind of clasp hands briefly over the bar enclosure rail whenever the two other bailiffs brought Doyle to or from the defense table. Maybe thirty or so, Lisa didn't dress to show off the rest of what Frank figured to be a dynamite figure under the clothes, but she couldn't do much to hide that face, even when she was bringing a dark hankie up to it—just so—to dab at her eyes from time to time. Eyes that hung back a little above cheekbones like Michelle Pfeiffer's, only with longish black hair, like Michelle wore hers in *Married to the Mob*. Which made Frank laugh a little, he had to admit.

Here Lisa Doyle reminds you of your favorite actress in that movie, and the poor broad actually *is* married to the mob.

Then Frank Rossi caught himself staring at her because he suddenly realized she was sending him a smile. Kind of a warm, dreamy one, which Frank held on to almost too long. Almost long enough for her husband to maybe turn sideways a little and notice. Which thank Christ he didn't, especially since, with Aaron Weinberg earning his money, Dennis the Menace was probably gonna walk out of the courtroom a free man.

TWO

In the bailiffs' locker room, Frank changed from his uniform to a flannel shirt and blue jeans. The jeans were loose enough at the waist to let him stick the Glock over his right hip under the shirt, which his late mother always thought looked sloppy but which made Frank feel a lot more secure. After he was done changing clothes, Frank left the courthouse through the employee's entrance, thankfully spared the "anti-terrorist" arch of metal detector that visitors had to go through on the other side of the building.

Hitting the open-air parking lot, he got into the old wreck of a Buick that had been his mom's and started the usual ritual. Drive to a bar, have a few pops while catching part of a ballgame on the tube, "Monday Night Football" that October evening. Then stop off at the video store to return last night's selection and pick up a new one to watch later in his apartment. From bed, fantasizing the VCR was letting him pull back the sheets for the best-looking woman in the flick. Frank saw a lot of guys renting the hard-core porn tapes, but half the bimbos in them were stone-ugly, and the other half were dense as a fucking post, the way they talked, if the director let them talk at all.

No, Frank preferred the real thing, somebody with a genuine personality. Kathleen Turner in *Body Heat* or Sharon Stone in *Basic Instinct*, if he was into flashy and dangerous. Sandra Bullock for good fun, Winona Ryder for sensitive—

Whoa, boy. Pay attention to the traffic. Plenty of time to make up your mind after you're on the corner stool a while.

And it was a while, sitting on that corner stool at the bar, before Frank noticed the blonde over in the booth, all by herself. She was wearing tinted glasses and a bulky turtleneck. He watched two guys try their luck, neither getting as far as sliding onto the bench across from her. Hard to tell much about the broad with the shades and sweater, but there was something about the way she was holding her head that rang a bell. She even looked over at him, more than a couple times, almost like that—

Hey, who you kidding now? You got Doyle's wife on the brain. Go back to your ballgame.

Which Frank did, for one more beer before leaving the change on the bartop and going out the door.

He didn't recognize the voice behind him because he'd never heard her yell before.

"Frank, you want to wait up?"

He stopped and turned. The blonde, with a walk he did recognize.

Frank looked around the block nervously. "The hell you think you're doing?"

"Trying to talk with you." Lisa was less than an arm's

length away now, her tone conversational. "Okay?"

Frank didn't think it was, but he couldn't tell her so.

She said, "I've been watching you in that courtroom for a week now. Found out your name, put on this wig and glasses, and followed you to that bar back there."

"Why?" was all Frank could manage.

"My husband. Aaron thinks he's going to get off on this murder charge."

Frank thought, "Aaron," not "my husband's lawyer."

Lisa said, "And I think he's right."

So did Frank, but what did that matter?

She leaned a little closer. "I can't stand being married to Dennis anymore, Frank."

He began to turn away. "You want a divorce, find your own lawyer."

Lisa touched his arm. Didn't grab it or even the shirt. Just a touch, nails long and pink. Frank felt something like electricity ripple through him.

All the way through him.

Lisa said, "I don't want to get divorced, Frank. I want to be widowed."

"You're talking crazy now."

"I'm not crazy, but I will be if I have to spend another night with Dennis. He's a pig, Frank. And I need somebody to take him out of my life."

"I don't do murder." Frank turned away. Partly to get away, sure, but partly—mostly—to see if Lisa Doyle would touch him again.

She did, and it stopped him because she picked a slightly different spot on his arm for her fingers.

Same feeling though.

Lisa said, "I can offer you money, Frank. And lots of it, once Dennis is dead."

"Okay, that's crazy just as it stands," Frank thinking he was sounding perfectly reasonable. "You expect me to kill a guy—a goddamned mobster—without being paid for it up front?"

That dreamy, Michelle Pfeiffer smile from the courtroom. "I've come up with a way to make it worth your while. I'm going to be staying at our beach house on the shore tomorrow night." Suddenly she was tucking a folded piece of paper into his shirt pocket. "That's the address, with my little diagram for parking at a shopping center five blocks away, so nobody'll notice your car. This time of year, none of our neighbors use their houses during the week."

Frank said the first thing that popped into his head. "What about your security?"

"Security?"

"That Eddie guy or his goons?"

The dreamy smile. "You watch too many movies, Frank."

Lisa Doyle walked away. Frank stood where she'd left him, following her with his eyes until she got into a silver Mercedes sports coupe and drove out of sight.

That's when he said to himself that he'd think about it. Just think about it.

But before heading north to his apartment, Frank Rossi stopped at the video store and rented a copy of *Married to the Mob*.

THREE

That next Tuesday, in the courtroom, Frank sat in his chair at the end of the jury box and watched Lisa Doyle. When he realized he had to stop watching her, he turned toward the witness stand and thought about watching her.

Absently, Frank felt sorry for Ellen Duchesne, her whiny voice botching the direct examination of a crime lab techie who'd run some tests on fibers found at the homicide scene. Just as Aaron Weinberg began slicing and dicing the techie on cross-examination, Eddie the number-two guy came in the courtroom, waiting until the morning recess to confer with Dennis the Menace. The two mobsters leaned toward each other above the bar enclosure like a couple of suburbanites chatting over a picket fence.

Once, when Frank turned back to Lisa, she was staring at him, mouthing the word "tonight."

That's when he turned away again, he thought for good. By the clock on the courtroom wall though, barely three minutes had passed before his eyes strayed over again. And again.

Frank Rossi found himself looking up at the clock often, thinking the hands must be moving backwards, it still seemed so long till four o'clock and quitting time.

After changing in the locker room, Frank tried to follow his usual routine. Walk to the car, drive to the bar, early hockey game on the TV over the top shelf. Midway through the first period and only one beer, though, he found himself going through the door. At the video store, Frank returned *Married to the Mob* and came out onto the sidewalk, breathing hard. Before he was behind the wheel again, Frank knew which way he was going to turn. South. Toward the shore.

Frank did a drive-by of Lisa Doyle's address at normal speed, nothing to call attention to himself.

It was a saltbox cape with weathered shingles, backing right onto the ocean. Her silver Mercedes coupe, snugged up against a garage door, glittered like a piece of jewelry. Frank could see a couple of lights in the cape, one downstairs, one up. The windows of the surrounding houses stood dark, though, and there were no cars in front of them.

Continuing along the street, Frank found the little shopping center right where Lisa's diagram put it. If nobody else was using the shore houses, enough other folks must be year-rounders, because the lot seemed nearly full, and his Buick could kind of hide in the crowd.

Frank turned off the ignition and sat for a while. Sat until he thought a guy alone in an old wreck might look suspicious.

Then realized that wasn't the reason he wanted to get out of his car.

Frank opened the driver's side door and heaved himself to his feet. After locking up, he started walking the five blocks back toward the house. Started huffing, too, and consciously slowed down.

Hey, you don't want to faint on her stoop, right?

At the cape, Frank moved up the path, the Mercedes to his right now catching some moonlight, the same moonlight that twinkled off the ocean water beyond. He was about to push the button on the jamb when the door itself swung open.

A table lamp deeper in the house turned her into a silhouette, the sheer body stocking the kind he'd seen only on women in mail-order catalogs.

"I've been waiting for you, Frank," said Lisa Doyle in a voice from one of his dreams.

FOUR

Wednesday morning, Frank Rossi couldn't believe how he felt, even just sitting in his bailiff's chair. Tingling all over, the way a real movie star must feel after a night with a starlet.

Only Lisa Doyle wasn't any kid, and she knew how to do everything perfectly. Not like the porn films he'd rented before growing tired of them, the bimbos looking like they were bored or faking or so obviously coked up it amounted to the same thing. No, Lisa was a . . . a sorceress, taking him to the top once, twice, and even Frank didn't believe the third time.

By the same token, there was no bullshit about her. He was going to enjoy her body and talents only until she got the money to pay him for killing her husband.

And Lisa Doyle had even come up with the perfect way to do that, Frank had to admit.

"So," she said as soon as he arrived for the second night, "let's run through it again."

Lisa had rearranged the dining room chairs in her living room, just like she'd shown him the prior evening. Four of the chairs outlined the courtroom's bar enclosure on either side of its center-aisle gate. One of the chairs represented the first gallery bench, where Lisa had sat throughout the trial, dabbing her eyes with that black hankie.

Now, in the beach house, she pointed to the small revolver she'd laid in Frank's hand. "Let's practice you passing it to me again."

He turned the gun over. "You sure the serial numbers are wiped off?"

"Positive. Dennis always said, 'You need a clean piece, this is the one you use.' "

Frank didn't think he wanted to know why Dennis the Menace would believe his wife might need a "clean piece."

Lisa said, "You've smuggled that through the employee entrance in the morning, where there's no metal detector and you're not searched.

"In the locker room, when nobody's watching, you put the gun in the side pocket of your uniform pants with the black hankie around it. Now, go ahead."

"Go ahead what?"

Lisa took a small breath before smiling. "Put the gun in the hankie and everything in your right pocket. Good. Now, make like it's just before court starts. You walk around the chairs like they're that bar fence, and I'll turn away from the gate."

As he had the night before, Frank felt a little silly, but he moved along the two chairs as though they were actually the bar enclosure. Using his left hand, he pushed on the imaginary "gate," stepping into the "center aisle."

Over her shoulder, Lisa said, "That's when I'll turn back around and bump into you, so the gun already has to be in the black hankie and in your hand for me."

"What if I slip up and put a fingerprint on the gun by accident?"

"While it's in your pocket?"

"Or while I'm pulling it out."

"Then just be sure you're the first one to Dennis."

Frank pictured what she meant.

Lisa frowned. "You okay?"

"I'm okay."

"You look kind of—"

"I'm okay, all right? Now what?"

Lisa smiled again, that dreamy . . . "Just like we did last night."

Frank shook his head, but he moved through the living room as though he were walking down the center aisle. After six strides, he said, "Judge'll be out in a minute" to an imaginary person before turning and walking back.

Lisa frowned a little. "You'll look more natural in the real courtroom, I think."

Frank "opened" the gate again and approached his usual "swivel chair" at the gallery end of the jury box.

"And besides," she waved at the surrounding walls, "there won't be any cameras to catch it anyway."

In the Doyles' living room, Frank sat down in the chair that was supposed to be his own.

"After that," said Lisa, "all we have to do is wait till the morning break, and—"

"Recess."

"What?"

"The morning recess, the judge calls it."

"Fine." That smile. "When she says it's time for the morning recess, you say 'All rise' like any other day. Then I lean over the bar rail to Dennis, and I push the gun into his hand."

"What if that Eddie guy is there?"

"Half the time he isn't."

"He might see you, though."

"Don't worry about it."

"Or Weinberg. He'll be right there, too."

"Frank," a little impatience maybe creeping through the smile. "I'll pass the thing so nobody sees me."

"But without leaving any prints on it."

"What the hankie's for, remember?" Lisa closed her eyes a moment. "That's when I scream, 'Dennis, no!' "

"And I yell 'Gun, gun, gun!' "

Lisa stopped, a hand rubbing the ear closest to Frank.

"That's how you're going to do it, three times like that?"

"It's the way they trained us."

"Fine, so that's what you'll do. And then . . . ?"

"Then . . ." Frank hesitated until the dreamiest smile yet about melted him. "Then I pull my Glock and shoot him."

"Just 'shoot' him?"

Another hesitation. "Kill him."

"Say it again."

Frank cleared his throat. "I kill him."

"Try it three times, loud, like when you yell about the gun."

"I kill him, I kill him, I kill him!"

A different smile. "Now you've got the idea."

Afterward, in bed, Lisa said, "You probably should leave soon."

Frank spoke to the ceiling, the sheets still caked to him all over. "When?"

"Say ten minutes. You want to shower, it's—"

"No." Frank shifted a little, but didn't get any more comfortable. "I mean, when do you think we'll do it?"

"Pretty soon. Aaron says he doesn't see that whiny prosecutor having much more to throw at Dennis."

What Frank heard was the "Aaron" part again. "You trust him?"

"Who?"

"Your husband's lawyer."

A sigh. "You've probably seen him in action more than I have, but yeah, I trust his judgment on the trial stuff."

Frank couldn't bring himself to ask anything more about Weinberg.

"Frank?"

"Yeah?"

"Don't worry. You'll be a hero. Believe me, Dennis really killed that guy. Not to mention a dozen others."

Right then, Frank Rossi was thinking less about the people Dennis the Menace Doyle had shot and more about the ones Frank himself hadn't.

FIVE

Thursday morning before court, Frank noticed that Eddie wasn't in the gallery. Doyle himself almost lounged in his chair at the defense table, joking with Aaron Weinberg like a salesman knowing he was going to close a big deal. At the first recess, Frank did a dry run with Lisa, not actually bumping her in the center aisle, but feeling out the distances and timing.

When the trial resumed, Weinberg started hammering at a Commonwealth "earwitness," as Frank liked to call people who heard something about a crime but didn't actually see the thing go down. By the time Doyle's attorney was done, the witness looked battered, and dumpy Ellen Duchesne looked beaten.

Lisa, on the other hand, looked beautiful. Just before lunch, she acted like she had something in her eye, using the hankie to hide her giving Frank a wink.

And that's when he knew for sure he was going to do it. All the doubts he'd felt—qualms, his late mother would have called them—just seemed to slide away inside his chest, and Frank genuinely relaxed in the swivel chair.

He was going to do it. Less for the money and more for Lisa, to get her free of that arrogant pig.

In fact, you look at it the right way, you're kind of *her* hero, solving this problem she has.

Thursday night, when Lisa opened the front door of the

beach house for Frank, she had on a dress instead of lingerie, but it was a different kind of dress than the quiet business ones she wore to court for her husband's trial. This was kind of skimpy, plain black and a little shiny, too. Like silk, maybe.

When Frank stepped into the foyer, he could see the dining room chairs arranged again in the living room. "We gonna do another rehearsal?"

"Passing the gun, you mean?"

"Yeah."

"Later," she said.

"Later?"

"After we go upstairs. I have a treat for you."

Frank could actually feel his knees shaking from excitement as he climbed the steps behind her.

Once in the bedroom, Lisa turned to him. The sheets were already pulled down, the lights muted. Frank kind of liked that she'd dimmed the lights because he knew he didn't have the greatest physique in the world, nothing like a male version of the body on her.

Lisa gave him the dreamy smile, her teeth the brightest things in the room. "Tear off my dress."

That stopped him, but excited him, too. "What?"

"Tear off my dress."

"I . . . I don't get . . ."

"Frank," reaching for his hand, "you've been a good guy through this so far, and I want you to have something special out of it tonight." She brought his hand up to her neckline. "I want you to tear this thing off me, get to see what I'm wearing underneath."

Frank could feel the silky material, could feel himself swelling below his belt buckle, bigger than he'd ever—

"Come on, Frank. I want you to."

And suddenly, irresistibly, he wanted to as well. He ripped the dress down the side of her body, then across, like a huge letter "L" with the foot kind of diagonal instead of straight.

Which was when he could see that what she was wearing underneath was nothing at all.

"It's tomorrow, right?"

After Frank had spoken the words to the ceiling, he turned away from Lisa and stared at her torn dress on the bedroom carpet.

"How did you know?" she said.

He turned back to the ceiling. "Because after it happens, we don't see each other again except for you giving me the money, and tonight felt kind of like . . ."

"A going-away present?"

Lisa's voice sounded thick to Frank, almost as if she was going to cry.

He said, "Something like that, yeah."

Her voice steadied. "Aaron told us today he doesn't think he has to put on much of a defense case, and for sure not call Dennis to the stand as a witness himself."

"So, if we don't do it at the morning recess—"

"We may not get another chance."

Frank could see it, feel it. Lisa was right.

In an even steadier voice, she said, "Tomorrow you're going to be a hero, Frank. And a week later, you'll be rich to boot."

Frank Rossi was conscious of hearing both things Lisa Doyle told him, but he realized it was only the first part that he cared about.

SIX

At five minutes to the morning recess, Eddie the number-two guy still hadn't shown up in the courtroom, and Frank let himself breathe a little easier in his swivel chair. It'd been a piece of cake getting the snubbie revolver wrapped in Lisa's handkerchief through the employee's entrance and, at his locker, into the side pocket of his uniform pants. And Frank had passed it to Lisa at the center aisle so smoothly, he'd felt like a feather as he floated down the aisle, exchanged a stupid crack with another bailiff at the rear of the room, and then walked back to his chair.

When the judge announced the morning recess, Frank stood quickly. Calling out, "All rise," he was aware of everybody else getting to their feet. But then the rest of it played out in a kind of slow motion, like one of those shoot-'em-up scenes from a spaghetti western.

Lisa, her hankie between her hands, leaning over the gallery rail to Dennis Doyle, like she always did. Him taking both of her hands in his, again like always.

Then Lisa jumping back as the two bailiffs casually approached the defendant, her mouth opening, her words splitting the air.

Somewhere between "Dennis" and "no!", Frank was bringing the Glock out of his holster, the two bailiffs jumping back themselves from Lisa's scream. Frank bellowed the magic word "Gun!" three times as he opened fire, the shots making his ears ring.

The first slug struck Dennis Doyle square in the chest, just as the man was looking down at the revolver in his own hand. The second caught him near the left shoulder, knocking the mobster off-center. The third bullet punched Doyle in the throat, carrying him back over his chair and onto the defense table. By now, everybody in the room except for Frank had dropped to their haunches, yelling like they were real excited about looking for a contact lens on the floor.

And then there was nothing but the smell of cordite hanging heavy around him, every living eye staring up at the hero near the gallery end of the jury box.

Funny, the thing you think will be the worst part turns out to be the easiest.

Passing that revolver to Lisa without fumbling it out of the hankie or putting a fingerprint on the frame was what had occupied Frank the most, but the thing he'd really worried about was the shooting itself. With a real human being in his sights, would he be able to pull the trigger?

But, turned out, everything felt exactly the way it did on the firing range. Frank had found himself not so much aiming as just pointing and squeezing off the rounds, seeing the little puffs of cloth and blood come up as the slugs impacted their target. There was no video of the scene to play back, of course, except the one in his head, which improved slightly each time Frank revisited it during his week's paid leave of absence from the job.

He'd also worried some about the Shoot Team interrogation, but that proved to be so routine he was almost embarrassed to answer their questions. The guys who really drew the heat were the two bailiffs who supposedly checked the defendant carefully each time they brought him into the courtroom, because—after all—that little snubbie had to come from *somewhere*.

Frank was less concerned about Aaron Weinberg. The defense attorney immediately told the press that there was "absolutely no reason" Dennis Doyle would have thought he needed to shoot his way out of the charge against him, especially given Weinberg's confidence "in the jury's eventual verdict." Obviously, Lisa had done a nice job of shielding the gun from her husband's lawyer.

In fact, as things unfolded, the biggest pain in the ass for Frank was all the fuss the media made over him. He stopped clipping the newspaper headlines—or even taping the broadcast stuff with his VCR—by the end of the second day. The fucking jackals, they camped outside his apartment around the clock, just waiting for him to go buy a loaf of bread or a six-pack of beer to pump him for "additional comments" or "after-shock feelings" on the incident which had made him "The Dirty-Harry Hero."

At least, Frank conceded, they'd gone with a movie he liked.

In the end, though, it wasn't till the fifth day—when two state troopers brought down a drive-by shooter after a high-speed chase—that the media picked up stakes and moved their circus to somebody else's front yard. Frank telephoned his superior, saying he figured he could come back in to work then, but still was told to wait until after the weekend.

Which washed fine with Frank. After the days he'd had with the media—not to mention the nights with Lisa before that—he could use the rest. He began to spend his time more normally, going out for a few beers, the hero stuff still there but starting to slack off in the bars. The way Frank saw it, he was getting his life back on track.

But what had happened in Lisa's bedroom and the courtroom had been a part of his life, too. And, starting up the old Buick to drive to her house for his money, Frank Rossi realized that he had no regrets about having lived those parts—and having been her hero—for real.

"It's open," was Lisa Doyle's muffled answer to his knock on the front door.

Frank entered the foyer, noticing that all the furniture from the dining room had been moved back to where it belonged.

"I'm upstairs."

He climbed the steps, thinking how differently he'd felt every other time he'd done so.

"My bedroom, Frank," in the dreamy voice.

The tantalizing thought of a "bonus" went through his head, and he walked a little faster to the open door of the room Frank associated with the best hours he'd ever lived.

Before what he saw stopped him dead.

"God, Frank, don't be shy now."

On the bed, a briefcase lay open like a clamshell, cash stacked inside it. Lisa stood next to the bed, fanning a pack of greenbacks with her left thumb, the right hand behind her, like she was pregnant and resting it on her butt.

But Lisa wore the silky black dress from their last night together. The torn one, only with a bra and panties clearly visible underneath.

Frank said, "I don't . . ."

"I thought it might be kind of fun to do it one last time." She gestured with the cash in her left hand. "On the bed, but with your money spread all around us."

Frank just stared.

Lisa took two steps toward him. "Come on, what do you say?"

He couldn't say anything, truth to tell, but he swallowed hard and began walking toward her.

When Frank was about an arm's length away—like they'd been that first time after she'd yelled to him on the street—Lisa Doyle brought her right hand out from behind her back and fired the gun in it three times.

Frank thought somebody had hit him in the chest with a sledgehammer. Then the walls and ceiling began to switch places. He felt the back of his head bounce off the floor, but somehow it didn't hurt.

Which seemed kind of funny, you know?

Stretched out flat, staring at the ceiling from a different perspective than he'd gotten those nights from her bed, Frank heard other footsteps and saw two faces superimpose themselves on the ceiling, looking down on him now. Lisa's, right side up and . . .

Eddie's, upside down?

Sure, thought Frank. Because he's standing behind you.

"I didn't kill him?" from Lisa's face.

"The fucking whale's got to bleed out," from Eddie's. "Way it's going, shouldn't take too long."

Your eyes and ears still work, but so hard to . . . breathe.

Lisa's face said, "Should I shoot him again?"

"No. Lab stuff from the cops wouldn't look right, the sex-crazed hero gets shot on the floor after you already popped him for tearing your dress off to rape you."

Frank wanted to say something, but could only burble out some . . . spit?

She turned away. "Jesus, he's trying to talk."

"I'll give you this, Lise," said Eddie. "The fucking guy never knew we were setting him up."

Coming from a new direction, Lisa's voice sounded bitter. "We wouldn't have had to, you'd done the frame on Dennis right from the start."

"Yeah, well, I didn't," said Eddie's face, grinning down at Frank. "Every day of that trial, the boss had me hustling my ass all over the fucking place, trying to find out who'd fingered him. But, once Weinberg got Dennis off in court, the boss would have figured why I was coming up empty."

"And figured us," from Lisa.

"Hey." Eddie looked away now. "Make sure you don't smear the whale's fingerprints on that fucking dress."

Lisa Doyle's face loomed back into Frank's vision, and he tried to muster a smile to thank her for the sight.

She spoke with those eyes as well as her mouth. "Sorry, Frank, but I needed you to make this thing work. Do you understand?"

Frank Rossi tried to remember which movie that reminded him of, but there wasn't quite . . . enough time . . . to . . .

The Safest Little Town in Texas

Alone in the stolen '92 Ford, Polk Greshen checked the rearview mirror. No cars behind him, period, much less one with bubble-lights on its roof. First good omen since he'd killed that gas station attendant over the Oklahoma line.

"Damn-fool beaner," thought Polk, focusing back on the road in front of him. "I tell him, 'All right, I'll be needing your cash,' and he makes like, '*Senor, no hablo* the English.' Only the beaner'd have to be blind not to see the nine-millimeter in my hand, me waving it at the register. What'd he think I meant? But no, the man has to be a hero, try for the tire iron he had on a shelf behind some oil cans. Well, now he ain't never gonna '*hablo* the English.' Or anything else, far as that goes."

Polk had boosted the Ford from a movie-house parking lot five miles from the station, so he figured it was still a pretty safe vehicle in terms of being connected to the killing. Radio didn't work, but the air did—praise the Lord. Also, he'd found a set of keys under the driver's seat that fit. "Damn-fool owner, might's well leave them sticking in the ignition." Only thing was, the Oklahoma police could have the license plate on their hot list by now, and Polk was pretty sure those computer things could run the tags on any car they stopped.

So after killing the attendant, Polk had driven real conservative-like, getting on U.S. 283 south and crossing the Red River into Texas north of Vernon. Maybe an Oklahoma stolen car wouldn't get onto the hot list for Texas, and he could always hole up with a cousin lived just outside Hobbs, New Mexico, which should be due southwest from where he was right now. "About got enough money from the beaner's till to see me through gas and food, long's I don't go hog-wild on things." Polk also figured it was smart to stick to the smaller roads, and so far he'd been right.

Until the Ford's goddamn oil light came on.

Polk used the heel of his hand to wham at the light, but that didn't do any good. Pulling over to the side of the road, he got out. The heat was like standing on top of a griddle, but Polk didn't plan to be in it long. He went to the trunk of the car, using the key that didn't fit the ignition to open the lid. A rat-eared blanket, two wrenches, and . . . a bird cage? Would you look at that.

But no oil. Figures.

Polk slammed down the lid. "Should of stole some from that beaner back at the gas station. It was an omen, for sure, him having that tire iron by the cans there."

The air frying his lungs, Polk tried to guesstimate where he was at. Hour or more east of Lubbock, probably. But he hadn't seen a soul along the road, not a house, nothing for quite a while. Looking west, there seemed to be some kind of signpost only half a mile on.

Back behind the wheel, Polk drove toward the signpost. Sure enough, it marked a small intersection, the arrow aiming north with "Bibby, 2 miles." Better bet than taking a chance on civilization suddenly sprouting up in front of him.

Muttering under his breath at the oil light, Polk Greshen turned right.

★ ★ ★ ★ ★

"Well, well. Do you believe it?" Polk expected Bibby to be no more than a crossroads, lucky to have a general-store with a pump outside it. Instead, just about the time he could make out a clump of buildings in the distance, there was this real nice mini-billboard on the side of the road:

WELCOME TO BIBBY
THE SAFEST LITTLE TOWN IN TEXAS
POP. 327

Another favorable impression as he approached the first few buildings along the main street. Old and mostly wood, except for the bank, which was yellow brick. But everything all spruced up with new paint and bright little signs like BIBBY CAFÉ and COLE'S HARDWARE and so on. Good omen, for a change. All the way at the end of the street, Polk thought he could see POLICE on a bigger sign with something else writ smaller beneath it, but it was too far away to read. "Don't think I'll be visiting that end of town, anyway, no-thank-you-sir."

There was precious little vehicle traffic, only a couple of people walking heat-slow past the storefronts. Fortunately, in the next block Polk spotted a filling station—not a national company, just "GAS"—but it had a couple of service bays. He pulled into the station near the pumps; and a mechanic came out from one of the bays, wiping grease off his hands with a rag.

The man was dressed in a white tee-shirt and denim overalls, all kinds of things sagging in his pockets. Polk thought he must be just about dying from the temperature, though the mechanic gave no notice of it walking over to the Ford.

Polk glanced down at his own clothes. New, tooled boots; sharp, stone-washed jeans; and a Led Zeppelin tank-top from that Tulsa rockshop, the nine-millimeter barely a lump where he'd stuck it in his belt under the top. "I'll probably look mighty city to these folks."

The man's overalls had a name patch on the left breast. "Sid," was what it said.

Without turning off the engine, Polk looked at him. "Sid, I'll be needing some oil."

A nod. "What weight you got in her now?"

Polk could hot-wire a car, but he didn't ever have one long enough to think of such things. "Not sure about that."

Another nod. "Your light come on, did it?"

"About three miles back, give or take."

Sid nodded again. "Let me take a look under her."

Polk had run some cons himself in the past, so he sure could see one coming at him now. He got out of the Ford, trying not to breathe the heat too deeply, and squatted down as Sid did about the sorriest pushup you've ever seen, face staring under the chassis.

"See that there?"

Polk used his hand to brace himself, nearly burning the skin right off the palm on Sid's hot asphalt. Following the mechanic's pointing finger, he could see the kind of drip-drip-drip you get from an old faucet. Only it wasn't water.

"Oil, huh?"

"That's what they call it." Sid got to his feet like a lame bear. "I'm gonna have to put her up on the rack, try and plug the leak."

"How much?"

"Won't know that till I get her up there."

Polk figured he could kiss what was left of the beaner's money good-bye. "How long, then?"

A sweep of the hand toward the other cars in the lot. "Got four ahead of you."

Polk considered grabbing this hick by the straps on his overalls, shaking him till he thought some about changing his priorities. But Polk was a wanted man driving a stolen car, and the less attention he drew, the better.

"Any place to eat?"

"Café. You must've passed her a few blocks back, way you were driving."

"Thanks." Saying it kind of flat.

As Polk began to walk, he adjusted the gun in his belt for strolling instead of driving. Passing two of the cars ahead of him for servicing, he automatically glanced at their steering wheels. Both had their keys still in the ignition.

Despite the temperature, Polk smiled, talking softly to himself. "Well, well. Old Sid tries to hold me up, leastways I can get myself some substitute transportation."

Heading south toward the café, he noticed keys in the ignition of most every parked car on his side of the street and felt his smile getting wider. "My kind of town, Bibby is."

"Afternoon."

As the screened door slapped closed behind him, Polk looked at the woman who'd spoken. She was dressed in one of those old-fashioned waitress outfits and a bulky apron. Chubby, with brassy hair and too much makeup, her nametag read "Lurlene." Polk thought about how convenient it was, everybody sporting their names for him, but he wondered how come they needed to, since in a town of 327, you'd think everybody would know each other. "Maybe their way of remembering who they are themselves," thought Polk, and laughed.

"What's so funny," said Lurlene. Not sassy, just curious-like.

"Nothing." Polk slid onto one of the chrome stools, resting his elbows on the Formica counter under a ceiling fan that might have been put up there in the Year One. He glanced around the café. Old skinny couple—wearing sweaters, dear Lord—in one of the booths, young momma and her yard-ape in another. Four stools away, the only other customer at the counter was a fat fart pushing sixty, his rump overhanging the seat cushion, a fraying straw Stetson angled back on his head.

"Get you something?"

Polk looked at Lurlene. "Coffee. And a menu."

She gave him a piece of orange paper, the items hand-writ on it, then poured some coffee from a pot into a white porcelain cup with a million little cracks on its surface, like a spider web.

"Lurlene, honey?" said the fat fart.

"Yes, Chief?"

Polk froze as she moved with the coffee pot to the other end of the counter. Then Polk, as casual as he could, kind of scoped out the man who might be a policeman.

Talking to Lurlene like she was a schoolgirl, but wanting to change a twenty. Polk noticed there was no gun on his belt. Maybe the fire chief? Un-unh. As the fat fart turned, Polk could see a peace officer's badge on the khaki shirt. Now what kind of damn fool wears a badge without toting something to back it up?

Lurlene came toward Polk, pawing under the counter for what turned out to be her pocketbook. Opening it, she shook her head. "Sorry, Chief. And I know there's not enough in the register yet."

Polk looked up at the clock on the wall: 1:15 in the p.m.

Must do one hell of a business, not enough change in the drawer after lunchtime to so much as cash a twenty. Briefly, he thought about helping the lawman out, and almost laughed again.

"Well," said the Chief, "I'll just ask Mary over to the bank. Be right back."

Polk watched the fat fart take about thirty seconds to make it off his stool and waddle out the door toward the yellow-brick building across the street.

Lurlene spoke to the back of Polk's head. "Decide on what you'll be having?"

He turned his face toward her. "Hamburger, medium. Fries."

"You got it."

Lurlene went through a swinging door, and he could hear her voice repeating his order. Left her pocketbook open on the counter, in plain view and an arm's reach from a total stranger.

When the waitress came back out, Polk said, "Hey, you forgot something here."

"What else you want?" Again not sassy, now just confused.

"It's not what I want." Polk gestured, feeling charitable. "Your pocketbook. Shouldn't be leaving it out like that."

Lurlene laughed and waved him off. "Oh, that's all right. Bibby's the safest little town in Texas."

Polk thought about the billboard he'd seen. "That why your police don't even carry a gun?"

"The Chief? Well, he don't really need to."

"Kind of odd, don't you think?"

"Not for Bibby. The Chief used to be the guard, over to our bank. At least until the bank realized it didn't really need a guard. Seemed a shame to have Harry—that's his name, Harry—be out of a job, so we kind of voted him police chief. Only he don't have that much chiefing to do, since he don't have any officers under him. But someone's got to process the paperwork those folks over to Austin make us file, and that keeps Harry just real busy."

Polk sipped his coffee, but he was really tasting all this information. A police chief without a gun or other officers, a bank without a guard. And himself, Polk Greshen, sitting here with a broke-down stolen car, a passing need for money, and a nine mil' under his tank-top.

Omens. Omens just everywhere you looked.

He said, "Sounds like y'all don't have much crime around here."

"None, really. Not since we also voted to—"

At which point the café door slapped shut again, and fatfart Harry the Chief returned to the counter, easing his haunches down on the stool he'd left and allowing as how he could use maybe one more cup of Lurlene's coffee before heading back to the office.

Which sounded to Polk like fine timing. Yes, fine timing indeed.

Polk was kind of clock-watching. Ten minutes since the Chief left the café and started walking up the street toward his station. The hamburger and fries Lurlene had brought weren't half bad, though Polk realized his immediate prospects just might've brightened the meal some.

The young momma and her kid got up to leave their booth, the old skinny couple in their sweaters having teetered out a little before that. Polk decided he didn't really want to be Lurlene's only customer in the café. You spend too much time alone with a person, they tend to remember your face that much better.

What Polk figured: I finish up here, cross the street, and slip into the bank. With any luck at all, won't be no crowd there, given how dead old Bibby seems to be. I flash the nine mil' under some teller's nose, then take what they got in cash and run to Sid's garage. Only a few blocks, and either he's got the Ford ready, or I boost one of the others. Hell, this town, I could jump in practically any car parked along the street, find the keys still in the ignition.

"More coffee?"

He looked up at Lurlene, poised with the pot over his cup.

"Just the check."

After leaving a dollar tip—right generous, too—Polk got off his stool and ambled outside, not wanting to appear like he was in a hurry just yet. The young momma and her kid drove by in a Chevy pick-up heavy on the primer, but the old skinny couple were sitting on a shaded bench a block toward the gas station. The woman jawing away, the man looking to be falling asleep. "Can't hardly blame him," thought Polk.

The rest of the street was almost deserted, Polk having to wait for only one car to go by before crossing to the bank. He entered the double doors, and it was dark enough inside that he had to let his eyes adjust some to the room.

High ceiling, with polished mahogany along the walls. The business counter was made of the same, three of those old-fashioned teller's cages like . . . like the bird-thing he'd found in the trunk of the Ford. Another omen.

One colored girl, maybe twenty or so, stood behind the cage closest to the doors. There was nobody else in the place, and no sound, either.

"Well, well," thought Polk. "All by herself for true, and not even bulletproof glass between us."

He walked up to the girl's cage, a little placard with "MARY" on the counter. Goddamn, but this is one well-identified town, Polk remembering Chief Harry saying that name back at the café.

"Help you, sir?"

Polk grinned, reaching under his tank-top. "You surely can, Miss Mary. I'll be needing some cash for my friend here."

The girl looked down at his side of the counter as Polk brought the gun's muzzle up, pointed dead center on her chest.

"You getting the picture, Miss Mary?"

"Yessir."

Said it real calm. Had to give her credit, didn't seem even a bitty-bit scared.

"All your money, now. And don't be pushing no alarm buttons, neither."

"We don't have none to push."

Polk couldn't believe this town. Wished he'd found it sooner in his life.

"The money, Miss Mary."

He watched as she opened a cash drawer and started stacking bills in front of him. Polk wasn't the best at doing sums real quick, but he could see lots of twenties and even some fifties in with the others. Might not have to hole-up with his cousin in New Mexico after all.

The girl stopped, closing the drawer.

"That it?" said Polk.

"Less'n you want the coins, too."

He grinned. Genuine brave, this Miss Mary. "No, they'd just slow me down." He gathered the cash, stuffing it into the pockets of his jeans. "Now, I'm gonna walk through your door there, and if you just sit tight and don't do nothing stupid, my partner out front won't have to shoot you. Got all that?"

"Yessir."

"Good. Pleasure doing business with you, Miss Mary."

Polk backed up a few steps, then turned to open the door, sticking the nine mil' back under his shirt.

From behind him, Mary said, "Sir?"

Polk turned back to see her leveling a pistol at him.

He barely had time to duck before the first round went off, deafening him and grazing his upper left arm, the flesh feeling like it bumped into a branding iron. Yowling, Polk barged through the doors just as a second round from Mary's pistol lodged in the jamb next to his head.

Outside, Polk drew his own weapon, looking up to see Lurlene at the door of the café, the old skinny couple rousting themselves from their bench. No problem, once I . . .

Out of the corner of his eye, Polk saw Lurlene's hand come up from the bulging apron, a small black—Goddamn, no!

Her first bullet whistled past his shoulder as he broke into a loose-limbed jog, the boots not really made for it, his legs feeling like they were taking an awful long time to get the message from his brain. He'd gotten about abreast of the old skinny couple when—

No. No, this can't be.

The man was down on one knee, sighting a long-barreled revolver, while the woman had a cigarette lighter in her—Wait, a derringer?

They opened up on him, too, and Polk felt something like a hammer whack him in the right thigh. He nearly fell, afraid to look down and maybe see his own—No, can't think like that. Got to get the car.

After what seemed to Polk like a mile of running through

sand, Sid was there, just ahead, by one of his gas pumps. Closing the driver's door of the Ford, as though he'd just rolled it out from the bay. Already gasping for breath, Polk began waving to him with the nine mil'. "Sid, Sid . . ."

The mechanic waved back with one hand, dipping the other into one of the sagging pockets in his overalls and drawing a snub-nose belly-gun.

"No!" Polk knew he was screaming as he dived to the pavement, the bullets whining in ricochet around him.

Struggling back to his feet, the pain in his thigh growing bad—real bad—Polk willed himself up the street. He could hear the sound of people coming after him, different kinds of shoes making different kinds of noises. "The police . . ." he thought. "I make it . . . to the station . . . Chief Harry . . . stop this . . . crazy . . ."

Hobbling like a man in a three-legged race, Polk got to within fifty feet of sanctuary when he felt something hit him in the back. More like a baseball bat than a hammer this time, and he pitched forward hard, his weapon clattering a body-length away from his hand.

The shoe sounds behind him were getting closer.

With the last of his strength, Polk managed to lift his face off the pavement, see Chief Harry standing with fists on his hips in the station's doorway. The smaller lettering under "POLICE" arched above the peace officer's head.

The sign read:

BIBBY, TEXAS: WHERE EVERY CITIZEN HAS A PERMIT TO CARRY.

Polk Greshen thought about all the paperwork that might cause, and why Chief Harry might be too busy to worry about toting a gun himself.

Rotten to the Core

Thirty-three years old, and I'm still working for my mother.

Life can really suck, you know it?

I mean, if we was still turning a profit growing apples, that'd be one thing. But ever since the old man bit the big one five years ago and the land came to be all hers, Ma's been getting fat around the middle and thin around the business.

Not that it's all her fault, mind. We ain't got but a hundred acres of trees, which used to be enough to compete, long as you had two strong backs to help out most of the year. Come picking season, we hire another twenty, plus enough grading ladies on the packing line to tell the good apples from the ones bound for cider.

Only now, it ain't enough to know how to *grow* good product. No, these days, the fruit's in over-supply. Washington State is killing us, and China is killing them.

Ma says to me, "Orrin, I don't how they can do it. I mean, whoever heard of *Chinese* apples?"

And I says to her, "Ma, how they can do it is if everybody in that country plants just one miserable tree, they've got four billion of them."

And she says to me, "Oh, I don't think there are that many people in China, do you?"

You see what I'm up against, a woman who can't keep her facts straight?

And, even without the overseas competition, the regional wholesaler here can play one of us little growers against the rest, which means we got to give away another dollar a box to keep that wholesaler's business. Only way to make a go of it at all is to build a pissy little retail store on the county road next to our packing barn, with apple jelly, apple potpourri, apple everything for sale to the dumbos up from the city, driving past and making believe they're some kind of country gentry by buying our stuff for twice what it'd cost in any supermarket worth its name.

Except that Ma don't believe in having a retail store. Nossir, not Mrs. Jeannette T. Weems.

She believes in baking apple pies. With her little "JTW" initials as a "mark of quality" in the center of the crust. But without preservatives or anything else "unnatural." And guess what that means?

Right the first time. It means I got to be on the road pretty near every day, driving this old panel truck with shelves in it that the Nissen Bread folks pitched away. One pie to a box, nine boxes to a bread rack, thirty racks to the truck. And drive that sucker I do, fifty, sixty hours a week, delivering Ma's fresh, unpreserved apple pies to gourmet shops and fancy restaurants. Even a few of the big estates, too, think it's cool to have a local peasant drive up to the servant's entrance with the "fruit of the land," I heard one of the whales in a whale-patterned shirt and tweed skirt say once.

Goldarnit, but I do hate the smell of apples.

You'd think working in a fish market or a slaughterhouse'd be worse, the stench of death all around you, getting into your clothes, your hair, even your skin.

But nothing's worse than apples when you can't get away from them, especially if one's rotten to the core. It's a stink that . . . penetrates, that's what it does. Goes *past* your skin, all the way to the bone. And it festers there, like some kind of infection, till it drives you near crazy.

As *you* drive over half the county in that goldarn panel truck with those goldarn racks of pies in the back.

I says to her, "Ma, you should just sell the farm for real estate development."

"Now, Orrin, your father wouldn't like that."

"Ma, the old man's got his own land. Measures about eight-by-three and six feet under."

Which naturally made Mrs. Jeannette T. Weems cry, to hear me bring up the truth.

Even so, though, I thought I had her leaning—I *know* I did—until that Earle Shay showed up two months ago.

We'd lost the other fella working the orchard with us to a selling job at the Wal-Mart, so Ma put an ad in the county weekly for "Hired Help, No Room or Board, Must be Clean and Polite and Willing to Work Hard."

And, wouldn't you know it, Earle had to be all three?

He's also black as coal, with a chest like a pickle barrel and a shaved head so shiny you dast not look at him on a sunny day without a good pair of dark glasses on you. I think Earle's around Ma's age—I can't never tell how old black people are, at least until they hit seventy or so, when their skin just seems to go into raisin mode and they start shuffling instead of walking right. But Earle's a long way from shuffling. He can work all day and keep Ma laughing in her kitchen half the night. She's been laughing so hard, Ma's dropped about ten pounds or so of that weight around her middle, and she's even taken to going to Bessie's Hair-a-Drome again, first time since the old man went in the ground.

But that's not the worst part.

No, the worst part is, Earle's got Ma believing we—and "we" don't mean just me and her—can run the farm at a profit again.

In that deep, booming voice he has, Earle says to Ma, "Why, Jeannette, all we have to do is put in a retail store, and devote a couple of acres to specialty veggies for the gourmet shops and restaurants."

"But Earle, who would tend this store and garden?"

"I've got relatives aplenty in the city who'd love to come up here, stay in the country for a time. Clean air, no crime. And Orrin's already visiting most of the places we'd sell the veggies to with his panel truck and your pies."

"Well," Ma says to him, "it might work."

Might work. And if it did, I'd be stuck in the goldarn panel truck for the rest of my natural life. Only then I'd have goldarn garden dirt under my fingernails to go with the goldarn apple stench in my bones. In fact, I couldn't hardly see a light at the end of the tunnel.

Until I finally got The Idea.

It happened on a cold, rainy day in late October, maybe a month after Earle'd used the John Deere forklift to stack the bins of MacIntosh eight tiers high in our C.A. room. The "C.A." stands for "controlled atmosphere." Basically, if you've got a hundred acres of apples, a lot of them are gonna get ripe in the same two-week stretch, so you bring in the pickers and box the fruit quick as you can. Unless you want the product breaking down and getting soft, though, you got to seal it up in C.A. storage. Where the air's maybe ninety percent nitrogen—like they must have on the planet Mars? But put in a refrigeration unit to cool and blow that

Martian air around the apples, and they'll keep preserved for a good five months.

I'd already parked the panel truck outside the packing barn, between the John Deere tractor that tows our AgTec crop sprayer—a big white thing, looks a little like a ten-foot dog kennel with tubes and nozzles at the back—and the Agway roto-tiller—which, long as I'm describing things, looks a lot like a gasoline-powered wheelbarrow with little propellers that dig into the ground. I walked past the brush chopper—this heavy flail mower that rolls behind the tractor, too, only it can chop-and-chip pieces of junk timber two-inches thick. In the barn, I was on my way to the little fridge where I keep some cold beers when I realized the packing line looked a little longer than the day before.

Jesus God, I remember thinking. They've gone and done it.

Earle'd been after Ma for weeks to spring for a waxing machine. Even she thought seventeen thousand dollars—seventeen *thousand!*—was kind of steep, but Earle kept pressing her and teasing her with that Darth Vader voice. His idea was that we—the "three we" again—could sell to the wholesalers who supply the big supermarkets that want their apples to sparkle like fire trucks. Takes another six-hundred dollars of wax to polish fifteen thousand bushels of apples, but they come out looking better than the one Eve must have flashed at Adam back in their Garden.

I had to sit down hard, on an old slatted crate in the packing barn.

Ain't no grower in this whole country—or, hell, even over there in *China*—that's gonna burn the price of a new pick-up truck for her one and only son if she's really leaning towards selling the land for development. As apple orchard, our land wasn't worth spit, and we didn't have the kind of houses around us already that'd let us carve off a small building lot here and there at the edges. But I knew we could divide the whole shebang up into "mini-estates," and get a fortune for every five-acre chunk. Sure, we'd have to put in a road and run the electric and arrange for probably half a dozen other things, but I knew it'd all work from the numbers side.

Only right then, sitting on that packing crate, I couldn't see it working at all, not with Ma doing whatever Earle told her he thought was made sense. Next thing'd be the designer veggies and a retail store, with even more "employees"—dark in color—on our land.

Or Ma's land, I guessed. At least until . . .

I jumped back up and ran outside. Our crop sprayer looked mean enough, but I didn't see how showering Mrs. Jeannette T. Weems with pesticide would solve my problem. The roto-tiller had those little prop blades, but at best they'd take off some toes or maybe a finger, if you got careless clearing a jam. Then I stared—long and hard—at our brush chopper. It'd do the job all right, but despite what Ma was doing to me, I couldn't quite stomach her being spritzed like hamburger over a row of our trees.

Scuffing my boots in the dust, I went back inside the packing barn.

And saw . . . the packing line?

No. No, even with the new waxing machine, the equipment at most might mangle an arm. And, anyway, with the crop already in storage, there'd be no reason to run the line nor for Ma to be fiddling with the different stages, not with Earle around.

But that's when I heard it. A simple little noise, though maybe more beautiful than any country tune Garth Brooks ever wailed.

The noise was coming from our C.A. room. That metal-on-metal shear of a bearing going bad in the refrigeration unit's blower.

I went over to the big steel door we have bolted on the storage. You got to keep the room sealed absolute tight, otherwise the nitrogen air inside would seep out, rotting the apples and maybe killing you, you breathed deep enough close enough. Of course, nobody could predict when something might go wrong with the refrigeration unit either, so we had a little kitty-cat trap door on the bottom of the steel one. The little door was hinged on top and bolted at the corners, too. But it'd give you a way in and out of the C.A. room in case some kinda repair was necessary. And we even had an old airpac Ma bought off the Volunteer Fire—the kind that rides on your back, like the tanks in this scuba-diving flick I saw one time? Our tank's yellow, with a hose running to the nose-and-mouth cover that you strap on over your head, the way fighter pilots do in those old war movies.

Right then, though, I pushed all the Hollywood stuff out of my head. Sitting down on that packing crate again, I closed my eyes to recollect the inside of our C.A. storage. Solid cement floor, ceiling twenty feet high, walls made from white insulated foam. Over the years, we'd spackled food-grade tar here and there to patch leaks, so the whole room'd look to you like the hide of a pinto pony. And most of the space was filled with those eight tiers of weathered-wood bins with the MacIntosh in them.

But every other cubic foot was ninety percent nitrogen. That only a Martian could breathe without an airpac.

I took The Idea as an omen. Especially since that same night—after driving my old pick-up over to Clete's Tap to celebrate—I met Honey.

Clete's ain't nothing more than a taproom, one of maybe ten in the county. It's about the only place where the races mix much, though, and so I wouldn't go there but for it's the closest by far to the farm, and I don't fancy getting stopped by a sheriff's deputy for Driving Under the Influence account of I'm already Driving Without a License from another such encounter.

Anyway, I go into Clete's that night, and the crowd—fortunately—is mostly white. Oh, there're a couple of big young bucks bellied up to the bar, but I move over to a table by itself and tell Amy the airhead waitress to bring me a bottle of champagne, they had one cold. She asks me if I was sure I wanted that and not a Miller's High Life, "the champagne of bottled beers." I say I'm sure, and as Amy turns away, airhead shaking like one of those ballplayer dolls on the TV, the stunner standing at my end of the bar turns a little.

The girl was black, technically, but her skin really glowed the color of honey, her hair maybe two shades darker. About five-five or so in jeans and a pair of those spiky cowboy boots, she was all legs and had just the cutest little rump I ever did see. She seemed to know she'd caught my eye, too, because before I could even get up, the girl'd click-clacked over to my table, asking if she could sit.

I says to her, "Honey, you can sit on anything you'd like."

All of a sudden, she looks sorta funny, like maybe I offended her kinda.

But all she says to me is, "How'd you, like, know that's my name?"

And I says to her, "What is?"

"Honey."

"Only on account of that's what you remind me of, girl.

A gorgeous itty-bitty thing just spun out of honey."

Which made her smile, and as Amy finally arrived with my champagne—in this spittoon with ice—I knew the chair acrost from me in Clete's Tap wasn't the only thing Honey'd be sitting on that night.

Honey says to me, "So, you're gonna kill your mama?"

It was afterwards, and now she's towards the passenger's side of my pick-up, still at the turnaround off the dirt road we'd parked at beforehand. To this moment, I can't remember how The Idea'd come up in our conversation. But it seemed natural enough, telling her about it. Especially since Honey'd already told me she was up from the city for just the weekend, visiting relatives until she had to get away from all the "My, child, how you have growed up" talk.

I says to Honey, "Well, yeah, I have to kill her. But like I said, I couldn't feature Ma scattered over half-an-acre by the brush chopper like so much ground chuck."

Honey looked a little funny again, but this time more like she might urp up. All she says to me, though, is, "How you gonna use that storage room?"

I told her about the bearing in the refrigeration unit, how I could hear it was going, and why we'd have to replace it or risk losing the fruit to a system failure.

"And your mama's just gonna, like, walk in there through that little trap door you have?"

I says to her, "No, Honey. All's I have to do is *tell* her about it when Earle ain't around. Then she'll have to go out to the packing barn with me and stand a ways off, because the safety rule is, Nobody goes into C.A. storage without somebody else being on the outside."

"Like Lassie."

"Huh?"

"Like Lassie," Honey says to me. "That dog who'd go get help when some person was in trouble."

I shake my head, but I says to her, "Yeah, like that. Only I'm not going in there myself."

"What are you gonna do?"

"I'm gonna wear that airpac, and use a wrench on the trap door, and then say to Ma, 'Come over closer, I need help with this last bolt.' And when she's close enough, I'm gonna rap her upside the head with that wrench. Once Mrs. Jeannette T. Weems is for sure out cold, I'm gonna open the kitty-cat door on its hinge, pushed her in through it, and close the door again."

"I don't, like, get it."

I close my eyes. She might have a body like spun honey, but the brain was more spun cotton. "I wait maybe two minutes, just to be sure Ma's a goner. Then I bleed out all that's left in the airpac, and I slide it off me. I take a deep breath, open the trap door again, and push the airpac inside. After that, I toss the wrench in, too."

Honey looked kind of sick again, but she says to me, "Oh, so everybody will think your mama was, like, trying to fix the bearing thing and ran out of good air."

"Right the first time. And, once the lawyers get through with doing her estate, I'm rich as that Trump fella."

Honey puts on a smile, a cousin to the last one she gave me at Clete's Tap. "You know, Orrin, I probably don't have to be back to my relatives for, like, another hour or so."

Omens. I'm telling you, they were everywhere for me, that afternoon and night.

Next morning in the kitchen, I says to Ma, "Where's Earle?"

Mrs. Jeannette T. Weems looks up from a pie she's making her little "mark of quality" in the crust of. "He said he had to run into town for something."

"Well, maybe Earle oughta spend a little less time running to town and a little more time checking the barn."

"Why, what do you mean, Orrin?"

"I mean, I was in there yesterday after I broke my back delivering all your pies, and I could hear this bearing starting to go on the C.A. blower."

"Oh, my goodness, no."

"Oh, my goodness, yes," I says to her. "I think you and me ought to go over there, quick as we can."

"Of course, Orrin. Let me just get this last batch out of the oven."

Last batch. I especially liked the sound of that first part.

"Ma," I says to her, over my shoulder and casual as can be, considering how the nose-and-mouth cover of the airpac's muffling my voice. "I'm having a little trouble with this last bolt."

Her voice comes from a corner of the packing barn. "Is it safe for me to join you there?"

"Sure it's safe. The room's still sealed. I just need a little help with the wrench is all."

"Well, if you really can't do it without me . . ."

"No, Ma," I says to her, my face against the trap door so she won't see me grinning ear-to-ear. "Take my word on this. I can't make it work without you."

I hear footsteps, only they're sounding heavy, like Ma was before Earle answered her ad in the weekly. I get ready anyway, figuring to just stand up a little and—

—I wake up in the dark, lying on my right side.

My head hurts behind my left ear. When I reach back there, I can feel a lump the size of a small hen's first egg.

I also feel the strap of the nose-and-mouth cover of the airpac.

I try to sit up, but when I do, the yellow tank part makes a scraping noise on the cold cement floor.

Cold? Cement?

"Orrin?" Ma yells to me from outside somewheres. "Can you hear me, Orrin?"

"Yeah," I says to her, muffled by the cover, but . . . echoing, too.

Like I'm in a room with twenty-foot walls.

"Orrin, I never believed you would consider doing such a thing to your own mother."

"What such a thing?"

"Murder for profit," booms Earle's voice to me, and I have a pretty good idea whose footsteps I heard coming up behind me on the other side of the kitty-cat door.

I says to him, "I don't know what you're talking about."

He booms to me, "Lucky thing that when I was in town this morning, my niece up from the city told me what you laid out for her last night."

"Laid" was the only word I really focused on.

Ma yells to me, "Orrin, how could you even have *contemplated* that?"

I says to her, "Ma, she's the one picked *me* up in Clete's."

"That's not what I mean, young man. I'm talking about killing your own mother."

I didn't like the way my air from the yellow tank was tasting. "Let me out of here."

"No, Orrin," Ma yells. "Earle believes Honey, and I believe Earle. What I don't believe is that you haven't even the decency to own up to the things they've said."

"Ma?"

"What?"

"Let . . . me . . . out . . . of . . . here."

Her voice goes different. "I couldn't bear to have Earle kill you the way he wanted to, after you'd planned to kill his beloved."

His "beloved?" Things were just getting better and better.

"So we compromised," Ma yells to me now. "We slid you in there with the airpac on and rebolted the trap here. I don't know how much time you have left, but at least you'll go quickly after reflecting on the horrible deed you intended."

"Ma—"

She yells this time till her voice about cracks. "And then we'll take a page from your book, Orrin. Earle will unbolt the trap again and toss in the wrench, so everyone will think the same tragic accident that you so diabolically aimed at me simply befell you instead."

"Ma, listen—"

Earle booms to me, "Poetic justice for a boy that just went rotten, rotten to the core."

I start saying a whole string of words Ma never liked to hear. When I'm done, neither of them's yelling or booming to me anymore.

So here I sit, in the dark and the cold. I really don't like the taste of my air from the yellow tank at all now. It's sour, like everything's going stale, and I practically have to whistle in reverse to feel anything reach down towards my lungs.

Then I remember something else from that scuba-diving

flick I saw. One of the jerks you know is going to die anyway runs out of air when he's maybe three hundred feet down. Even though he knows it's stupid, he pulls off the mouthpiece from under his mask and starts breathing in water.

I guess it's like a reflex or something. Which means that, pretty soon, I'll probably be doing the same thing.

Which oughta bother me a lot, but somehow it don't. No, what does bother me is something else.

I'm in a controlled atmosphere storage room. When I take off the nose-and-mouth cover and draw in that first—and last—breath of Martian air, I'm also gonna smell . . . *them.*

The last goldarn thing on God's green earth I'll ever experience is the goldarn stench of goldarn apples.

Didn't I tell you that life can really suck?

Off-Season

A Mystery Novella

PROLOGUE

My gecko of the day, a mottled lizard three inches long, ran about a foot up the wall before pausing. Its throat began puffing out and in, out and in, like a mirror image of Dizzy Gillespie blowing his horn.

We play a little game, the geckos and I. They look for food—a fly, an ant, whatever—and I try to spot the target first. I'm getting pretty good, but then it's been nearly . . . no. No, don't go there yet. Better to start at the beginning.

Or almost the beginning.

ONE

I didn't catch his title when he said it, but another officer had called him "Inspector," so I did, too. His nametag read "Gant," and the uniform—dark blue pants and an almond safari shirt—was precisely tailored and crisply pressed. About six-two and black as ebony, the fortyish Inspector sat behind his desk like a West Point plebe at dinner. Above our heads, a ceiling fan turned slowly enough to distinguish each blade, maybe because, like everything else on a Caribbean island, electricity was so expensive. The fan barely moved the muggy, Saturday morning air and looked ancient, although the cinder-block police station in Macaroon's capital city of Ste. Marie seemed newly-constructed. A radio monitor erupted sporadically in the next room, sounding off like an electronic parrot.

I did my best to relax in the hardbacked chair. One of Gant's men stood behind me, in effect barring the door. I could hear that officer breathing through his nose.

Gant was holding my passport in one hand and comparing it with my Boston Police shield and I.D. card in the other. We went through some recent history. I had come down to the island on Thursday, two days earlier. After six weeks spent breaking a mob killing, I'd needed a rest. I told Gant that I'd heard Macaroon's varied heritage (at different times British, Dutch, French, and even American) before becoming independent made for a perfect vacation spot. Also, even with Carnivaal just ending, ten days in June cost about as much as three days in January. My small joke about the off-season didn't bring a smile.

I was staying at the Bayview Hotel, but had spent the night before with a British woman who ran a French restaurant in the old Dutch quarter. The Inspector hadn't yet reached my sex life, though.

Gant folded my shield case and slid it back to me, his long fingers retaining my passport. I didn't like that.

"Mr. Kevin Malloy, I am sorry to impose these questions, but a violent death does terrible harm to the very foundation of our community here. Especially two such deaths." Gant was very somber, his eyes engaging me in the searching stare of the cop who knows the person he's watching has something to hide. I decided to give him a peek.

"Inspector, I was with a woman last night. She lives on the island, and I'll identify her before I leave your office if you believe I should. But first, can you tell me what crime it is you're investigating?"

A smile toyed with the corners of his mouth. "My men mentioned nothing to you?"

I thought back to the brusque but polite way I was spirited from the hotel lobby as I came through the front entrance at 5:45 a.m. "You've trained them well."

"Thank you," a little insincerely and with no apology for making me wait until nearly 8:00 a.m. to see him. He drew a breath and began. "Last night Mrs. Faith Bressler, the woman staying alone in the room next to yours at the Bayview, died. It would appear that she had met and invited to her room a young islander named Tony de Weeter. When the other guests at the hotel heard loud noises in the night, they called the front desk. A member of the staff, Mr. Kepper, went up to the room."

I could picture Kepper, a middle-aged islander who seemed officious.

Gant motioned with both hands. "There were several people milling about in the corridor. Mr. Kepper opened the door to Mrs. Bressler's room to find de Weeter dead of two gunshot wounds. He was . . . completely undressed. In de Weeter's left hand was the shoulder strap of Mrs. Bressler's purse. In his right hand was her wallet as well. Mrs. Bressler was lying in the bed, also nude and also dead. We found one bullet hole and accompanying powder burns on the pillowcase near her head wound. The weapon was in her hand. You are the only guest of the hotel who was not reached last night. Therefore, my men were told to await your arrival and identification by Mr. Kepper at the desk."

I rolled things around in my mind. "Inspector, Macaroon depends on tourism?"

"That would be a fair statement, yes."

"Then I don't believe you'd publicize this incident any further than you felt was professionally necessary. You wouldn't be interested in the other guests, me included, unless that action-panic-murder-suicide sequence didn't seem odd to you."

This time Gant gave me a real smile. "You must be a very effective policeman in Boston, Mr. Malloy."

"Are you aware that I had dinner with Faith Bressler the night before last?"

"Thursday?" He tented his fingers on the desk and leaned forward until his chin lightly rested on them. "Yes."

"Are you aware that she and I went up to her room together after that?"

Now Gant just nodded.

I said, "She was a very troubled lady." It sounded a bit hollow. "Separated from her husband."

Gant didn't raise his chin from his fingers, reminding me of a chess master studying the board. "On her driver's license there is a residential address in Chicago, Illinois. The telephone number has been called. Mr. Bressler, a building contractor, will be arriving late this afternoon."

Neither of us spoke for about a minute. I conducted a mental inventory and cleared my throat. "I'd like to give you the name of that woman now, the one I stayed with last night."

Gant straightened up, and I told him.

He reached for his parade hat and inclined his head toward the man at the door. "Let us see her."

★ ★ ★ ★ ★

Sophie Travers froze solid behind the bar of Sophie's Soupcon when she saw me enter with Gant and his driver. Her face, pale for a blonde who lived under year-round tanning rays, lost what color it did have.

I thought I should jump first. "Sophie, the police just want to ask—"

"Thank you," interrupted the Inspector, "but I would prefer to conduct my own interview."

Sophie looked from me to Gant and back again to me before wiping her hands nervously on her jeans. The only sound I heard was the low hum of the big food-refrigeration locker downstairs.

Gant said, "Do you know this man?"

"Of course I do," said Sophie, regaining some of her color. "His name is Kevin Malloy, and he's a policeman from Boston." She looked to me for confirmation. "What's all this about, now?"

Gant ignored her question. "Did he spend any part of last night with you?"

Sophie glared at me and then turned her back on us. Over her shoulder, she said, "Bragging to your copper-colleagues, you bastard?"

"Soph," I said, "There were two shootings at the hotel last night."

She spun around, her mouth wide open.

Gant said, "Mr. Malloy, I really—"

"Murder?" said Sophie, again looking from one of us to the other. "At the Bayview?"

Gant lowered his voice. "Sophie, was Mr. Malloy with you last night?"

"Yes." Now to me. "Yes, from about 7:30 into this morning. He left—oh, sometime around 5:00?"

Gant rubbed his chin, then shook his head. "Mr. Malloy, I am sorry. You realize that I am required to investigate all possibilities."

It wasn't a question. "Of course, Inspector. No hard feelings."

Sophie said, "Paul, who was killed?"

Gant seemed almost relieved to hear her use his first name. "An American woman named Bressler, and Tony de Weeter."

"That bitch, with him?" said Sophie, surprise showing through.

Gant gave it a beat. "You knew Mrs. Bressler?"

"You bet I did." Sophie stomped to the other side of the bar, picking up a wet rag to wipe down the old mahogany top. "She was here last year, about this time. Just before the Bayview did some . . . housecleaning."

"Housecleaning?" I said.

"Yes, luv. New owners came in and cleared out a lot of staffers who were," she winked at Gant, "trading on the tourists?"

"Prostitution?" I said.

"Mr. Mal—"

"Sorry, Inspector."

Sophie paused with the rag. "Anyway, the Bressler woman comes in here one night of her 'week in paradise,' as she called it, and proceeds to talk my bloody ear off. Then she makes a big play for this Dutchie naval officer I was sort of sweet on. When I found out she was successful, I kicked his ass out."

"The officer's name?" said Gant.

Sophie paused again, a bit longer this time. "Eric Volker, off the *Alliance*. I figured the Bressler tart was a little . . . crazy for sexual gratification, shall we say?"

I said, "Seems to me like the murder/suicide is sounding stronger."

Sophie laughed nervously. "Not exactly, luv."

I looked at her. "What do you mean?"

Paul Gant handed me my passport, then motioned his driver toward the door. "You see, Mr. Malloy, Tony de Weeter was homosexual."

Sophie set a piña colada in front of me and leaned her elbows on the bar. We were alone in the place and starting to relax. I tasted the drink and smiled my approval.

"You know," I said, putting down the glass, "given what Faith Bressler did to you, I'm as much your alibi as you are mine."

"Not likely, Kev. If I were going to kill her, I'd have done the job last year, when she hurt me."

TWO

I took a cab back to the Bayview just before noon, hand-strung ropes of flowers from Carnivaal flapping sadly in the full daylight. Sophie's restaurant didn't serve meals in the off-season, and I wanted to clean up and change before lunch. Crossing the lobby to the elevator, I noticed Mr. Kepper, impeccably dressed and groomed himself, give me a distasteful look from behind the registration desk.

I got off the elevator on the fourth floor and walked down past a police guard at Faith Bressler's room. Hers was 412, mine 414. We both had a beautiful view of Grand Bay, as did all the off-season guests at the hotel. I guess the management felt that as long as the place was nearly empty, every tourist should have a water view and be on the same floor. The policy probably promoted a sense of community among us and eased the chambermaid's burdens as well.

Inside my room, I stripped, showered, and shaved. I was halfway into a pair of khaki slacks when somebody rapped firmly on my door. I zipped up and opened it.

"Mr. Malloy," said Inspector Paul Gant, smiling sheepishly, parade hat cradled in the crook of his arm. "May I speak with you for a moment?"

"Sure. Have a seat."

He settled rather uncomfortably on the desk chair, the hat in his lap. I sat on the edge of my bed. Neither of us spoke.

Then, "I find myself somewhat embarrassed in that I do not recall your police rank in Boston."

"Sergeant Detective, which is the reverse of what most American forces call it."

"Ah, the reverse, yes. However, in our initial interview, you told me one of your duties is the investigation of . . . homicides?"

"Yes," I said, cautiously. "For the last three years."

Gant ran his right hand through his short-cropped hair. "Sergeant Detective, my problem is—"

"Not to interrupt, but 'Kevin' will do just fine."

"Thank you," relaxing into the chair. "And I am 'Paul.' " His voice grew formal again. "I have been in charge of the police in Ste. Marie for nearly four years, and on the force for nearly twenty. However, I have never myself had a homicide to investigate that was not—how would you say it, 'open-and-shut' clearly? The same is true of my officers, and the most capable of them already is on special assignment. While there is a procedure for summoning the help of police agencies from the larger islands, it has always been . . . politically discouraged."

"Especially because that kind of publicity would impact the tourist trade?"

Gant smiled grimly. "Precisely so. Therefore, I would ask a favor of you which I have not the right to request."

"If you want some help on the Bressler case, I'd be happy to give it."

A better smile. "My deepest thanks, Kevin. I shall try not to impose on your vacation too greatly." He picked up his cap and walked to the door. "May I suggest we view the scene?"

"As soon as I pull on a shirt."

"Of course," said Paul Gant, and left me.

The bodies had been removed, the sooty blood stains on the bedding and rug as memorials. Feathers were scattered all over the place.

I said to Gant, "The feathers from that pillow you mentioned before?"

"Yes."

When he didn't say anything else, I began moving around the room with my hands in my pocket. "Kind of odd, Faith shooting this de Weeter first, then after that noise, silencing her own killshot."

"Precisely my concern."

"On the other hand, I've known suicides to be pretty erratic, especially after gunning down another person."

"Certainly that is a possibility as well."

I looked back at the door to the corridor. "I assume the chain lock wasn't on?"

"That is correct. Only the knob lock was engaged when Mr. Kepper arrived."

I thought back over my last few trips through the lobby. "Sounds like he puts in a long day."

"Mr. Kepper lives on the premises, and he was notified by the night clerk on duty downstairs."

"Convenient." I walked over to the interior, connecting door, which had a twin opening from my room. "Was this door locked from Faith's side?"

"Mr. Kepper did not know. When my men arrived and tried it, however, it was unlocked."

I turned and faced the opposite wall. "How about her door into the other adjoining room?"

"Locked. The occupant of 410 is a Mr. Neil Coughlin of New York City. He heard the shots and was the one who initially raised the alarm."

I looked at Paul Gant, who was watching me carefully. "Sounds like someone was hoping I'd be home for a set-up."

"That thought had occurred to me, Kevin."

I leaned against a wall. "What's the origin of the weapon?"

"Unknown. It is a Smith and Wesson, point-three-eight caliber, five-shot revolver. Horribly effective, but not especially available on Macaroon."

"A credit to your gun control."

Gant shook his head. "No. A good bit of arms smuggling goes on, but usually of larger pieces. Even those are often of European manufacture."

"Faith certainly couldn't have gotten a hand-gun past the metal detectors at the airport in the States."

A small smile. "It would seem that Mrs. Bressler arrived in Macaroon by ship, Kevin."

I went through what Faith and I had talked about on Thursday night. "She never mentioned any cruise to me, but it argues in favor of her providing the means, which sounds more like murder/suicide again."

"But no chain lock on the door to ensure privacy, and a most inappropriate choice of lover, and . . . ah, now you see why I need your help."

I looked around the room again. "How about the bag and wallet being in de Weeter's hands. A rip-off?"

Gant looked puzzled. "I'm sorry?"

"Could de Weeter have been trying to rob her?"

"Ah, 'rip-off,' yes. But I think not." He reached for the bag.

"Paul," a little warning in my voice. When Gant looked up, I said, "Fingerprints?"

He smiled and grasped the shoulder bag by the strap. "My laboratory officer has already checked the leather. No prints at all except for de Weeter's own."

"Not even Faith's? Or smudges?"

"That is correct. Rather unusual for someone to wipe off her bag entirely, is it not?" Gant hefted the thing. "Tony de Weeter was of my height, and his hand held the strap here." Gant let his arm drop to his side, the bag resting on the floor now with slack in the strap. "Not likely he would have tried to carry it like this, is it?"

"Not if de Weeter were going to carry it. But I thought he was found with the wallet already in his other hand?"

"He was, but notice." Gant lifted the bag by the same point on the strap, stopping with his hand a little above his belt. "You see, de Weeter would not have held the bag at this height to rifle it for the wallet." Gant raised his hand until it was over his head a few inches, the bag now waist high. "And, at this height, he could have groped in the bag with his free hand, but why do so when it would be so awkward for his strap hand?"

I smiled. "Nicely done, Paul. And no prints but de Weeter's on the wallet, too?"

"Precisely so. Otherwise wiped clean. And we would have to believe that he would continue to clutch it after receiving two bullets in the chest."

"Someone was gilding the lily."

Gant cocked his head.

I said, "Doing more than he needed: adding robbery ineptly to make it look like Faith killed de Weeter, then herself."

"Ah, yes."

"How about suspects?"

"I have been struggling for a sensible approach to that problem, Kevin. Macaroon seems an inconvenient place to arrange the shooting of a building contractor's wife from Chicago. Therefore, I assume that the murder must be connected with the island and presumably spontaneous. Mr. Kepper is one of the few hotel staff remaining at the hotel since the . . . 'housecleaning.' He informs me that Mrs. Bressler stayed here approximately this time last year. At my request, he is therefore going through all the guest invoices from then and comparing them to this off-season's to determine which of those who might have met the woman last year had the opportunity to commit the crime this year."

"Two problems with that approach. First, what makes you think it was someone Faith met last year rather than this year?"

"Because Mrs. Bressler was killed within thirty-six hours of her arrival, and you are the only person she seems to have spent any time with."

Kind of a conversation-stopper. "Okay. Even assuming that's so, your hotel guest comparisons won't include a lot of people who could have met her last year. Ships' passengers, guests at other hotels, et cetera."

"I agree. And I would appreciate your giving the 'et cetera' as much thought as you can. But I must begin somewhere, and the ship's captain assured me by wire this morning that when he departed Ste. Marie Thursday afternoon, Mrs. Bressler was the only one of his passengers who chose to remain on Macaroon."

I didn't like where my next point might lead. "How about the Dutch naval officer Sophie mentioned this morning?"

A tired sigh. "I do not wish to affect a man's career by a clumsy inquiry. I have, however, advised Mr. Volker to be in my office today at 6:00 p.m. for questioning about an incident 'on shore.' "

"You usually schedule appointments that late?"

"No, but I have no choice, which leads me to ask a second favor of you, Kevin."

"Go ahead."

Gant glanced out the window at an overcast sky. "I should meet Mr. Bressler's plane, which arrives at 4:45 p.m. I would feel far more at ease with him if you could accompany me."

I walked toward the corridor door. "Be glad to, on one condition."

"Certainly."

"We don't tell him I had dinner and . . . dessert with his wife Thursday night. I have a career back in Boston to think of, also."

Inspector Paul Gant nodded gravely. "I will do my best."

THREE

A police car would come to pick me up at 4:15. Since there was no sunshine, I decided to get some lunch.

Crossing the lobby and entering the bar, I realized that most of the few guests were in the hotel rather than out shopping or sightseeing. I'd seen the same reaction in apartment buildings back home after a violent death. Nobody wants to be involved, but nobody wants to miss anything, either.

I was finishing a chef's salad when a slim man in his high thirties with horn-rimmed glasses slid onto the stool next to mine and ordered a white wine. He wore a new Lacoste shirt and preppie, tattersall pants with cuffs. His hand shook violently as he lifted the wine glass.

Without turning in my direction, the man said, "Me, drinking before noon. But it's such a terrible, terrible thing, don't you think?"

A reedy voice, not made for easy listening. "The shootings?"

The base of his glass clattered on the bar as he straightened his eyeglasses with the other hand. "Of course, though that's an odd way to describe it."

"What do you mean?"

"Well, that woman, having to kill that . . . man, and then . . . suicide . . ." He took a gulp of wine.

"Why do you think that's what happened?"

The reedy voice rose a notch. "Why? Because I was there when they were *found*. I'd called down here to the desk, and—"

Extending my hand, I said, "You must be Neil Coughlin."

He jumped on his stool and absentmindedly shook with me. "But how . . . ?"

"My name's Kevin Malloy. Inspector Gant mentioned you while he was questioning me this morning."

"Oh," said Coughlin, suddenly withdrawing his hand, the veins taut against his dry skin. "I heard about your . . . uh, that is, the police . . ."

He seemed to have trouble finishing his sentences. "Maybe 'arrest' is the word you're looking for, but they just wanted some information."

"I see." Coughlin apparently had more questions because he fiddled with his now-empty glass without ordering another.

I decided life was too short to spend much more of it talking with him. I signed my name and room number on the tab and walked through the French doors to the patio.

Given the clouds and a breeze, the air was almost cool. The pool was to my right, Grand Bay in front and to my left. A few hardy souls were stretched out on lounge chairs or playing cards around the pool apron. A gecko skittered across my path and under a shrub. I started down toward the beach.

"Figured the next time I saw you it'd be in a ball and chains."

One of the loungers—overweight, fifty-something, and off by himself—was beaming up at me, an index finger keeping his place in a Jeffery Deaver thriller. The guy at least seemed to have a sense of humor, so I walked over and took the chair next to his without being invited.

"Christ," he said, "but you look like a cop."

I smiled and leaned back. "Good guess. What's with the 'ball and chains' remark?"

"You kidding? One school teacher who's up at the crack of dawn spots the locals hauling you off this morning, and by 10:00 a.m. only my cousin back in Philly didn't know about it."

"Just routine questioning, that's all."

He lowered his voice. "Listen, pal, a guy my age . . . Well, he sort of notices beautiful women. And in the process, guys who are with them. Faith Bressler may have been a scorpion, but she was still a stunner. And you were with her two nights ago. Rose and me—" He jerked his head toward a female version of himself squealing "Gin!" at one of the card tables. "—That's Rose. Her and me saw you two together. Then Faith ends up dead, and you end up with the cops. 'Just routine questioning?' "

"You're starting to bore me as much as that yuppie at the bar."

The fat man swiveled his head, looked inside, and grunted. "Christ, if I'm getting as bad as Coughlin, I'd better lay off. Buy you a drink to make amends?"

"Piña colada, please."

"Good." He waved to the youngster who hovered around the pool and put in one for himself. "By the way, Stan Dalberg."

"Kevin Malloy, Stan." We shook. "You're from Philadelphia, then?"

"Rose and me both. Built a plumbing supply company to where we can take a week off while her idiot nephew fucks up the paperwork but somehow gets the stuff out. This is our third year on Macaroon. You?"

"First visit."

Our drinks, in plastic cups, arrived quickly, Dalberg signing for them. The youngster thanked him and left us.

Raising his cup, Dalberg said, "Great service, and the best people in the Caribbean. 'Course, that's mainly on account of it's being the off-season and all. You know, the staffers have to do extra to get extra from the fewer of us down here. But still a great place."

"You knew Faith Bressler, then?"

Dalberg stopped in mid-sip, then finished, the drink leaving a little white mustache on his upper lip. "Some. Rose and her got talking on the beach last year. Turned out her husband's in construction, too. General contractor, though. Chicago."

"You come to the Bayview every June?"

"More or less. There's a bunch of us. Coughlin, Janice Dorn—she's the screwy schoolteacher saw you get picked up—a few others. I was kind of surprised to see Faith here again, though."

"Why is that?"

"Well, most of us are people who have a set time off, you know? We come to Macaroon because it's exotic, but we sort of . . . know the place, I guess? And in the off-season, it's reasonably priced. Faith, now, for what she was looking for, I'd of figured she'd be more the flit-from-island-to-island type, not caring much about the cost."

"And what was Faith looking for?"

Dalberg snorted into his drink. "Pal, you didn't find out Thursday night, you blew a great dinner."

"She genuinely chased around, did she?"

Dalberg set down his cup, as though he were trying to weigh things and speak fairly. "We had lunch with Faith one day last year, and she was really . . . nice, you know? It was kind of crazy, because I'd seen her the night before feeling up the tennis pro from another hotel in our bar. Whoring at night, then next day acting the perfect wife, like her husband had just left the table to take a piss and she was filling in the conversation till he got back. Crazy, you see what I mean?"

I nodded. Dalberg shook his head.

"The tennis pro," I said.

"What?"

"The tennis pro. What's his name?"

Dalberg shrugged. "Who knows?"

"He still around, Stan?"

The plumbing supplier eyed me suspiciously, then grinned. "You really are a cop."

"That's right. Which hotel was he from?"

"Whispering Winds, next one north. They're heavier into sports than this place, which is mainly for fat fucks like me who just eat, drink, and gamble. And I don't know if he's still there. I sure haven't seen him so far this year."

I finished the p.c. "Well, thanks for the drink."

"Hey, you're welcome. Any time."

Rose yelled "Gin!" again.

Standing, I said, "Think I'll get some sleep, away from all the action."

Dalberg grunted again. "Some action. So long."

I took a step, then turned back. "By the way, you wouldn't have been after Faith Bressler yourself, would you?"

A laugh from Stan Dalberg and another signal to the drink boy. "I thought about it, sure, but Rose convinced me I wouldn't be exactly entrancing with two broken legs."

FOUR

Paul Gant's driver called me from the Bayview's front desk at exactly 4:15 p.m. When I got downstairs, we walked to the gray Toyota sedan in the driveway.

Gant was in the back seat and pushed open the left rear door. "Please, join me."

I did, and the Toyota bounced over speed bumps on the hotel's access road before turning north onto a main drag to the airport.

Gant shifted in his seat. "Kevin, I want to thank you again for coming with me."

"No sun to be missing, anyway."

"The weather forecast predicted better conditions for tomorrow."

Going no more than thirty miles an hour, we paralleled the ocean, about a hundred feet above the tide-line. Hibiscus and elaborate, orange-flowered flamboyant trees dotted both sides of the road, a few pigs feeding on litter under the branches. At one point, we had to stop completely as a skinny kid pushed, pulled, and kicked about twenty goats across the pavement.

"By the way," said Gant as we waited for the goats, "Mr. Kepper has compiled his list of those whose vacations overlapped with Mrs. Bressler's last year."

"Do you have it?"

Undoing the button of his breast pocket, he fished out a folded paper and opened it. "Dorn, Miss Janice. Dalberg, Mr. Stanley and Mrs. Rose." Gant refolded the paper.

"That's it?"

"No. There were seven, actually, but during our initial investigation last night, we discovered all the others have perfect alibis."

"And these three don't."

"Mr. Dalberg says he was gambling at the Petite Bay Casino. His wife says she was in bed, sleeping through the shots and the discovery of the bodies. Miss Dorn says she was in the bar of the Whispering Winds, a nearby hotel.

205

However, no one remembers seeing either Mr. Dalberg in the casino or Miss Dorn in that bar."

The goats finished their crossing, and the Toyota started up again. "Paul, I don't know Dorn, but I've met Dalberg and seen his wife. Neil Coughlin's not on your list?"

"No. Why?"

"He sat next to me for a while today. Tried to pump me for information."

"As I told you, Mr. Coughlin is the one who raised the alarm, but he is not on Mr. Kepper's list."

"What about the other lists, airlines and so forth?"

"I have requested them, but this is, after all, Macaroon, and just after Carnivaal, as well. Mr. Kepper's efforts in compiling his list were superhuman by our standards."

"I may have someone who won't appear on any list. Stan Dalberg told me today that the tennis pro at that Whispering Winds place was seen with Faith Bressler last year."

"Ah, Chip Burrington."

"Great name for a tennis pro."

"Sorry?"

"Nothing."

An uncertain nod. "He will be checked. However, Kevin, I too have the name of a non-tourist to include on the list. Corey Raines."

Droplets of water began to splat against the windshield. The driver turned on the wipers, which rubbed on the still mostly dry glass, making the barking sound of a seal.

I said, "Man or woman?"

"Man. A guide, of sorts, and a heavy drinker. It seems he also was a friend of Mrs. Bressler. And of Sophie."

As evenly as possible, I said, "Seems like my latest love has a pretty active past."

"Oh, no, Kevin. To the contrary, Sophie is one of the

most respected women on all of Macaroon. Respected in every way. It is just that . . . Well, both Raines and the Dutch naval officer Volker saw Mrs. Bressler last year and had the opportunity to see her again this year."

"This Raines works on the island, then?"

"In a sense. He operates a small outboard boat from Little Macaroon, across the bay." Gant gestured toward the small cay that was visible on a clear day but not through the rain. "As I said, a guide of sorts."

"By 'of sorts' I take it you think he uses his boat for more than fishing?"

Gant allowed himself a rueful smile. "What I think and what I can prove are, alas, two separate matters. We do know Raines was on Macaroon last night though, because a fisherman spotted his boat tied to the public dock in Ste. Marie before dawn this morning. It was still there a short time ago."

"Any leads on where this Raines might be?"

"Not as yet. He was seeing Sophie until recently. But now, who can say? We shall find him eventually. Macaroon is too small a place to hide for long."

The driver turned into the airport. We got out in front of the low, open-walled terminal to wait for Bressler.

Charles T. Bressler, to be exact. Faith had referred to him as "Charlie." She'd described him, too: fat, bald, and given to double-breasted suits. Gant and I beat his slightly overdue plane by fifteen minutes, but we remained silent, standing together near the expectant limos, cabs, and hotel vans.

The people from the flight began to file into the terminal from the Customs area. The passengers walked left, then right, then finally looked around the way disoriented tourists do. I focused on a squat, balding man squeezed into a loud, glen-plaid suit. He caught me looking at him, glanced at Paul's uniform, and bustled over to us.

"Gant," he said to me, "I would have thought you could've worn a tie, considering."

I started to speak, but got cut off. "Mr. Bressler, I am Inspector Paul Gant. This is Mr. Kevin Malloy, whom I've asked to be here as he is a countryman of yours. We are both deeply sorry to meet you under such circumstances."

"Oh," said Bressler. "Sorry, I thought . . ." A look to me for help.

Gant said, "No difficulty, Mr. Bressler," smoothly glossing over the man's embarrassment at realizing his assumption. "Have you any luggage?"

"Yeah, a suitcase."

Gant nodded and began to walk toward a simplistic conveyor belt just beginning to spit out bags of all shapes and colors.

Bressler lagged behind and leaned into me. "Hey, I really appreciate your coming out like this, but, uh . . ."

He was obviously trying to decide why I really was with Gant. "I'm a police detective from Boston, and Paul's asked me to help him on the case."

Bressler's eyebrows knitted. "What do you mean, 'case'? Faith committed suicide, right?"

"I guess maybe the Inspector should explain things to you."

"Christ on a crutch," said Charles T. Bressler as he scooped his luggage from the belt, declined Gant's offer to carry it, and half-followed, half-led us out to the car, spraying questions like a garden hose.

Bressler said, "Definitely suicide."

He was mumbling now, not really to me, and slurring his

words. The two of us were in the bar at the Bayview. An hour before we'd been at van Broeck's Funeral Parlor, viewing the fresh-frozen remains of his wife. At the undertaker's, Bressler had said nothing except "That's Faith" and "I'd like to go to my hotel." Since arriving at the hotel, he'd said only "Scotch, straight up." Four times.

"Scotch, straight up."

Five times.

Bressler pushed the empty glass away from him. "She was nuts, you know?"

"I didn't know her," figuring a lie to be kinder than the truth.

He gave me the sidelong glance of a shrewd drunk. "That's funny, she liked your type." His elbows on the bar, his head went from bowed to rocked back. Bressler never looked straight ahead, as though there was no notch in his neck for that setting.

I said, "Why are you so sure it was suicide?"

"I told you. Faith was nuts." He roused himself a little. "Not from the beginning, though. Sixteen years back, she was just kind of neurotic, you know? Needed a job, but couldn't type or nothing. Insecure, too, even with her looks and that body . . ." Bressler shrugged. "Hey, I was no Burt Reynolds, but when I met Faith, she really needed an anchor more than a job, and I was it. And Faith, she was everything I'd . . ." Another shrug, and he slugged back half of his fifth scotch.

"Charlie, what happened to change things?"

A laugh that didn't quite come off. "Faith started to catch up to me. Agewise, I mean. She was telling everybody this year she was thirty-four. Last year it was thirty-five. Faith was really almost forty-one."

"She was stunning for her age."

209

The sidelong glance again. "Thought you said you didn't know her?"

Time to back-pedal. "I didn't, but I saw her in the lobby before that night. A beautiful woman."

"Yeah." Then a bit quieter. "Yeah, Faith was that. Stupid to say she had everything, but she did. I had to tell my surety company little white lies so they'd bond me for enough jobs to keep the cash flowing to cover her 'trips.' I knew what Faith was doing, but I couldn't help her and I couldn't stop her and . . . oh, hell . . ." The tears began, real ones it seemed.

Charles T. Bressler recovered long enough to sign the tab, and I helped him back to his room.

FIVE

Eric Volker sat in the same chair in Paul Gant's office that I'd used early that Saturday morning. I could feel fatigue seeping into me, and I wondered if I looked as uncomfortable then as Volker did now.

He was tall, a good two inches over my six-one. Trim, too, with the long, non-showy forearm muscles of the truly strong man. His hair was close-cropped and very blond, the eyes almost white-gray rather than blue. And nervously darting.

"I appreciate discretion in this thing," Volker said in a thick accent.

Gant nodded, folding his lips in a toothless smile as though to say "Mmmmm" after tasting a delicious dessert. "Perhaps you would detail your activities of yesterday for us?"

"Yes." Volker straightened in the chair and began his

story, clearly rehearsed. "I am duty on the *Alliance* before sixteen hundred hours. I change then from uniform to clothes, civilian, and come to city on small launch. I dinner in one restaurant, then drink in bar. Then I . . . sleep with girl for night."

A lot of that going around. "Her name?"

Volker eyed Gant. "Necessary?"

The Inspector nodded.

Volker searched within for another English phrase. "Confidential to us, yes?"

Gant nodded again.

Volker let out a breath. "Elleta Menner."

Gant wrote something down. "When did you return to your ship?"

"On early launch, oh-six-hundred hours."

"You were with Ms. Menner until then?"

Volker's turn to nod, my turn to ask a question.

"Do you know of any reason anyone would want Faith Bressler dead?"

Volker started a bit, looking at me, then Gant. "I am marry in Netherlands, wife and one child, big with second."

I became part of the nodding epidemic.

"Faith Bressler woman, she write me letter, say she will be with one she love forever. Here, on Macaroon."

"How long ago was the letter?" I said.

Volker held up his hands. "Letter take time to get to my house. I tell to Faith Bressler last year that I live in Amsterdam. Her letter get to there, and teacher-friend of my wife read the English to her." Volker started kneading his cap, alternating hands. "Bad."

"Do you still have the letter?"

"No. Never see letter. Wife rip all up, then rip me all up." A weak smile.

"Is that all you remember?"

The hands again. "All wife tell me. She think I am the 'one lover.' " Volker suddenly became firm. "But not me, and I do not kill Faith Bressler woman."

"Do you know who the 'one lover' was?"

Volker's head seesawed, side to side. "I think she have many, even here on Macaroon."

We were all silent for a moment.

I decided to underline my neutrality. "Do you think Sophie Travers could have anything to do with it?"

Volker half came out of his chair, his English going south. "Sophie, oh no! No, she me friends, better than friends, but no kill Faith Bressler woman."

Gant tented his fingers on the desktop and spoke to me. "Anything else?"

I said, "No," and Volker left us.

After the door closed, Gant sighed. "I am tired, Kevin, as you must be. But I feel we should discuss soon where we are now and where we are going. May the police department of Ste. Marie take you to lunch tomorrow?"

"Sure."

"Perhaps Sophie's at 1:00 p.m.?"

I stopped. "Only for a drink, Paul. She doesn't serve food in the off-season."

Gant mockingly struck his forehead with his palm. "Of course. The Coconut Café, then, on Front Street?"

"I'll find it."

"Excellent." He stood and returned the case folder to a file cabinet.

"By the way, given Volker's jitters, is this Menner woman married, too?"

"No, but quite young," said Paul Gant, his back toward me. "And black."

★ ★ ★ ★ ★

Walking to Sophie's that night, not a lot of people were on the street. Maybe the end of Carnivaal had left everybody broke and tired. Or maybe the news of the killings at the Bayview had squelched the local spirit.

Across from the Soupcon, a young islander sat propped against the wall, brown-bagged bottle to his lips. Dark-skinned, he was only about twenty-five, but his clothes were so dirty that you wouldn't want to approach close enough to smell him.

Sophie had fish cooking in her apartment over the bar that night. Even outside her door, I could hear it crackling. I knocked and went in.

She was wearing a fetching halter top over a print skirt. Sophie handed me a Grolsch, Dutch beer that came in brown bottles sealed with hermetic, rubber-and-plastic stoppers like miniature cheese jars.

"Well," she said, "and how did it go?"

"As well as it could. Gant and I met Bressler at the airport and interviewed Volker at the stationhouse." I filled her in on the rest as we filled our plates, then our stomachs, with yellowtail snapper and ratatouille.

A little later, we slipped out of our clothes and between Sophie's sheets. Harbor waves slapped vaguely against the pilings below us, and a gecko climbed the wall toward the windowsill.

I slid my hand up Sophie's thigh. She blocked its path for a moment with her left. "Kev, do you think we have anything to worry about?"

I said, "Not so far," and Sophie Travers let go of my hand.

SIX

Leaving her building the next morning, something bothered me, and I called Sophie from a payphone on my walk back to the Bayview. I spent the rest of that Sunday morning lying around the hotel's pool, soaking up the sun and trying to work things through. Neil Coughlin fidgeted some on a lounge nearby, but he left without approaching me directly.

Down the beach, three youngish islanders, two of them female, were playing in the water with three children. The older ones would hold the kids by the waist, swinging and dunking them in the mild surf. When the wind was right, you could just hear their squeals of delight. An old fart a couple lounges away from me looked at them, frowned, and straightened his *Wall Street Journal* as though he were riding a metropolitan commuter train and the islanders, heaven forbid, had sneaked aboard.

Up the beach, three tanned boy-men were jogging long-leggedly toward me. As they drew even, I could see their short blond hair and black Euro-briefs, younger clones of Eric Volker. Speaking to each other in excited, though not winded, Dutch, they seemed to be in depressingly good shape. I noticed the old fart at first admiring them, then catching himself and straightening his paper again.

Beginning to feel drowsy, I counted up how little sleep (as opposed to sack-time) I'd logged in the last few days. Just before closing my eyes, I saw a couple of large, wasp-like insects hovering at the edge of my lounge. They never seemed to attack people, instead burrowing in the sand like six-legged prairie dogs. Macaroon was remarkably free of biting insects, maybe because the wasps kept down their annoying cousins.

I was nearly asleep when a warm, long-nailed hand

rested on my left shoulder. "You're looking very relaxed for a murder suspect."

I opened my eyes to a plain, thirty-something female face on a traffic-stopping, twentyish female body. Smiling coyly, she kept her hand on my shoulder.

I said, "That's a common misconception."

The woman sat down on the edge of my lounge chair, shifting her rear end so that one cheek was now brushing against my right leg. "The cops I saw arresting you were no 'misconception.' "

"Kevin Malloy, Ms. Dorn."

She took her hand from my shoulder and squeezed mine, a bit harder and longer than was, strictly speaking, required for introduction purposes. "Are you a good detective, or a mind reader as well? And by the way, it's 'Janice.' "

Dorn made no effort to give the hand back, so I dropped it to my thigh, carrying hers along. She began rubbing little concentric circles with the nail of her middle finger on my right leg.

"You'll give me an odd kind of tan that way," I said, a mite hoarsely.

"You look like you've had enough sun for one day already." A purring voice, nestling her rear more solidly against me.

I looked down at my legs. They did seem reddish, especially the right one. "What's your room number?"

Dorn locked onto my eyes, then made them follow hers to my thigh and her finger. She traced 4-2-4 on the skin.

"Fifteen minutes?" I said.

"Make it ten," trailing her finger up my leg toward my trunks as she rose and walked back into the hotel.

I cleared my throat, then cleared it again. I waited all of five minutes, then followed her.

★ ★ ★ ★ ★

Janice Dorn greeted me at the door of her room. She'd changed to a see-through nightie, and there were two plastic cups atop her bureau, amber liquid in each.

"It's brandy, but . . . before or after?" Dorn said, closing the door with her left hand and gesturing demurely toward the drinks with her right.

"Let's play it by ear." I tugged the little supporting bow at the back of her neck. The nightie slipped down as she came into my arms.

Dorn immediately thrust her tongue into my mouth. Then she yanked out four or five of my pubic hairs by violently tugging my trunks down over my butt.

In bed, Dorn was acrobatic, too much so for my taste. Back in Boston, I'd seen women in discos with great bodies moving mechanically, as though they'd learned to dance by watching silent movies of others and then imitating them. Dorn reminded me of that, moving correctly but not in time with the music.

When we were done, she rolled out from under me and walked, swinging her hips, to the bureau. Carrying back the brandies, Dorn said, "To Macaroon."

I held out a hand for mine as she took a gulp of hers, coughed, and smiled oddly, almost shyly. Then the smile went to coy again, and Dorn dribbled the rest of her brandy just south of where she'd yanked out the hairs.

The purry voice said, "I like playing it by . . . ear."

"Hey, time to get up."

I blinked awake. Janice Dorn was wearing a tennis outfit, brushing her hair in front of the bureau mirror.

"What time is it?" I said, shaking my head.

"Twenty minutes before my tennis date. Move."

I felt like a third-grader whose lunchbox and books weren't packed in time to catch the school bus. "I'll get dressed after you leave."

"Not . . . a . . . chance." Dorn tossed my trunks over to me. "That's all the dressing you need to do."

"I've never been this rude to anyone in my life, much less somebody I just slept with."

She turned, angry, then softened. Coming over to the bed, Dorn sat on it the way she had on my lounge by the pool.

"Look, lover. Back in Middle America I've got an image imposed on me by the people who pay my salary. I'm tenured, sure, but the 'baby boomlet' has passed through the grade I teach, and the 'reductions-in-force' are going to start any time now. I can't afford to live it up much in a small town because some kid's older brother or sister would spot me and then tell the kid or the parents who'd go to the P.T.A.—"

"Then why not move to a big city?"

A slow shake of the head. "Because I wouldn't enjoy living in a big city. I like small towns. It's just that they have certain limitations you have to observe while you're there. So I come here and other places on my vacations and, well, exceed those limitations." Dorn gave me another coy expression. "If you know what I mean."

I reached for her hand, but she popped up from the bed.

"Sorry, lover, but I've got just three days left down here, and I'm making the most of them. You've been, and may be again, a nice part of my vacation, but for now . . ."

I swung my legs out from under the sheet and pulled on the trunks. Dorn gathered up her tennis racket and gently pushed me into the hallway. As she locked her door and turned to go, I asked her who she was playing.

"A guy named Chip. The tennis pro at Whispering Winds."

I watched her turn into the exit stairway and wondered.

It was just after noon when I got to my room. I showered and dressed semi-nicely for the semi-official lunch with Paul Gant. He hadn't said he was sending a car, so I walked downstairs and stopped at the front desk. Mr. Kepper smiled twice at me, the first a warm one before he recognized me, the second a cold one like you'd use on a friend who hits you up for money.

I decided not to disappoint him. "Have the police been asking around for me this morning?"

"They have not, sir."

"If they do, tell them I decided to walk into town, will you?"

"Certainly, sir."

"That's Malloy, Kevin."

"Yes, sir. I know."

I started to walk away, then thought of something I'd intended to ask about the day before. "By the way, is there a good scuba-diving operation on the island?"

"There are several, sir." Kepper turned to a display rack within reach of both staff and guests and nimbly plucked three brochures from it. "I'm sure you'll find any of these suitable."

I took the brochures.

"If I may, sir, were you planning to dive at any particular time?"

I was a little surprised by his interest. "Yes. Tomorrow afternoon."

"Ah, in that case, I recommend you call ahead, right now if possible, to ensure a place on the boat, even out of season."

Kepper was smiling warmly now, and I smiled back. "Thanks."

He lifted a telephone up onto the counter. "I recommend Yelton Pierce, sir. He is the best on the island."

It occurred to me that Kepper might be setting this up *a la* the other guests pre-"housecleaning," but I pulled out Pierce's brochure from the batch and scanned it quickly. It said he provided all the equipment and would also rent it if you weren't interested in diving with him.

Pierce's promotional promises met all my requirements, so I dialed his number and by chance reached him just as he was coming in from the morning's dive. We talked for a few minutes, Pierce making sure I was certified by a course in Boston, me making sure of his prices. He said he'd even pick me up at the Bayview the next day.

I hung up, passed the phone back to Kepper, and bumped into the driver Gant had sent after all.

SEVEN

My "date" was sitting at a corner table in the Coconut Café, what looked like a piña colada in front of him. The place was decorated in every way a palm tree and its fruit could be used.

I said, "Please, don't get up," as Paul Gant started to rise. A waitress appeared instantaneously, and I ordered a p.c. for myself.

"Great service," I said after she headed toward the bar. "Befitting a police inspector."

Gant grinned. "Befitting an uncle, rather. Taren is the daughter of my sister."

The drink came, and Paul raised his glass. "To a

successful solution, Kevin."

We sipped. I said, "No problems with your drinking on duty?"

Gant wagged his head. "No rum in the glass. I have found I prefer the taste of the coconut this way."

Taren brought menus and patiently awaited our order. I asked for a recommendation, and she suggested the grouper rijstaffel.

After Taren walked to the kitchen, Gant said, "We found her car."

"Faith Bressler's, you mean?"

"Yes. Parked at the Bayview, in fact."

"I didn't know she'd rented one."

Gant took some more of his drink. "She had not. Not exactly, that is. You see, according to Mr. Kepper, last year when Mrs. Bressler stayed at the hotel, she made a fuss over a car not being ready for her upon arrival. So, this year, Mr. Kepper arranged one as soon as he received her telephone call making the room reservation."

"And when was that?"

A smile. "Just seven days ago."

"Spur-of-the-moment trip, it sounds like."

Gant nodded. "The rental agency insists upon giving out the cleanest of cars. They wipe down the entire interior before delivering one to a hotel. The only fingerprints in this vehicle are Tony de Weeter's and the rental agency driver who drove it to the Bayview. And the steering wheel was wiped clean."

"Like the handbag?"

"Precisely so."

We drew down our drinks.

Then Gant said, "I had an interesting experience this morning."

I thought, Me, too. "What was it?"

"Mr. Charles Bressler."

"He came to see you?"

"Yes. It seems Mrs. Bressler left a suicide note."

I almost choked into my glass. "A note? We missed a note?"

"No, Kevin. Mr. Bressler claims to have found it in Chicago, in his bedroom." Paul added quickly, "It appears they were not legally separated, although each maintained a bedroom in the house."

"What did the note say?"

Gant set down his drink. "We do not know for certain. That is, Mr. Bressler destroyed the note when he found it. In a 'blind rage,' according to him. However, apparently his wife wrote that she was leaving to be with the one she loved, in life or death as the case may be."

"I don't remember our Mr. Bressler mentioning any note yesterday."

"Nor do I, Kevin."

"On the other hand, it sounds enough like the letter Volker said Faith sent to Amsterdam that it rings true."

"Agreed."

"Only we also have two bodies, and a tidal wave of circumstantial evidence that points away from suicide." I took another sip of my piña colada. "Have you considered the possibility that Old Charlie may have hired someone to push the wayward Faith into the next life?"

Gant frowned. "I have, but discarded the thought. First, Mr. Bressler seems entirely sincere in his devotion to his wife and in his belief that she committed suicide. Second, and more objectively, I would think it highly unlikely that he would have a killer follow her to Macaroon on, as you say, the 'spur of the moment,' to kill her. If your country's cinema is to be believed, violent deaths are far less unusual, and more easily commissioned, in Chicago than here."

Taren arrived with our entrees, and we ate in silence except for my compliment about the food. Gant seemed to be on top of things, which might mean he'd wrap up the investigation even sooner than I'd hoped.

After Taren cleared the plates, the Inspector and I ordered coffee. We exchanged small talk about the best beaches on the island until the cups and saucers were in front of us.

"By the way," said Gant. "We now have our 'master list' of suspects." Taking a folded paper from his pocket, he spread it out so I could read it.

"As you can see Kevin, there are twenty-three possible contact persons with Mrs. Faith Bressler last year who are here this year. For example, Eric Volker. Like Volker, all but six have alibis which have been confirmed, and therefore the letter 'A' has been placed next to their names. Those who met her only this year—for example, Neil Coughlin and yourself—are in the group at the bottom. The crossed line between your name and Sophie's indicates that you and she are alibis for each other."

I looked down at the six names without an 'A' next to them, providing my own characterizations:

Chip Burrington, tennis pro.
Albert Kepper, hotel staff.
Janice Dorn, the bizarro OUR MISS BROOKS.
Stanley Dalberg, plumbing supplier.
Rose Dalberg, wife of same.
Neil Coughlin, the tiresome wimp.

I said, "Two comments?"

"Yes?"

"First, when I spoke with Coughlin over a drink yes-

222

terday, I had the impression that he'd never met Faith. He kept referring to her as 'that woman.' What makes you think Coughlin knew her this year?"

"Mr. Kepper distinctly remembers seeing Mrs. Bressler on the afternoon of the night she was killed, speaking with Mr. Coughlin very briefly in the lobby. While he may never have been introduced to her by name, he is therefore on the list of those who 'knew' her this year."

"Very thorough, Paul. However, my second comment is kind of the opposite. Haven't you left a name off this list?"

Gant frowned again and examined the paper carefully. Slowly, he said, "I do not believe so."

"The guide? Baines or Raines . . ."

"Ah," Gant struck his palm mockingly on his forehead as he'd done once the day before. "Of course. This list was compiled by me from interview lists submitted by my men. Since Corey Raines has not turned up as yet, he had not been interviewed."

"How about Burrington? What did he have to say for himself?"

"The report submitted by my officer was . . . incomplete. I thought I would try to see Mr. Burrington this afternoon myself."

Nodding, I wondered instead about the real reason Paul Gant had overlooked a candidate as obvious as Corey Raines.

EIGHT

I declined the Inspector's invitation to visit Chip Burrington for two reasons. The one I told Gant was the truth, that I wanted to snorkel a bit to warm up for my scuba dive the next afternoon. The one I didn't tell him, also the truth, was that if Burrington didn't look exhausted post-Janice, I'd begin to feel pretty old.

Gant had suggested I try Petite Bay, which was close to my hotel and which he assured me had a great rock formation along its southern peninsula. I thanked him for lunch and accepted a ride back to the hotel.

At the desk, Mr. Kepper told me I could check out a mask, fins, and snorkel from the pool boy. He added that if I found a mask that suited me, I could take it on my dive the next day. I thanked him, too, deciding everybody on the island was suddenly being awfully nice to me.

As I walked away, Kepper said, "Oh, Mr. Malloy, I am so sorry, but I almost forgot. There are two messages for you. One is from a Captain Hanrahan in Boston, the other from Mr. Coughlin, who would like to speak with you in his room."

Both of the messages could wait until after my "snork." Upstairs, I changed to trunks and running shoes. At the pool, I started trying on masks. Two years before, another captain on the Boston force had suggested I get certified in scuba. The proper way to select a mask is to hold it up to your face, then inhale through the nose to see if the mask "sticks" without the strap holding it on your head. If the mask sticks, that means the seal on the inner, rubbery edge fits the features, and you won't get water leaking into your mask when you dive.

Two of the pool boy's masks passed the test, me choosing the one with the best lens visibility. Snorkels are pretty generic, and the fins just depended on foot size, since they were "tropicals," like shoes, rather than "powers" with back straps. The tropicals are supposed to protect your feet from stinging or chafing creatures and plants in warmer waters.

I slid the snorkel's strap over its spout, then threaded that strap through the left-hand side of the mask's strap until the snorkel lay comfortably vertical against my temple and in my mouth. I nodded to the pool boy, who began writing a rental receipt for the equipment. I noticed a laminated five-by-eight card with miniature paintings of reef fish captioned with the appropriate names. I asked the kid if the card was waterproof, and he said yes. I tossed the card in with the other stuff, signed for everything, and walked the mile or so to Petite Bay, reading both sides of the card along the way.

Reaching the jetty arm where the snorkeling was supposed to be best, I waded out until the water was waist deep. I put on my fins and stuck the fish card into the top of my trunks. Swishing my mask in the water, I then spit on the inner surface of the glass and rubbed it around with my index and middle fingers. Something in the spit (protein, I think) keeps the mask from fogging under water. I rinsed the mask in the water, repeated the spit ritual, and rinsed again. Slipping the mask strap over my head, I mouthed the snorkel and eased forward in a splashless dive.

Even in the shallow water, there were at first dozens, then hundreds of fish whirling around. I pulled out my card and identified a French grunt, two kinds of goatfish, and a barjack. As I kicked out, the schools parted and ran from me, like caribou before a bushplane. I remembered my scuba instructor telling us that if we'd just hang in the water, we wouldn't scare the fish, our bodies' natural buoyancy allowing us to breathe by keeping within snorkel height of the surface. I stopped kicking and just floated, spread-eagle.

I could breathe easily, and the fish stopped running and resumed their idiosyncratic patrols. I kicked a little farther out, and the bottom began to get farther away and rockier. There were sea urchins everywhere, black pin cushions whose spines were like glass pick-up sticks and which could give you a nasty wound and infection if you stepped on one. I was pretty sure the tropical fins would deflect the spines, but I decided not to experiment personally. Then I tracked a couple of barracuda, the length of my arm and one-third teeth.

Half an hour later, I was back on the jetty, the equipment I'd signed out having worked so well I decided to keep it for the next day's dive. As I walked back to the Bayview and through the main entrance, I caught sight of Neil Coughlin just a heartbeat too late. He began waving frantically to me from his sentinel post in the bar. I shrugged and waved at my appearance.

Awkwardly, Coughlin stepped off the bar stool and moved quickly toward me. "Didn't you get my message?"

"Yes." I headed for the staircase.

"But I need to speak with . . . someone."

"Then you need to wait till I've changed, Neil."

"I'll come up with you."

"No. The bar in half an hour."

"But that's not private enough."

Almost whining. "It'll have to do," I said, opening the staircase door.

In my room, I showered and shaved. After putting on a dress shirt and slacks, I dialed the switchboard, giving Kepper the Homicide Unit's number in Boston. After three tries, the call went through, the connection scratchy.

"Homicide, Ciccio," said a female voice.

"Joan, it's Kevin Malloy."

"Hey, Kevin. We thought the sharks got you."

I thought back an hour and then again a year, when Joan

Ciccio put a slug in the shoulder of a wild-eyed kid trying to brain me with a tire-iron. "Just barracuda. Is the Cap' in?"

"Yeah, wait one."

I could hear her yell, then a different voice on the other end of the line said, "Malloy. I was hoping the sharks got you."

"Sorry, Cap'," I said, wondering who had started that hopeful rumor. "How can I help you?"

"Well," I could hear him rustling paper. "It's about the Boivin case. You know, the doctor stabbing."

"What about it?"

"The D.A.'s office says it's coming to trial Friday, and the assistant tells me she needs you as first witness up."

"Cap', that shaves two days off my vacation time. Besides, Tom Hering was supposed to prosecute this one, and I told him I wouldn't be available till the—"

"I know, I know, but Hering's got hepatitis, so he can't try it. And the signals got crossed somehow by Judge Stipple's clerk, and you know as well as I do that Ruby Stipple won't grant a continuance for a lawyer's vacation, much less a cop's."

"Yeah, yeah." I liked Bill Hanrahan, with his six kids and beer gut. The problem with him was his old-fashioned attitude about what was moral and immoral. And the fact that he ran his squad and promotion recommendations that way. On this one he was right, though. Stipple was so by the book she made Hanrahan look like a sodomite.

"By the way, Kev, I'm not supposed to tell you this, but to sort of make up for your vacation and all, I asked around about the lieutenant's list."

The anticipation surged inside me. "And?"

"And it looks like you'll be on it. That Nufano hit you broke was the icing on the cake. Just keep your nose clean till September, and you're in."

"Thanks, Cap', I really appreciate it."

"Enjoy the vacation, but see you Friday, huh?"

"I'll be there."

We hung up. Friday. I needed at least one night after finding Faith Bressler's killer, and now Hanrahan had shortened my deadline by two full days.

NINE

I slung a lightweight blue blazer over my shoulder and went downstairs. Pressing my luck, I asked Kepper to inquire into an earlier flight with the airlines. He was very pleasant, saying he was sure it could be arranged and would leave me a message.

"Enjoy your dive, sir."

"That's not till tomorrow."

"Yes, that's what I meant, sir. I hope you will enjoy it."

"Thank you," I said, then braced myself for Neil Coughlin.

Only he wasn't there. I looked once around the bar, walked out to the pool. I could see Stan Dalberg in a lounge, Rose playing cards near him, and Janice Dorn doing an unnecessarily complicated dive from the board. But no Coughlin. I watched Dorn perform for a few minutes, then walked back through the hotel and toward downtown.

I stopped at Sophie's, the wino across the way seeming to have passed out hours before. Inside, she was doing a brisk drink business, mainly shoppers. With no employees in the off-season, Sophie could manage only a disjointed conversation with me, and we eventually decided that I'd see her that night. No reason to tell her of my accelerated schedule till then.

I had a terrific meal at a place Sophie recommended, then a boring after-dinner drink with a cloying middle-aged couple from New Jersey at the rectangular bar. I begged off a second round, saying I was meeting someone else. The man winked as his wife said, "Oh, Phil."

I walked up Front Street and noticed that, like retail strips everywhere, the Carnivaal decorations stayed up past the event itself, hoping to retain in the tourists a sense of free-spending. Passing the Bayview, I continued on to the Petite Bay Hotel, which advertised a casino.

Unfortunately, the marquee failed to mention that the casino didn't open till 9:00, so I tried the cocktail lounge across the lobby. There was a guitarist picking away to the delight of four college girls in one corner. A few couples huddled at barely-lit tables. But more obvious, at least to me, was Neil Coughlin.

He was seated, if you could call his posture that, at the far end of the bar, oblivious to everything except the glass of white wine he was cradling in the joined fingers of both hands. I thought about dodging him, but I had time to kill, and he'd find me sooner or later. When I ordered a beer, the sound of my voice seemed to break Coughlin's trance. He first glanced at me, then smiled shakily. He got up even more shakily, holding his glass in one hand and sliding the other along the brass rail for support.

"Coughlin," I said.

He settled onto the stool next to mine. "Oh, please, you called me 'Neil' this afternoon."

Coughlin was slurring his words like Charles Bressler had after the funeral home. "Neil, then." I put a twenty in front of my delivered drink.

"Why wouldn't you talk to me today?"

"I looked for you in the Bayview's bar, but you weren't there."

"I wasn't there?" Coughlin raised his voice, indignant. "You, policeman, you weren't there when I needed you. Policemen never are." He tanked his drink, and the bartender gave me a sour look, holding me responsible whether the guy's condition was my fault or not.

"Well?" said Coughlin.

"I'm an officer only in the city of Boston, Neil. We're not there, and you're not even from there."

"Boston? Boston? Who's talking about Boston? I'm talking about here, and dead bodies, and . . . Oh, God." He began to sniffle, then sob.

Great. I took a breath, waving off the approaching bartender. "Neil, let's call you a cab, okay?"

I put my arm around his shoulder to ease him from the stool, but he threw me off and jumped down himself, knocking over his empty glass.

"No!" Coughlin tried to focus his eyes. "You're just like his Eminence, you know? He never has time to listen, either. He's a crummy priest, too. Just plain crummy."

And Neil Coughlin stumbled out, banging a shoulder into Stan Dalberg as he was entering the bar. Dalberg said something to him that I didn't catch and even started after him, but Coughlin was running now, and Dalberg didn't even try to catch up.

Instead the plumbing supplier came toward me, his head inclined toward the door. "What the hell got into him?" Dalberg said, taking the stool on the other side of mine.

"Aside from too much Chablis, I don't know."

"Chablis?" said Dalberg as he pointed to my beer and waggled two fingers at the barkeep. "I never saw a guy get drunk on white wine before."

"You know much about Coughlin, Stan?"

"Not a hell of a lot. Rose and me—oh, thanks." He picked up his glass. "You see, Rose and me, we take our vacations mid-week to mid-week on account of the airfare break, but Coughlin, he has a job where he has to go weekend-to-weekend. So, we overlap maybe two, three days max with him each year."

"Where does he work?"

Dalberg took a deep draw of his beer, smacking his tongue against the roof of his mouth. "New York City. He's an assistant something-or-other for this Cardinal in the Catholic Church. In fact," said Dalberg, now a little conspiratorially, "I always figured Coughlin for kind of a busted priest himself. You know, somebody who starts studying for it but never gets through?"

I nodded and took a sip of beer.

Dalberg changed the subject before I was quite ready to let it go. "I understand you and Janice are pretty close now." A sly grin.

"Somebody gossiping?"

"Just Janice herself. She gave you very high marks in . . . Phys Ed?" He giggled into his glass.

"Getting back to Coughlin—"

A ship's bell sounded twice.

"Post-time!" said Dalberg jubilantly, downing his drink. "Come on. Even in the off-season, the blackjack tables fill up early."

He hopped from the stool and threaded his way through the sudden crowd. I lost him in the minor crush at the casino doorway. Fat American males in Hawaiian shirts, trimmer ones in polo shirts, a few others with placket-collared, ill-fitting shirts that had any one of several Macaroon logos emblazoned on the pockets. There was only a sprinkling of women, mostly middle-aged, with rolls of quarters in their fists.

Past the entryway I found a room about fifty by a hundred. Ten blackjack tables were arranged in a long, narrow ellipse, five on a side. Dalberg was saving me a seat at Table Three on the left. Nearly every slot machine around the perimeter of the room was already occupied, and cocktail waitresses floated through the eager gamblers. I noticed that the management provided no chairs away from the tables. Not being able to sit without betting probably promoted both gambling and drinking.

I slid in next to Dalberg.

"See what I mean?" he said. "Like when tickets go on sale for the Series. This is the only casino I come to, but it's the best in town."

The dealer, a striking, chocolate-brown islander, brought over the shoe of cards. Dalberg put two fifty-dollar bills on the green felt in front of him.

"Good evening, Vera," he said.

"Good evening, Mr. Dalberg." Dazzling smile.

"Vera, this is my friend, Kevin Malloy."

"Good evening to you, Mr. Malloy."

We traded smiles, but I got the better of at least that deal.

Vera gave Dalberg twenty black chips, placing them in one of two card-shaped outlines in front of him. I took a twenty from my wallet and in my thoughts kissed it goodbye. Vera was nice enough to give me two blacks and five reds, a sign behind her indicating that two dollars, or one red chip, was the minimum bet.

The four other players around our table received chips in exchange for cash, three low-rollers like me. The fourth, a slim, older black in a burgundy safari shirt, laid out three hundred-dollar bills.

As we began to play, each bettor put a chip or two on the felt inside one white outline. Vera dealt the cards, one down, one up, onto the other outline. She was very fast and very smooth.

Under the house rules, the dealer had to display his or her own hand face-up. The dealer also had to take another card if holding up to sixteen, but wasn't allowed to hit at seventeen or more. Nevertheless, I remembered reading somewhere that the house still held a wide statistical advantage.

You couldn't tell that by Vera, however. Dutifully hitting each of her below-sixteen hands, she went bust each time. Dalberg, who had been betting first fives and then tens, was up nearly fifty bucks already. I'd been betting twos, my black fives shaming me, so I was only twelve to the good. The guy in the burgundy shirt had already made enough to pay for my airfare down and back.

After her eighth disaster, in which Vera stayed at seventeen and all but one of us held higher, she smiled around the table, turned her head, and said, "Peter?"

A man in a vested tuxedo outfit with a jacket nodded and beckoned to a man in a vested tuxedo outfit without a jacket. "Without" took Vera's place as dealer. Dalberg watched Vera leg away from us.

"Good evening, folks, my name is Raymond," said Without.

"Good evening, Raymond," said Dalberg.

"Good evening, Mr. Dalberg," said Raymond.

This time I wasn't introduced. Raymond did a bit better than Vera, but not much. I wondered if the casino would rig the first shoe of cards to let the yokels win and thereby hook themselves, but I couldn't figure out how the house could do it. We all watched the cards being shuffled, Dalberg cutting the first shoe and the black high roller the second.

After ten or so hands with Raymond, I had nearly fifty bucks, even my black chips having danced twice in front of me. The house was comping drinks for the table, and I was seriously considering asking Safari-Shirt if he was interested in financing a condo for me with his winnings.

Then Raymond also said, "Peter?"

Looking a little pissed this time, Peter beckoned to a woman who made even the dazzling Vera look a touch weak.

"Good evening, gentlemen, my name is Tanya."

"Tanya."

"Mr. Dalberg."

Dalberg flicked his head toward me. "Kevin Malloy."

Big smile from Tanya, but eyes that reminded me a lot of the barracudas I'd tracked snorkeling.

Dalberg leaned over to me and whispered, "Fasten your seat-belt."

Tanya's long fingers were a blur. I'd had only two drinks, but I really couldn't see her hands moving. A man at our table, realizing the situation, collected his chips after just one round and moved on. Nobody took his place, despite the fact that there were people standing behind us and no other available chairs in the room.

Tanya's luck was as awesome as her coordination. I went from betting fives back to twos again. I still got slaughtered. Dalberg dug out another fifty, Safari-shirt another three hundred. Losing my last chip, I felt like a seventeen-year-old punk after facing Wyatt Earp.

I leaned over to Dalberg. "Maybe later, Stan."

Never looking up from the cards, he said, "Right. Take it easy."

As I rose, Tanya said, "Come back again, Mr. Malloy."

I smiled and carried my beer around the casino for twenty minutes or so. In that time, Dalberg must have dropped another fifty and Safari-Shirt another few hundred. My seat and the other vacated one were finally taken by a couple in designer jeans who dipped a thousand each.

Leaving the casino, I wondered about Stan Dalberg, a guy who flew mid-week to save fifty bucks on airfare only to drop two hundred in one sitting—just an hour, really. I also wondered why, the night of the killings, nobody in the casino remembered seeing the plumbing supplier there when everybody in the place seemed to know him by name.

I took a cab to Sophie's. The young derelict was still across the street, looking like he'd slept the day away.

Inside, Sophie and I talked casually at the bar until the last single guy in the place gave up the ghost for the night and trudged out as coolly as possible. I helped with the clean-up, then we went upstairs.

"Any progress on Faith's death?" she asked as soon as we were in her apartment.

"Hard to say, but I do have some bad news."

A troubled frown. "What, luv?"

I told her about my call to Hanrahan.

"Oh, Kev, we'll never make it, will we?"

"Sure we will," I said, taking her into my arms and putting more reassurance into my voice than I truly felt.

Sophie tilted her head back, managing a smile. "So long as Faith's killer doesn't outwit the famous Boston detective."

"And so long as there's no power failure."

She shuddered, and I was sorry at once that I'd said that.

TEN

Sophie and I had breakfast on her porch overlooking Grand Bay. I told her I'd see her the next night for a late dinner.

It was almost 10:00 a.m. by the time I got back to the Bayview. Walking past the desk, I heard Kepper's voice behind me.

"Mr. Malloy?" He beckoned me closer. "Inspector Gant telephoned you yesterday evening at 7:00 p.m. He would be pleased if you would call him."

"Thank you."

"Would you like me to postpone your diving trip?"

I searched his eyes for sarcasm. There was something there besides warmth, but it wasn't sarcasm.

"No, thanks. I'm sure I'll still make it."

"Good. Enjoy, sir." Kepper turned back to his paperwork.

Upstairs, I sat on my bed and dialed the police.

"Ah, Kevin, thank you for getting back to me," said Gant, a brightness in his voice.

"Something come up?"

"No. No, I'm afraid not. I thought I might brief you, though, while you enjoyed some real island cooking. Tonight, if convenient. My wife will be going to the market at dockside soon."

"That sounds great, Paul. What time?"

"I will call for you myself at 7:00."

"Can I bring some wine?"

"That would be so thoughtful. A white, perhaps." He paused. "Please do not expense yourself, though. I fear many of the better wines either do not travel well or are mistreated by our merchants upon arrival."

236

"I'll be guided by that. See you here at 7:00."

"Excellent."

I hung up and decided I would have to begin accelerating the pace of Gant's investigation. I changed to a pair of trunks and headed downstairs to rattle some poolside cages.

"Didn't expect to see you still here," I said quietly in the bar, signaling the keep for a drink.

Charles Bressler looked up at me, eyes bloodshot but otherwise steady. "Fucking red tape. Can't release the body without somebody's stamp and seal. We're set to go on the flight to Miami tomorrow afternoon."

The "we" made me stop for a moment.

"You okay?" said Bressler.

"Yeah, fine." I held out my hand as my piña colada arrived. "Take care of yourself."

"Yeah," and he shook my hand as his left grabbed my drink check. "And, thanks for, uh, being there. The airport and here and all. It wasn't your problem, and I appreciate it."

I nodded and released his hand. Picking up my glass, I tried not to feel too hypocritical as I continued to the pool.

At one corner, Janice Dorn was lounging with a guy who looked like Troy Donahue in his prime. Dalberg occupied his usual position, a crossroad which allowed him to scope both the women walking to the beach and the women walking to the pool. Rose's gin game was going full tilt, but Neil Coughlin was nowhere in sight.

I decided to start with Dorn, since I knew Dalberg wouldn't be moving very far. Despite how close they appeared from a distance, the Troy-friend got up with a mean smile on his face while Janice looked worried.

She said, "Please, Chip—" but friend cut her off with a

wave of his hand, then extended it to me.

"You Malloy?"

"That's right." I shook his hand. Vise-like grip that comes from playing lots of tennis. I asked anyway.

"Chip Burrington." He looked around behind me. "Can I talk to you for a minute? Privately."

"Sure."

Burrington walked away. I followed him down behind the pool, but we went right into the shrubbery instead of left onto the beach. He stopped and turned to face me.

I got out "What's on your—" before his sucker punch caught me just below the left eye. I went down hard, conscious but with arms and legs not responding to the urgent message from my brain to rally and defend.

"What's the idea telling people I was with that fag de Weeter?" said Burrington.

I hunched up on my side.

He kicked me in the shoulder. "Huh?"

I awkwardly got back on one elbow.

"Do you realize what that would do to my rep around the fucking hotel?" Another kick, this one only a glance off ribs. "Around the fucking island?" Burrington was reaching down for me and pulling up on my hair for another punch. "Around the whole fucking Caribbean?"

Suddenly the edge of a reddish, beefy hand cracked down on his left wrist. Burrington yelled, in pain this time, and let go of me. As I slumped to the ground, I saw the tennis pro, enraged now, throw a right at Stan Dalberg. The plumbing supplier stepped in toward Burrington, parried the punch up and away, and drove his right hand, fingers curled, high into the guy's stomach. Burrington grunted and sank down, Dalberg bringing the side of his left hand this time hard onto Burrington's nose, the face exploding into a cloud of blood and snot.

My legs started working again, but Dalberg and Janice Dorn were already lifting me up. Someone yelled for an ambulance.

"I'm alright," I said. It came out "aw-rye," so I said it again, a little better.

Dalberg hawked and spat. "Not for you, Kevin. For him."

"Where . . . ?" I started over. "Where did you pick that up?"

"Oh," said Dalberg, looking down at his hands. "Army. Back in Vietnam, I was a Ranger. Guess it's like riding a bike, you never forget the reflex, you know?" He rubbed his right hand. "Only thing is, I don't remember it hurting then."

At poolside, Paul Gant arrived just before the ambulance. He spoke first with Mr. Kepper, who by then had been summoned. They turned to Burrington, who was holding a now-crimson Bayview towel to his face and shaking his head sullenly. Gant started walking toward me as the ambulance driver appeared. Dalberg was sitting to my right, alternately holding up fingers to be sure I was focusing. Rose, who turned out to be a nice woman with a far more extensive vocabulary than "Gin!," was holding an ice-filled towel against my left cheek.

"Are you alright, Kevin?" said Gant when he reached us.

"I will be."

"Burrington started it," said Dalberg. "Janice came running over to me and said he was going to get Kevin because of some note, and I turned the corner just in time to see Burrington throw the first punch."

Gant let him finish, then nodded. "Mr. Burrington has

admitted as much. He indicated that he would not prefer charges against Mr. Dalberg so long as you, Kevin, do not prefer charges against him."

"Prefer charges?" shrieked Dalberg, jerking his thumb to his chest. "Against me?"

"Easy, Stan," I said, patting him on the forearm. "That's fine with me, Paul, though I want to talk with you about some . . . aspects of it later."

"Will tonight still be convenient?"

"Fine. Same arrangements?"

Gant nodded, then moved after the ambulance driver and Burrington. The Dalbergs tended to me until I told them three times that I was fine. Finally getting up, I took a few steps, then jumped up and down lightly. Okay. I thanked everybody and headed back to the lobby.

At the entryway, Kepper fell in beside me. "Mr. Malloy, I wish you to know that I shall see to it that Mr. Burrington is never again permitted upon the grounds."

"It's not your fault, Mr. Kepper."

"Nevertheless, please enjoy lunch—on the house—as we say. Shall I take any action regarding your scuba dive today?"

"No, I'll be fine for that. And thanks for the lunch offer."

Kepper smiled and walked off. Damned interested in my diving, I thought, climbing three flights of stairs to survey the damage. The mirror in my bathroom showed just a faint discoloration now, but it would be a beaut of a black-and-blue mark tomorrow. The mask fit around the bruise without pain, though when I breathed out through my nose the pressure of the mask made the cheek sting.

No matter. I still had to regain the hang of using the equipment.

★ ★ ★ ★ ★

I went down for an early, 11:30 lunch. Janice Dorn came over to my table and said Burrington was a pig. I was noncommittal and mentioned that I hoped it wouldn't spoil my native dinner that night. She agreed and got up to leave.

"Janice, one thing. When you went to Stan out there, what did you say?"

Dorn looked at me oddly. "I told him I was afraid Chip might hurt you. You see, there was a note for Chip at the Whispering Winds this morning. It said you were saying . . . well, implying anyway, that he and de Weeter were . . ."

". . . both gay?"

"I guess so. Anyway, Stan was already up and out of his lounge, and—"

"Wait a minute. Stan was already up when you told him about Burrington?"

"Yes. And he said he'd keep an eye on things. Then . . . well, you know."

"Before Stan got up from his lounge chair, had you told Stan why Burrington might be after me?"

Dorn frowned. "You mean about the note?"

"Yes."

She looked off into space, concentrating. "No. No, I didn't."

True to his word, Yelton Pierce was waiting for me at the desk by 1:15. We bounced in his rusty Chevy Vega over the mostly paved road to Becalmed Bay, named for the dead air created by the sheltering mountain to the west. Three other people—a mother, a father, and an early-teens son—were already standing by the dive shack. Yelton fitted each of us with an air tank, a weight belt (to counteract the body's, and the air tank's, natural buoyancy), and a buoyancy compensator (a life vest whose air supply could be adjusted to keep you hovering just over the ocean bottom). While the equipment seemed as old as his car, Yelton was very thorough about safety, including the buddy system, hand- signals, and other underwater communication methods. Carrying our equipment, we crossed the beach to his mooring line and waded out to a modified Boston Whaler with two monster outboards.

Yelton, who had the slim but muscular build of an avid diver, cranked up, and we whined for a mile before hitting some chop. He slid the engines to neutral and looked over the side until he spotted a patch of glacier blue in the dark waters. Tossing an anchor off the bow, he tugged the line tight and told us to saddle up. I was to "buddy" with the son.

We dropped over the side one at a time. I descended, sucking on the rubber mouthpiece of the air regulator and swallowing dryly to allow my ears to pop in constant adjustment to the increasing pressure. The five of us kicked up a little sand as we met at the anchor, Yelton pantomiming the counting of noses and checking our equipment again. He signaled us to follow him, and we did, through a world that would remind you of the best Jacques Cousteau specials.

Learning how to dive in the Boston area, ten-foot visibility was considered good and a bulky wetsuit necessary to minimize, but not eliminate, the icy chill of sixty-degree water. On this reef, however, the water temperature, even at a depth of forty or so feet, was in the seventies, and the visibility must have approached a hundred-fifty in every direction. We finned over magnificent fan and elkhorn coral formations teeming with schools of improbably-colored fish. We crawled single-file through coral tunnels, spiny lobsters (without claws) scuttling ahead of us. When we emerged from one tunnel, Yelton pointed up, and we raised our faces. The sunlight was partially blocked by the outline of the boat and partially filtered by the water, but there were a hundred or more barracuda, each a yard long, hanging almost still, each facing a different way, sentries turning slowly at their respective depths like weathervanes in a light wind. The ones I'd seen snorkeling were no smaller, but this many of them in one place gave you reason to breathe a little harder.

We stayed down about forty-five minutes, pausing on our ascent by clinging to the anchor rope at ten feet below the surface to allow accumulated nitrogen from the depths to dissipate and thus avoid even a mild case of "the bends." Each of us was a little awkward climbing back into the boat after Yelton, but exhilarated as we talked about what we'd seen. I felt, for the first time in days, as though I were really on vacation.

Back at the dive shack, I arranged with Yelton to rent me equipment for a dive on my own. As we drove back with it, he recommended several spots that were good but not much frequented by the dive boats.

We pulled up to the hotel entrance, and I eased the gear from the backseat of the car. As I closed the door and thanked him, Yelton said, "Now remember, mon, don't you be diving by yourself."

"Don't worry, I won't be."

ELEVEN

I leaned the scuba equipment against the wall outside my door and stuck my key in the lock. It wouldn't turn. Reflexively, I glanced up at the room number: 414, and mine, alright. I now twisted the knob itself. The key hadn't turned because the door was already unlocked.

I looked up and down the hallway. No one.

Pushing my door open a little, I kicked it viciously so that I got a quick glance of the room while hopefully stunning anyone who might have been waiting behind the door.

I didn't like what I saw in the quick glance. There was no one behind the door, but a body was lying face down between the double beds, hands stretched out in mute supplication.

Kneeling down, I knew there was no need to check the pulse. He'd seemed a smart man, but with his brains showing like that, I had to change my opinion.

Standing, I pulled the bed linen down a little, using the floppy end of a pillowcase to pick up the telephone. "Connect me with the police, please," I said to the switchboard, my voice sounding very calm.

A noise like someone saying "bring" with a stammer. A woman's voice answered, and I said, "Paul Gant, please. It's Kevin Malloy."

A pause, two clicks, then Gant's voice. "Kevin, I hope you are not calling to cancel our dinner?"

"No, Paul," food the furthest thing from my mind. "Mr. Kepper's in my hotel room. He's been killed."

My story was easy to tell, even easier to check. Gant didn't bother. The same ambulance driver, this time with a helper, arrived wheeling a gurney. Flashes from the police photographer's strobe erupted intermittently, then stopped.

"Paul?" I said.

"Yes?"

"I could still use dinner."

He smiled in fatigue and looked at his watch. "It may be a late one."

While the doctor's autopsy report would not be ready until the next afternoon, Kepper had last been seen alive around 2:00 at the front desk, when he'd told his assistant he'd be gone for a while. The assistant said Kepper often spot-checked the hotel for hours at a time, and she did not feel, therefore, any concern about him.

Everyone had an alibi for most of the afternoon, none for all of it. There were gaps ranging from Neil Coughlin's twenty-five minutes to Janice Dorn's hour and a half. We found no weapon, so we assumed all had means as well as opportunity. The question then became one of motive.

TWELVE

Paul Gant set his rum punch down on the little rattan table beside his chair on the porch. We weren't screened in, but two squat, musky candles kept the mosquitoes and even the no-see-ums away from us. Though far from beachfront, his house perched on a high hill with a spectacular view of the sea. The sun was just a red and purple memory beneath the horizon-level clouds.

"Would you care for some more punch, Kevin?"

Already on my second, I wanted to be sharp tonight. "No, thanks."

There was an occasional clatter in the background as Marianne, Paul's wife, prepared dinner. The aroma helped to block brief flashes of Kepper's opened skull. I sipped my punch.

Paul took up his drink again. His eyes still followed the trail of the sun. "I would be most appreciative, Kevin, if you could favor me with your view of the situation." He sounded more tired than he'd been at the hotel.

I'd been organizing my information ever since I'd gotten over the jolt of finding the body. "To begin with the obvious, I can't believe Kepper's murder and Faith Bressler's death aren't connected. I also believe now that de Weeter was just the wrong man in the right place. Overlap your list of suspects for Faith's death and the possibles for Kepper's death. That gives us Janice Dorn, the Dalbergs, and Neil Coughlin. I'm assuming that Eric Volker will have been onboard his ship and therefore a scratch. I also assume that Chip Burrington will have an alibi, or will look so conspicuous with the broken nose that he'd never have been able to slip through Kepper's edict of excommunication from the hotel."

"I am following you so far."

"I also figure this Corey Raines, if he's hiding as well as he seems to be, wouldn't venture to the Bayview in broad daylight where he'd look out of place and be easily recognized. I'm toying with the idea that Charles Bressler should be added to the list, since he was the original source of the suicide slant and since Kepper might have been a contact here for arranging Faith's departure."

"Which brings us to motive," said Gant. "Who, besides possibly her husband, would wish to see both Mrs. Bressler and Mr. Kepper dead?"

I shook my head. "No, Paul. Let's stick with Charles Bressler, even if only to eliminate him from consideration. What comes to mind is Bressler contacts Kepper, Kepper arranges with Corey Raines to kill Faith, and Raines follows through, rigging it with de Weeter to look like the suicide plan Charlie proposes when he arrives, allegedly bereaved."

Now Gant shook his head. "No, Kevin, too many inconsistencies. First, Mrs. Bressler's letter to Volker's wife supports the suicide theory. Second, how does Mr. Bressler, who appears never to have been to Macaroon before, even *know* Mr. Kepper to contact him?"

"Well, both of Faith's supposed notes have been destroyed. If Bressler knew of Volker, he could have sent the note to Amsterdam, although it seems unlikely that Bressler could rely on the wife telling her husband and then destroying the evidence. As to your point about Kepper, maybe it was the other way around: Kepper sees Faith playing kissy-face last year, and contacts her husband about it."

"Who, enraged by his wife's betrayal, then waits an entire year to have her killed? By an islander like Raines who would know de Weeter was homosexual and thus the worst possible choice for implication?"

"Good point. Bressler admitted to me he knew Faith played around, and the de Weeter choice certainly seems to eliminate Raines." I thought for a moment. "Or any other person familiar with the island."

Gant smiled and drank some punch. "Please be at ease, Kevin. You are Sophie's alibi."

"And she's mine, though I was thinking of Burrington."

"So, that leaves us with only . . ."

I counted them on my fingers. "Janice Dorn, Rose Dalberg, Stan Dalberg, and Neil Coughlin."

"Let us begin with Miss Dorn."

"A very active person, sexually speaking."

Gant arched an eyebrow.

I confirmed what he was thinking. "But, Janice desires no attachments and seems to have formed none. Therefore, no motive for killing Faith or Kepper."

"Temporarily agreed. Mrs. Dalberg?"

"I don't know her very well. Her husband says she'd break both his legs if she caught him fooling around, but I sensed his remark was more toward her being deeply hurt than moved to violence. Also, Stan denies knowing Faith in the biblical sense."

"But his wife might not know that."

"No, but that still leaves Kepper. Why kill him?"

Gant seemed to mull it over. "Mr. Kepper could not have seen anything the night Mrs. Bressler was killed because he was in bed in his room, found there by the night clerk."

"And the note to Burrington?"

"Yes, someone clearly wished you harm by him."

"Maybe, but let's go on to Stan Dalberg." I downed the last of my drink, but now didn't object when Gant reached for the pitcher to refill my glass. "Dalberg has no alibi for the night Faith was murdered. His vacations last year and this year overlapped with hers. Yet, he has no apparent reason to have killed her. Or Kepper."

"Which leaves us with Mr. Coughlin," said Gant, frowning.

"Who didn't have an opportunity to know Faith last year and who was seen by Kepper speaking to her this year for only a few minutes in the lobby. Not much motive apparent there."

"No."

"Volker's and Burrington's alibis for Faith's death check out?"

A nod. "Elleta Menner—the girl Volker was with—was too frightened to lie to me. Too frightened I would tell her parents, that is. And Burrington was with a vacationer at the Whispering Winds all that night."

"Which leaves us with three alternatives. One, it was

Raines or someone else, for whatever motives the person had. Two, we have a hole in our reasoning about somebody on the list. Three, we don't have a complete list."

Gant shook his head vigorously. "I would dearly love to speak with Corey Raines, but in view of the de Weeter choice, I must exclude him from consideration."

It seemed to me too early to completely ignore Raines. "Unless he was the first de Weeter."

Puzzled look. "I don't understand, Kevin."

"Well, I hadn't thought of it before, but try this. Someone kills Faith, for whatever reason, and goes looking for a dupe to use as the red herring in the rip-off/murder/suicide theory. The someone finds Raines, who's been drinking heavily, and tries to use him. Maybe Raines isn't too drunk to realize what's going on, or maybe Raines is foxy enough to try turning the tables and rolling the someone. Anyway, Raines is killed, away from the hotel, and then maybe dumped some distance out of town."

Gant shook his head slowly this time. "Mrs. Bressler's rental car showed only five kilometers expired. That is barely Bayview to the capital and back."

"Alright then, the someone dumps Raines in town, then goes a-hunting again, this time finding de Weeter. You can take it from there." I had a long draw from my punch.

Paul scratched his throat. "It is possible, but again, only a stranger to Macaroon would have picked the homosexual de Weeter as the second dupe, as you say. And a stranger could not, I think, have found a secure place to hide the body of Raines within the confines of the expired mileage." A smile. "After all, in our summer heat, a body would begin to make itself known rather quickly. And, given the un-locked door into your not-then-occupied adjoining room the night Mrs. Bressler was killed, I believe you were intended to be the 'first de Weeter,' as you say."

"Okay. Let's pass the soundness of our reasoning on the people already on the list, and concentrate on whether there are more who could be on the list."

Paul's eyes went left to right rapidly. "First, there could always be islanders, here last off-season and this, who met Faith Bressler both times, but of whom we have no notice. It is, after all, impossible to completely reconstruct even one visitor's weeklong vacations a full year apart. However, de Weeter was well-known here, and I cannot believe any islander preparing the deception in the hotel room would have chosen him for the reasons we already discussed."

"Which brings us to your Customs list."

"Not directly. First I had all the hotels on Macaroon prepare for me lists of those guests here with Faith Bressler last year and this. I used the Bayview's to compile the group we discussed on the way to picking up Mr. Bressler at the airport. Then I gave the original lists to Customs so that they could quickly eliminate anyone who already had been screened by the hotels. To have Customs do the overlapping list directly would have taken days, believe me. They are so slow in—"

"Wait a minute, Paul. If the hotels had made a mistake, your Customs people wouldn't have caught it."

"What do you mean?"

"Look, what if there was a guest in a given hotel this year who *did* know Faith last year, and the hotel involved fouled up, missed that fact. Since that person would have been only on this year's guest list, Customs would have interpreted his or her name as 'already checked by hotel,' right?"

"Yes, but you see, such a mistake would be terribly difficult to make. For tax purposes, all the hotels maintain sequentially numbered invoice systems, with each day's lodging and meals and drinks entered on a continuing series of pages. An entire day or days in the stay of such a guest would have to be ignored, and the date the guest checks out would be a control on such an oversight. Unless, of course," Gant began to rub his chin, "the guest checked out of the hotel *before* leaving the island . . ."

". . . or the hotel employee checking the records for you falsified them or lied, for a price, and then tried to gouge more . . ."

"Mr. Kepper," said Paul.

I leaned back and reached for my drink. "He did seem awfully interested in whether and when I was going scuba diving. And if he were arranging a blackmail meeting, my guaranteed empty room would make a good conference site."

"Why not just use an unrented room at the hotel?"

"To keep our someone in line, maybe?"

Gant nodded once, then twice quickly. "I shall call the night clerk at the Bayview immediately to re-check last year's and this year's guest invoices." He rose.

"Paul, would you also make another call?"

"Certainly. To whom?"

"The Petite Bay Casino. I'd like to know whether Stan Dalberg goes there tonight, and if he does, what time he arrives and what time he leaves."

Inspector Paul Gant looked at me strangely, but went off to make the calls.

THIRTEEN

The telephone awakened me at 9:00 the next morning. I reached for it blearily. Marianne Gant's dinner the night before had been wahoo with a varied salad, washed down by a white Bordeaux I'd brought. I hadn't gotten drunk, but I did fall asleep as soon as my head hit the pillow.

"Hello?"

"Kevin, this is Paul. We have experienced a delay."

It seemed that there was confusion at the Bayview. Kepper had kept things pretty much to himself, and the night clerk had no key to the room where the old records were stored. The police, of course, had a key among the effects of the late Mr. Kepper, but the night clerk didn't think to call them. The assistant day clerk did have a key now, Gant having gotten Kepper's over to her, and she was checking through the records.

Gant also received a call from Peter, the man in charge of dealers at the Petite Bay Casino. Stan Dalberg had entered the casino at 9:00 p.m. on the button, played for an hour, and left at 10:05, never to return.

"Kevin, does Mr. Dalberg's schedule have anything to do with the case?"

"I'm not sure, Paul. I may be able to tell you after I've talked with him."

"Very well. I shall keep you advised on the Bayview. I have also asked the clerks at the other hotels to similarly recheck their records."

"Good. Speak to you later." I hung up and reached for my trunks.

Walking through the lobby, I saw Neil Coughlin at the front desk, wallet in hand. He darted a nervous glance at me, then shifted his feet uneasily as he watched the clerk tapping on a desktop calculator.

I moved toward him. "Last day already?"

Coughlin put on a martyred expression and rolled his eyes. "Who can stand to stay here? Three deaths in three days! I'm so upset I called the airline and got an earlier flight back. I'll spend the rest of my time off in New York City."

"Where it's nice and safe."

A glare. "At least no one has ever been murdered in my apartment building."

"Murdered? I thought you were on the 'suicide' side?"

Coughlin curled his lips, then shook himself and turned back to the clerk. "Will you please hurry with that bill? My plane leaves in three hours, and I still haven't eaten breakfast."

Walking away, I said, "Take it easy, Neil. You're on vacation, remember?"

Outside, Dalberg was reclining at the edge of the pool, facing away from the beach and reading his Deaver novel intently. One striking woman in a bikini walked across his peripheral vision, but he never even glanced at her.

I drew even with him. "Must be some book."

"Huh?" Dalberg looked up at me. "Why?"

I jerked my head toward the receding woman. "You never even twitched."

He looked at her quickly. "Boy, yeah," drumming up enthusiasm. "Stunner." Then back to me. "How are you feeling?"

"Much better. Enjoy the casino?"

"Yeah, yeah. Lost a hundred and a half, but what the fuck, last night on the island and all, you know?"

"A hundred and fifty. Hope you made it last."

"Three, four hours."

I let the lie settle for a minute. "Why do you suppose somebody would send Chip Burrington a note like that?"

"Who knows?" Dalberg returned to the book, tracing his place with an index finger.

"Stan," I said quietly, "you have a choice. You can level with me, or you can level with Gant."

Dalberg pursed his lips, then closed the book slowly without marking his place. "Let's go some place quiet and talk."

"After yesterday, I think right here is fine."

He managed a smile. "Okay, okay. Along the beach, then. Out in the open, but where nobody'll hear us."

I nodded and followed him down to the water's edge. We walked north, away from the bathers but in plain view of twenty or so people.

I decided to start things rolling. "Janice Dorn never told you about the note. Nor did anybody else."

"I heard Burrington hollering about it while he was kicking your teeth in."

"Only about what I supposedly said, not that it was in a note."

Dalberg thought it over and shrugged. "So, I sent the note to him. No crime, is it?"

"Not in itself."

We walked a while.

Dalberg let out a breath. "You aren't gonna say much, are you?"

"If I did, I'm afraid it'd sound like locker-room talk pretty quickly, and I don't think it is that way. At least for you."

"It isn't," he said, digging his thumbs into the top of his trunks, incongruously like an Indiana farm boy. "Though for Janice, I'm not so sure."

"You were with her the night Faith was killed, too?"

Dalberg sniffed and nodded. "Yeah."

"When did it start?"

"Two years ago. Janice flirts a lot, but when she's with

254

you, it's like you were all that mattered. And she flirts different from the way Faith did. There's no, I dunno, *malice* with Janice."

"So, why the note?"

"Well, Rose decided she didn't want to come here again next year. I'm pretty sure she don't know about us—we been real careful, and Janice wouldn't tip her off or anything. But it's like Rose sensed it in the air. Anyway, last night was probably the last time I'd ever see Janice. But she said that, well, she was gonna go out to dinner with that Burrington. I'd met him last year with Faith, and he was a capital, grade-A shit. I couldn't let my last chance bounce over to him so . . ." Dalberg pulled his thumbs out of the waistband and spread his hands, "I sent the note."

"To get Burrington disgraced and busted up, leaving Janice for you."

"Uh-huh."

"Required a neat bit of timing on your part," I said, an edge in my voice, "making sure to let him get started on me but not kill me, I mean my being a friend of yours and all."

Dalberg shook his head. "I didn't plan it that way, Kevin. Honest. Sure, I knew Burrington'd go for you once he got the note. But I figured, with you being a cop and all, you'd handle him no sweat, busting him up for me in the process."

I felt my face redden. We turned around and started walking back to the hotel.

Dalberg said, "Janice was good to cover for me like she did, after Faith was killed. So Rose wouldn't know about us, I mean." A pause. "Rose doesn't have to know, does she?"

I thought about Dalberg and Dorn. If Faith knew about

them, then Faith might have threatened to tell Rose, giving Stan a solid motive. "I can't promise that, but I'll do my best to see that nothing comes out."

We walked in silence after that, him maybe pondering his sins and me doing the same with mine.

After Dalberg turned toward the pool, I stayed on the beach for another hour and a half. Eventually, Stan and Rose both came out in their "plane-clothes" to say good-bye. I hadn't seen Charles Bressler or Neil Coughlin, but I didn't really expect to. Since only the identity, and not the capture, of Faith's killer mattered to Sophie and me, I wasn't too concerned about the exodus by air.

The heat, though, was triggering a piña colada every thirty minutes or so. I was midway through my fourth when the drink boy came up to me.

"A little early yet," I said, swirling the ice in my big paper cup.

"Please, Mr. Malloy. The telephone is for you. The police." He blinked rapidly.

I stood up. "Where?"

He pointed to the lobby.

The assistant clerk for days was behind the desk, her nametag reading *Cobley*. She fumbled with a manila envelope and beckoned me over. "Inspector Gant is on the telephone. He wishes you to speak with him about these." Cobley handed me a sheaf of yellowish invoices with pre-printed numbers in red at the top.

I picked up the telephone and began to flip through them. "Paul?"

"Kevin, Miss Cobley called me a few minutes ago. She had reviewed all of the guest invoices which overlapped Mrs. Bressler last year and this. As you know—do you have them in front of you?"

"I have a bunch she handed me. I'm looking through them."

"Excellent. As I told you, each hotel maintains invoices on each guest for room charge, meals, drinks, tax and so forth. Now, please examine the invoices for last year, and see if anything stands out."

I went through the twenty or so. One was a slightly brighter yellow than the rest. I looked at the name and smiled. "I'm holding an invoice from last year that looks pretty new."

"Now look at the invoice number of that page and compare it to the others in the group."

It jumped out at you. "The newer, brighter one is four thousand numbers beyond the other old ones. Kepper did cover for him. The brighter one shows him checking out two days before Faith arrived last year."

"That is what Miss Cobley said."

I handed the sheaf back to her and winked. She smiled shyly and returned the invoices to the envelope.

Over the telephone, Gant said, "Would you like to be there when we take him into custody?"

I glanced up at the clock. "Will you have time to pick me up on your way?"

A brief hesitation. "On my way where, Kevin?"

I actually looked into the receiver. "To the airport. Didn't Ms. Cobley tell you?"

The clerk looked as panicky as Gant, for a moment, sounded. "The airport? He is running?"

"He is leaving, Paul. He checked out."

Gant said, "But Miss Cobley—"

She made a helpless gesture and pointed to the back room. I said into the telephone, "Ms. Cobley probably wouldn't have known because of working in the storage room on the invoices."

"We will be to you in two minutes."

"Can you hold the plane?" I asked, but he was already gone.

I considered going upstairs for a shirt and pants, but I didn't want to delay Gant and maybe cost him his collar. I waited at the main entrance. My guess is that the police car was there in a minute and a half, the driver and a second officer in the front, Paul in the back. The siren was whooping and the tires were squealing. The driver looked scared, as though he might never have driven that fast before.

If not, he'd have done the Petty family proud on the way to the airport. We took the high, winding curves over the ocean on the mid-lines of the road, poaching into the oncoming lane so as to downshift and brake less frequently. I said a silent prayer that goatboy had his charges well into the pastures.

I also suggested that Gant call to hold the plane.

"I gave orders as we left the station to do just so. We received a radio message as we approached your hotel. The number of the airline is busy, and the control tower will not answer its telephone during mid-day because of the heavy air traffic then arriving and departing." Gant clenched his teeth. "I tried to reach my officer at the airport, but he is not at his post."

I could see the driver's face in the rearview mirror. He grimaced at the last remark, as though he might be the partner or a relative of the presumed goldbrick. No wonder he'd looked scared before.

We roared up the approach road to the terminal, Gant leaning forward and muttering something. The driver reached down and flicked off the siren.

Pulling near the building, he honked to freeze cab

drivers as they tried to ease into our lane from the parking zone. We stopped in front of a double doorway. Gant, the shotgun guard, and I piled out, the driver staying in the car.

The three of us entered the terminal. An air-conditioned cocktail lounge, duty-free shops, and rental car booths were located haphazardly around the outer perimeter of the interior.

I spotted Charles Bressler almost immediately. He was at a ticket counter and started involuntarily on seeing us. We must have been quite a sight: two black cops in starched uniforms and a slightly sunburned white tourist wearing nothing but a pair of blue trunks.

I began to move toward Bressler as Paul waved his man to the other side of the airport. The recent widower looked around for a moment, almost wildly, as we moved through the crowd.

"What . . . What's going on?" he said.

"Nothing to worry about, Charlie," I said quietly. "Have you seen—"

I spotted him, uncomfortably engaged in small talk with Rose.

He saw me, then turned and sprinted toward Gate 3. A police officer, I assumed the goldbrick, came around a corner unexpectedly, and they collided, both going down.

"Neil! Stay where you are."

Coughlin scrambled to his feet and started running again, pumping his legs toward the gate door. He threw himself against it, but it wouldn't budge.

I stopped five feet from him, Paul and the shotgun guard pulling up beside me a few seconds later.

Softly, I said, "Just calm down, Neil. There's nowhere to go."

He looked at me bleakly, then dropped his head down onto his chest and began to cry.

We got the whole story on the way to the station. Gant told Coughlin a few times that he need not speak "for the record" (the Macaroon version of a *Miranda* warning, I guessed), but once Coughlin started, he went on like a faucet with a broken handle.

"In the beginning, Mr. Kepper was so smooth about everything. The very first year I was here, he said at the desk, 'I have a perfect room for you, sir,' and he put me next to a chef, a female chef from San Francisco. She was, well, a delightful person, but she was tied to her city and I to mine, and especially to the Cardinal. I didn't have the grades for a seminary, and it took me twenty-one years to reach the highest lay position."

Apparently not appreciating the pun, Coughlin went on. "Anyway, last year Kepper called me—*called* me, understand—in New York, two weeks before my vacation started. He said that a beautiful, charming woman would be at the Bayview that summer during my week, but unfortunately the rooms next to her were already taken. However, he said, for fifty dollars he could 'rearrange the accommodations.' I knew he was holding me up, but I'd had such a wonderful time the year before, I agreed. That woman was from Florida, a journalist, and so, oh, aware of the world, but she was leaving two days before I was. And she did."

Coughlin's voice dropped a register. "Then came Faith. She arrived the night before I left. Kepper put her in the journalist's room. Faith—well, there is no other word for it, she picked me up in the bar after dinner. We went up to our rooms, to her room actually, and . . ." Coughlin just waved his hands. "It was wonderful, a different *magnitude* of experience. Faith told me she felt young again, that I satisfied her spiritually.”

A deep sigh. “When I got back to New York, Faith called me and said she was coming to visit. She did, and Faith let drop when we were in bed again, and not before then, that she was married. *Married!* Can you imagine what that would do to me, what that would do to twenty-one years of service? I told Faith that she would have to go, that we could never see each other again. She screamed and yelled and cursed at me. Even packing her bags, Faith maintained that I was her ‘one true love.’ I told her that my job was gone, my whole *career* was gone, if the Cardinal ever found out that I was seeing a married woman. We went on for an hour or more. Then Faith took a cab to the airport, and that’s the last I saw of her.”

“Till this summer,” I said.

Coughlin nodded. “That’s right,” tonelessly. “She wrote a few times, telling me I was her spiritual match, and so on. I burned her letters, of course. Then I came back to Macaroon this year. I shouldn’t have, but I needed a rest, and Mr. Kepper said—he’d called again and charged me the same, fifty dollars—he said there was a lovely lady arriving two days after I did. Well, she arrived, alright. Faith. God knows what she’d paid Kepper. But Faith didn’t call me until the next night, Friday. She told me to come into her room, through the interior door. And right away, or she swore that she’d call the Cardinal long-distance and tell him about us. I was petrified.”

Coughlin’s voice dropped to a whisper. “I went through the adjoining doors into her room. Faith was lying on the bed, the sheets up to her waist. She wasn’t wearing . . . anything, except a dreamy smile, and told me to come sit beside her. I did, and Faith started stroking my thigh with her left hand. She said she couldn't live without me and asked if I felt the same way. The woman was talking so weirdly that I said yes, I did. Just to buy some time, you see, just to think. Faith said she had the room and a car for the week, but she wouldn't be needing them that long. Faith also said she'd sent notes, notes to her other lovers, telling them she just wanted to be with her 'special one,' me. She even told me she'd left a note for her husband. I was trying to start her talking rationally when Faith said she'd finally come to realize that I was right about what the Cardinal would do about us."

A grunt from Coughlin that might have been a laugh. "I sort of brightened up at that point, believing that she'd asked me in to, well, apologize before going back to Chicago. Then Faith said that she'd 'tested our love' by spending Thursday night with another 'attractive' man." Coughlin turned to me. "You, Kevin."

Then he shook his head. "But Faith said it just confirmed what she'd already known. So she'd also come to a decision, one she knew I'd share. I asked Faith if she'd told her husband or you my name, and she shook her head slowly from side to side on the pillow, the way you see a mother being patient with her child. Then Faith said that she understood that I would need help with my side of the decision. I started to ask her what decision she was talking about when she drew her right hand out from under the sheet. Faith was holding a gun, a *gun,* and aimed it at my chest. She cocked back the hammer with her thumb and said, 'Poor us.' I grabbed her wrist and pushed it away from me. The gun's muzzle went into the pillow. Faith twisted around, there was a dull, snapping sound, and at the same time the pillow just . . . exploded. I inhaled a few feathers and coughed and then gagged as the feathers fell and I saw her, saw her . . . head."

Coughlin put his hand up to his face, fingers splayed, and kept it there. "I didn't know Faith was going to have a gun, going to push through this, this *suicide* pact she'd made with herself. I stood up and tried to decide what to do. I started to leave the room, then thought about fingerprints. I couldn't allow myself to be caught, you see. My job, my career, would be gone even faster than before. I realized I had touched only the two doors between our rooms and of course, Faith's wrist. I forced myself to look at her. I knew the death would be investigated, and that she'd told her husband something about somebody, and I didn't have any alibi. I finally decided to take the gun and 'plant' it on someone credible."

"Me again," I said.

Coughlin took his hand from his eyes and looked at me. "Yes."

"But I wasn't in."

"No, so I decided to wait for you. I even unlocked Faith's interior door to your room, but you never came back. I don't remember now if I relocked it."

"You did not," Gant said, speaking for the first time in a long while.

Coughlin bobbed his head. "Well, I decided I had to find someone who'd known Faith last year, and I prayed— Oh, God, I did pray, do you know that? I prayed to God to help me while I sat in that room with her body. I prayed that I could find someone to pass for the other person in her suicide pact. I got the rental car keys from Faith's pocketbook, then wiped the pocketbook clean. I took the gun and went out through my room and down the backstairs.

"The keys had the license number of her car on the tab. I found the car in the hotel lot and drove slowly into town.

It was late, but a lot of people were on the streets from Carnivaal. Mostly couples or small groups, though. Then I finally saw one man by himself, walking as though he were a little drunk and had no place to go. I called him over, and he told me his name, 'Tony.' I realized I didn't have any, well, story to tell him, to get this Tony to come with me. I felt the gun in my pocket and just blurted out that I had something I needed help with back at my hotel and that I'd pay him well. To my surprise, Tony smiled and said he'd be glad to help. It wasn't until afterward, when I found out who or what he was, that I realized why Tony'd agreed so quickly, what he must have thought I meant. We went back to the hotel—"

"Excuse me," said Paul, "but was Mr. de Weeter the only man you approached that night?"

Coughlin looked at Gant as though he didn't understand the question. "Well, yes. He was the only one by himself."

Gant nodded. "Please continue."

Coughlin said, "We parked and went to the backstairs and came up to my room. No one saw us. I motioned Tony into the next room, Faith's. He smiled, well, lasciviously, and strolled in. I took out the gun, and Tony saw Faith on the bed. He wheeled around on me. Waving the gun, I got him to move to the other side of the room. Tony stumbled backwards. I told him to get undressed, but he didn't move. I told him more harshly, and Tony unbuttoned his shirt and took off his pants and . . ." a blush ". . . he wasn't wearing any underwear. I forced myself to look over at Faith, to be sure I had to do the next part. That's when Tony lunged for her pocketbook and came at me, swinging it by the strap. I remember feeling the gun jump twice or three times in my hand, like it was alive. I don't remember hearing any noise this time, but it must have been louder than with the pillow before. All I remember is Tony going down, backwards."

Coughlin licked his lips. "I went to Faith, wiped the gun handle on the pillowcase, then rubbed her fingers all over it. Then I ran into my room, stripped and changed to pajamas, then came back through the adjoining doors, locking the one on Faith's side and coming out her front door, letting it lock behind me as it closed. No one was in the hall, so I assumed no one had heard the shots. I slammed my hand into the wall twice, then shouted a little, then began knocking on her door wildly. By this time, a few people were in the hall—Stan Dalberg, I remember him—and someone got Mr. Kepper and well . . ." suddenly all the air seemed to go out of Coughlin, "that's about it."

I gave him a moment. "And Mr. Kepper?"

Coughlin almost laughed again. "Oh, yes. Him. He came to me later, told me that the police wanted him to tell them all the guests who had been on Macaroon with Faith last year. Kepper told me he could fix the records so it would look like I wasn't here with her then. Since we overlapped by only two days, he said it would be easy. I was sure he thought I'd killed Faith. I also realized by then that the man I had chosen—Tony—was not, well, suitable for the suicide pact, so I thought I had to cover up my knowing her last year. I agreed to pay Kepper five hundred dollars, all the cash and travelers' checks I had." Coughlin looked at me. "That's another reason I had to leave Macaroon early."

"But Kepper wasn't satisfied with the five hundred, was he?"

As we were pulling into the station lot, Coughlin shook his head. "No. I was so stupid. When I paid him that much, Kepper must have known that he had me. The man demanded I speak with him, in your room, Kevin. He said he knew it would be free yesterday afternoon. So I met him there, and Kepper said there was pressure on him, that he was sure I would understand that he would need more money, at regular intervals, to protect his position. I said what did he mean by 'more money'? Kepper said he realized I was not a wealthy man, but three hundred dollars a month seemed fair to him. I couldn't believe what I was hearing, and I told him no. He said, 'Very well, I shall simply have to notify the authorities here, and of course, your Church in New York.' Then Kepper stood and turned to go. I lifted the lamp from your night table and hit him with the base of it. He fell forward, and I looked at the base. It was . . . disgusting, but Kepper had a master key, so I exchanged the lamp with one from an unused room, wiping both of them off. I put his key back and left your room."

The Toyota came to a stop. Paul opened his door.

Coughlin seemed reluctant to get out. "I had to do these things, don't you see? Faith was an accident, but de Weeter and Kepper, I had to. I had to protect myself, my *career*." He turned to me. "Kevin, you understand, don't you? You understand what I mean."

I thought, Boy, do I ever.

FOURTEEN

That night, I paused in the basement of Sophie's Soupcon, just inside the door to the refrigerated food locker, staring at the covered lump in the corner.

Behind me, Sophie said, "Go ahead."

"Okay, okay." I leaned against the door jam, took a deep breath, and moved toward the body.

Stooping, I tried to make sure the old tablecloth would stay over him as I lifted. I got a grip on his cold, stiff left arm and, squatting onto my haunches, levered his upper body off the floor. He wasn't too heavy for me, but the rigor made the whole of him move. It was like trying to lift a cafeteria table by yourself, just awkward, dead weight.

I said, "You're going to have to help me."

"I can't," said Sophie, her voice cracking as she tried to keep it low.

I took another breath, then heaved him up. The cloth fell from his face, and Sophie strangled a scream as Corey Raines' blued and grayed face flashed her its now eternal smile.

I fumbled with the cloth, covering his face again and trying to think of what had happened so far to take my mind off what I was doing.

Sophie and I had been asleep in her bed above the bar the night Faith Bressler died. Raines had used a key to open Sophie's apartment door, but he was drunk and raring for a fight. I jumped out of bed, half asleep and naked. Raines came at me before I knew what was happening. He swung a roundhouse right at my head, but I caught his punch on my left bicep. Stepping into him, I pushed his jaw back as Sophie started to yell. Raines went over, cracking his skull on a corner of the woodwork. When I checked him, he wasn't breathing, and there was no pulse in his neck.

I sank into a chair, forcing my brain to work.

I imagined myself trying to explain what had happened to Captain William "the Moralist" Hanrahan. I pictured the headline as "Naked Cop Kills Lover of Bar Owner." I saw my promotion going up in smoke. Then I realized I was jumping ahead, overlooking the immediate problem of being prosecuted on an island I didn't belong to, for killing a probable love rival I didn't even know. I decided I had to cover it up, and Sophie went along. I would have taken him out that night, dumped him in an alley and banged his head against some sharp corner. But Sophie said, no, there'd be too many people out and about from Carnivaal.

So we got Raines down to the locker, Sophie having to turn it on since she didn't serve meals during the off-season and so didn't keep food in it. We decided I'd go back to my hotel and change, then rent a car. Back at Sophie's that next night, I'd load him into the trunk and dump him along the cliffs, let the sea cover up where he came from. I told Sophie to act naturally till then, and I took off walking to the Bayview, where Gant's men were waiting, scaring the shit out of me until I realized Paul was investigating the deaths of Faith Bressler and Tony de Weeter.

Sophie and I figured to wait an additional day. We would have moved that night, too, except the derelict is-lander outside her place bothered me. My call from that pay phone on the way back to the hotel was to Sophie. I de-scribed the derelict and asked her to look him over. She came back from her window nearly hysterical to tell me he was one of Gant's best officers, obviously staking out her place. I decided the police suspected there was something funny about Sophie or me, probably tied to Faith's death somehow. I also decided that we'd have to wait to move Raines until Faith's death was closed, and the police stood down. So I pitched in to help Gant and intensified my effort after Hanrahan's call told me I'd have fewer days on Maca-roon to see Faith's killing solved and my problem resolved.

Now, as Sophie guided me up the stairs from the base-ment, I shifted Raines' body on my shoulder and forced my thinking to return to the present. The rental car was parked outside the back door, nicely shadowed by her building. I had the scuba gear from Yelton in the back seat. Given the amount of time that had passed since Raines had died, I felt

I had to create a reason for him not being found quickly. We decided to drive to a cliff Sophie knew and drop him off it. Then I'd shinny down the easier slope with my gear, don it, and swim him out, wedging him under a ledge in the rocks somewhere. Either he'd float up eventually, by which time I'd be long gone and my actions not reliably traceable, or the creatures would reduce him to bones first.

Sophie was now standing in the exterior doorway of her building, looking both ways several times before waving me out frantically and scurrying toward the trunk with the key in her hand. I stayed in the doorway, shifting Raines again to carry him like a curved tree trunk.

Sophie was shaking badly, cursing under her breath because she couldn't get the key into the lock. When she finally did, the click of the trunk lid sounded abnormally loud in the humid, silent air. "Alright," she whispered.

I'd taken three steps toward her when the flashlight beams struck my face, blinding me.

"I am so sorry, Kevin," said a familiar voice as footsteps sounded all around us. "Please do nothing foolish."

A police officer was already at my side, helping me to ease Raines down to the ground.

"Do I have your word you are unarmed?" Gant said, now squarely in front of me.

I nodded. "It was self-defense and an accident. Paul, I swear it. I was trapped into this cover-up by my career, just like Coughlin was by his."

Gant didn't reply.

I said, "You knew. From the beginning."

"No," abruptly, then, more softly. "No, I only suspected something was amiss. When I brought you here to Sophie's that first morning, I heard the refrigerator motor humming from the basement. I thought that odd, since I was reasonably certain Sophie served no meals at this time of year, and the electricity to run the locker is so terribly expensive. I also thought your involuntary visit to my office somehow more . . . intellectually planned than I would have expected and certainly more careful than spending the night with a woman would have required. I considered having you followed, but I felt that you would easily realize that was happening. So I decided instead to have one of my best men, the one on 'special assignment,' watch the building here, on the theory that Sophie being your alibi, she must be involved as well. But when he reported to me that he feared Sophie had recognized him, I decided to believe you did have something to conceal."

"Which I confirmed by helping you out on Faith's death."

"Yes," said Gant, one of his cars pulling in behind the rental. He gestured politely with his hand to show me the way. "I thought it unusual for a policeman on holiday to be quite so cooperative and generous with his precious vacation time, especially one so harried that he had to wait until the off-season to visit us."

I got into the back seat next to a uniformed officer. "Maybe I should have seen Macaroon in the high season."

Gant closed the door, looking down at me. "Kevin, I fear you may have the chance."

EPILOGUE

I get glimpses of Neil Coughlin from time to time in the prison yard. They have to keep an eye on him. Word has it that he's tried to kill himself more than once.

Sophie was transferred to a prison on another island, I'm

not sure why. Paul Gant comes to visit me ("Upon occasion, Kevin"), and Captain Hanrahan even wrote, though just a note enclosed with my letter of termination from the department. But Gant's visits are getting more and more "occasional," and there isn't a lot to do when they can't trust you to work outside the fences.

Today's gecko is starting to climb the wall again. It's after a fly, but this time I spotted the target before the lizard did.

Long before, I think.